THE STRANGE DEAD

DAVID DUNWOODY

SEVERED PRESS

HOBART TASMANIA

THE STRANGE DEAD

ONE | SUMMER 2048: THE FIELD

Nightfall would bring the dead, and Death. But the sun was still pinned to the bright blue of Heaven's firmament, pitched only slightly westward, away from the mountain wall against which Potter's Field was buttressed. The warmth of midday was offset by a pleasant breeze, and it was in all-too-brief moments like these that Claire thought she must be feeling what it was to be alive, really alive.

She stood in a wide field at the foot of the mountain, separated from its steep, mossy slope by a high stone security wall. The field itself was fenced off to prevent livestock from wandering into the nearby "suburb," the encampment's tent city where residents made their homes. This was the calm part of Potter's Field, an area graced now and then by gentle laughter, even silence. The suburb had intentionally been set apart from the community's business end, where the soldiers trained and where, beyond the forward security wall, there was no mountain but a flat expanse of infertile earth which stretched to the horizon like a scab. The unspoiled land of the Field was the mar on this world where nature was rot.

Claire focused on the green grass beneath her feet and the smells on the air. Her horses had just been released from the stable and were fanning out in her direction. A couple trotted directly to her, and she looked up to receive a wet nose in the crook of her neck. Claire jumped with a laugh and patted Boy Blue's head. Smoothing the black hair matted atop his crown, she thought he needed more than a brushing; all twelve of them, in fact, were probably due for a trip with Claire to the edge of the reservoir. "You can lead a horse to water, but you can't make him wash his ass." One of Andre's many *bon mots*. Andre hadn't been by today. Claire cast a glance toward the gravel road which ran beside the fence as she fished through a burlap bag fastened about her waist. She offered Boy Blue a palmful of feed. His younger brother, Rocket, nosed into the exchange, and Claire fetched another handful for him. It was meager in both amount and nutrients, but it was the best she could do for her kids most days. The little bit of farmland the Fielders had managed to cultivate and maintain was

1

used to grow food for the people. Claire had been granted a little corner and a pittance of grains. Despite the importance of the horses – motor vehicles were an indistinct memory, almost like something out of a campfire tale – she received little aid in tending her crop. Andre, when he was on KP (which was more often than most, thanks to his *bon mots*), would sometimes sneak some carrot shavings into his pockets and bring them to the stable. "Rules are for those who need them," he'd say. "It's an equalizer, Clarissa." Clarissa wasn't her real name, and he knew that, but she allowed it. "Rules," he'd go on, "keep the sharks and snakes in check around the mice. For the rest of us, those who just know better than to eat their own, rules are meant to be bent."

Claire wasn't sure if she agreed with that. But half the time, even after all these years, she couldn't tell if Andre was completely serious or not. Fifteen years she'd known the man, most of her life. She'd been seven when he pulled her out of the MCM. Everything before that was a blurred tapestry whose designs only took shape in her worst nightmares. Andre, who was in his twenties then, hadn't known her before the MCM, and he'd had no luck tracking down anyone who did. But that was the way of things. Sometime around 2028, a big cleaver had fallen from the sky and severed history's vein.

The other horses had gathered around Claire, and she gave each equal attention. They ranged in age from five to fifteen. Blue was the oldest, and though he may have had many years ahead of him in the world before, Claire was seeing the signs of age. It was her job, had been for half a lifetime. Blue had been her first charge, and she knew he would be the first she lost. She took the brush from her belt and began combing it through his mane. "You're an old boy," she said, and smiled a little. Blue stood still, his eye fixed on her, as she worked her way down his coat.

"These guys get better treatment than a general," came a voice from behind her. She recognized it and chose not to acknowledge it. She heard the man rapping his knuckles on the wooden fence. "Hey, Claire! You in there?"

"Just enjoying the silence," she called over her shoulder. The man let out a thin laugh. She heard the fence creaking under his weight and bristled. The horses stamped their hooves; it was gentle, but a warning.

"Best stay back, John," Claire said.

"Why don't these guys like anyone but you?"

"They like plenty of people," Claire said, putting the brush away. This wasn't going to end anytime soon. If there was one thing Johnny Idaho could do, it was talk. Didn't mean he was any good at it.

She finally turned. Idaho was dressed in his weathered fatigues, though his shirt was open. He cocked his blond head and offered a leery grin. "They like the people *you* like," he said.

"They're good at reading people," Claire said, brushing a few bits of feed from her palms. "And like I said, you best stay back. Can't just come walking into their house."

"I'm one of the reasons they have a home," Idaho said. His grin was still half-there but, as usual, it didn't take much to wind him up. "Nice big field to shit in. Some of the families would like the schoolhouse relocated up here by the suburb. Potter says no way." Idaho hitched up his pants. "I agreed with him."

"That must have helped."

"Young lady, a lot of people don't think about anyone but themselves. I'm a soldier. My job's about everyone *but* me."

Claire nodded, slowly, then said, "Can I ask you a question?"

"Shoot."

"Are you ever going to leave me alone?"

Idaho snorted, shifting his weight from one boot to the other. At Claire's shoulder, Blue offered a snort in reply.

"You know what else?" Idaho said, steamrolling right over what she'd asked. "Some people think your animals are a health risk."

"I don't need to hear it," Claire said. "There's never been a case of a horse being infected. Or a dog, or a bird, or anything else. The bugs don't work inside animals."

"Lots of stories, though."

"If I believed everything I heard, I wouldn't allow you within fifty yards of me or this field," Claire said. She hadn't intended to flare up like that, but she wasn't about to hear any baseless rumors about her horses.

Idaho looked taken aback. His countenance darkened and he said, "Lots of stories, kid. And people who aren't so willing to gamble with their lives on these dumb things."

Claire steeled her expression and said nothing. If it weren't for the terrible consequence, she would have already sicced Rocket on him. He didn't know just how loyal her kids were.

Idaho shrugged. "Just wanted to let you know. I think you do good work. Thought you ought to know some of us still appreciate you."

As if she were some pariah in the community. Claire wasn't about to let any of this jerkoff's implications take root in her mind. She turned her back to him and began checking Rocket's eyes and teeth.

She had the feeling that Idaho was retreating when she heard him call, "Hey, Dozens!" *Shit.* Hell of a time for Andre to show up.

"What're you doing in there, Johnny?" Andre called back. Claire heard him clamber over the fence. The horses didn't react to Andre's approach. "Hasn't Claire told you these beasts will bite your dick off?"

Andre stepped into Claire's view, patting Rocket's head. "KP?" Claire asked.

"K is for carrot," Andre said with a smile. He emptied the pockets of his fatigues. Luckily, he knew how to hold out offerings for the horses to take, otherwise Rocket's lunging bite would have snapped off a few fingers.

"What's that you've got there?" Idaho asked. He didn't step any closer, though.

"Relax, Idaho, this is what they threw out from the mess tent. Unfit for human consumption." Andre winked at Claire.

"Probably tastes better than what I had for breakfast," Idaho retorted.

"Don't let Potter hear you say that," Andre replied. "You know they're going to name the mulch-wich after him."

Claire watched as Andre fed the other horses. As unkempt as their manes looked today, none held a candle to Andre's afro. General Potter was strict as they came, but he'd taken a liking to Andre, as most did, and had let him keep his hair. Idaho had a regulation cut and razor burn all over his chin and neck. Kept you from being snatched by the hair, they said. Kept your sights clear. Less chance of picking up lice. But Andre was an unapologetic individual, something he'd passed that on to Claire.

Natural that someone like Johnny Idaho would resent that, and Claire knew he did, but Idaho was always tagging along after Andre like some lost puppy. Maybe he was hoping some of that goodwill would rub off on him. In truth, Claire pitied Johnny. She wished he could see that. Maybe then he'd leave her alone. Then again…he had a short fuse. Perhaps it was better just to hold him at arm's length where she could keep an eye on him.

General Potter, for his part, figured anyone assigned to an isolated encampment like this one was capable of handling their own problems. Andre had approached him once about guys giving Claire a hard time – not that she'd asked – but Potter wasn't hearing any of it. For a general to be running the show out here, there had to be much bigger fish to fry. It was about the old power station on the mountainside. That was why the Field had been established here.

As Claire turned these thoughts over in her head, she and Andre made small talk. She knew Idaho was still loitering somewhere behind them. He'd get the message. Probably.

#

Once he had, Claire relaxed and Andre told her about the goings-on around the Field. "Couple of guys from the Church with a capital C came by the gate this morning," he said. "A *botar* and a *feder*. Wanted to set up a tent show inside the wall."

"Missionaries must be going out of their way to witness here," Claire said. She batted at a fly that was doing aerial stunts around Rocket's face. Rather than flee, it set about bothering her. She tossed her shoulder-length hair from side to side until the insect was gone.

"You look more and more like your kids every day," Andre said. "No offense."

"None taken, shrub."

Andre let out a hearty laugh that startled the horses grazing at the other end of the field. "You talking about *my* hair? This fro is a historical landmark."

"It's starting to look its age," Claire said with a wry smile. "You can really see the gray when the sun's just overhead."

"Well, now I'm depressed." Andre shoved his hands into his pockets in mock reproach. "You cut deep, Clarissa."

He scratched at the stubble beneath his nose and said, "Yeah, we're well off the beaten path for *feders*. But I'll bet they prefer it that way. People tend to be more on edge out in the middle of nowhere. More open to…'answers.'"

"So what happened? Were they turned away?"

"Eventually. Potter talked to them for a bit, but you know he wasn't about to let them in."

Claire shrugged. "Would it have been so bad?"

"I hear that once the Church gets a foot in," Andre said, "they start wanting to be involved in strategy and then economy. It's less about guiding specific people than 'the people' altogether." He made finger quotes as he spoke, and Claire nodded.

Andre went on. "Besides, the way they tell it, God's already everywhere. You want to talk to Him, talk to Him."

He set about beating the dust from his pants, which meant he was about to go off on some long tangent. Claire didn't mind so long as the horses didn't.

"You'd find it hard to believe, but there was a time when people *wanted* this," Andre said. "I mean the fall of Man. God's got a lot of faces and He's made a lot of promises. People were tired of waiting for Ye Olde Apocalypse for the return on their investment."

"Investment?"

"Faith, works, whatever. And I don't guess it's just those people – a lot of folks who didn't believe in God at all wanted to see the End Times come and go without so much as a fart from the heavens, wanted to know that they were right."

"What does it matter when this is the world we get now?" Claire shook her head.

"Amen," Andre said. "But if you feel like the world you got is a wash and it's never going to do right by you, you might just feel desperate enough to hunger for the end."

Hunger. Nice choice of words. Claire shivered in spite of the weather. Andre caught it and grimaced. "Sorry."

She shrugged it off, and there was an awkward moment of quiet. Then Andre said, "Balls."

"Come again, Corporal?"

"If Idaho or anyone else ever tries to get too cozy. I've probably told you this before."

"Oh." Claire nodded. "Yeah. Eyeballs, testicles. Whichever you can get at. I know. Yes, sir, you've told me a few times."

"Okay, okay." Andre held his hands up in surrender. "Maybe I just like saying 'balls.' I know you handle yourself just fine. I just…you know."

"I know."

Nightfall would bring the dead, and Death. But for now, in the encampment designated Fairfield but affectionately known by another name, there was light and warmth and a comfortable silence.

BEFORE | FALL 2033: AT THE MOUNTAINS OF MOTOR CITY

The bus jostled Andre as he tried to secure the straps on his arm guards. He wished the things weren't so damn light. Then again, they made hoofing it a helluva lot easier. Couldn't have it both ways. He buckled the last strap into place and wiggled his torso. Chest plate felt a little loose. He'd lost ten or twelve pounds since the armor was molded for him. "I can't wear you anywhere," he cursed under his breath as he undid the chest plate's buckles.

"Look alive!" Sergeant Easterling barked. Hanging onto one of the ceiling bars, he swept his free hand in front of each soldier's face. "We're just about at our destination, people. Standard recon bid. Reminder! There is nothing standard about a standard recon bid!" Easterling looked behind him at Elrod, who was piloting the bus. "Slow 'er down and kill those lights!"

Returning his attention to the four soldiers in the back, the sergeant said in a subdued growl, "Ready check."

Andre finished tightening his chest plate and planted the butt of his M4 in his lap. He mouthed along as Easterling said, "Ammo up. Armor up. Eyes up. Nut up."

Andre glanced across the aisle at Corporal Bradford. Her eyes met his and he grinned, mouthing "Nut up" again.

"You two passing notes in my classroom?" Easterling snapped. "Focus, people. MCM is considered up for grabs at this point. That includes slimes. If we can secure this stretch, we'll have a full unit camped here by sunup."

The bus slowed to a stop. It was one of those short rides that used to ferry seniors from the old folks' home to the country buffet. It had been repurposed into a military transport that could withstand the IEDs that were typical along these eastern thoroughfares. Most of the roadside explosives were crude, many quite old, forgotten by those who'd planted them. Andre was glad most of this trip had consisted of off-roading. Now they were in the shadow of the Motor City Mountain, and it was time for new anxiety.

"Suppressors are golden," Easterling said, "but I prefer actual silence. Bullets don't grow on trees out here. Use BFT whenever you can. Of course I'm talking slimes." BFT – blunt force trauma. Breaking a slime's neck with a well-placed blow to the head wouldn't risk waking the other dead, so to speak. And if it did…

"Let's make 'em deader," Easterling said, his requisite sign-off, and the rear door of the bus opened as the vehicle came to a stop.

Andre hopped out, followed by Bradford, Kessler, and Mink. He was immediately dismayed to see that the fog was still clinging. It was early evening, but visibility was ten yards at best thanks to this shit. He adjusted his helmet and spoke softly into the mic by his cheek. "Two by two. No one goes solo without authorization from the sarge. Kessler, you come with me. Bradford, take Mink. Sweep east."

The fog wasn't very high, and Andre could see the looming Mountain – a Great Wall of skeletonized cars, scrap metal and rebar, more a Great Pile upon closer inspection. About three miles long, it was several cars tall and probably just as many thick. The National Guard had helped Detroit authorities throw this heap together two years ago, perhaps hoping to later use walls and cement to fashion a formidable barrier. As it stood, the MCM was a creaking labyrinth of steel. It still held value as a control point, not only against the dead but against anti-military militias in the area: those who blamed the government for what had happened, and who did things like plant roadside bombs. Securing the Mountain would be a lot of work, though. This preliminary sweep was just the beginning. While the decaying city beyond the Mountain had been determined by aerial recon to be virtually clear both of life and unlife, that was only the streets. Quiet streets could be a bad omen.

Andre and Kessler headed west along the wall of cars. Every patch of fog hid jutting rebar and shattered windows. The interiors of partially crushed vehicles were perfect camping spots for either men or slimes. Andre pointed the M4 into each dark space he came across, boots crunching in gravel and glass. He grimaced at the sound, as well as the occasional distant groan of metal. Open window, open windshield, missing door. Clear. Clear. Clear. The Mountain seemed to be composed more of yawning, empty spaces than any actual substance. It was a wonder the heap stood at all.

Another far-off groan. Andre froze.

Kessler was beside him. "Slime," he breathed.

Indeed, just a few yards away, Andre could see a thick, ruddy slick atop the earth. The two men advanced in silence. The trail was spotty, but it was fresh. That meant the thing had fed recently. And fed well.

When the dead's innards began to fall apart and their distended bellies were no longer able to hold what they'd crammed down their gullets, the fruits of their vile labors had to go somewhere. If it wasn't out the ass, the abdomen would eventually perforate and provide release. The slime wasn't really digested tissue – just rotten, like the dead who'd eaten it, too stupid to know when they were stuffed. Andre had once seen a dead guy whose throat was filled to bursting with half-eaten fingers. There'd also been a pulverized eyeball dangling from between his butt cheeks.

It was one of those things that made one wonder how much longer this could go on. The bugs inside the dead, which had brought them back to life and somewhat slowed their decay, weren't enough to sustain the savages. How long would it be before the last dead man just disintegrated?

The answer was simple and terrible. *The world won't run out of them until it's run out of us.*

Andre moved forward in a low crouch. The slime trail angled toward the cars. Where it ended, the crumpled door of a station wagon was smeared with handprints. It looked as if the slime had crawled through the window. Had it heard the bus's approach and sought shelter? Andre switched on the tiny halogen light atop his gun and trained it on the open window. Past the station wagon, he saw a tangle of metal hanging down, the undercarriage of another vehicle. Beyond that, he saw the bumpers of two trucks facing one another. There was enough space in between for a person to squeeze through. The thought of attempting to navigate those narrow, lightless crevices made Andre's stomach turn.

He keyed his mic. "Sarge, you got my twenty?"

Easterling's voice came over his headset. "Ten-four, we've got you. What've you found?"

"Slime," Andre muttered. "Looks like a loner, but I can't be sure. Trail goes cold at the Mountain."

"You mean the sumbitch went inside?"

"Right."

"Great. Thought this might happen." Easterling sighed loudly, making Andre wince. "Come on back. If we're going to hunt, I want to wait 'til the fog clears."

"It may be night by then."

"That only helps us, soldier. Remember, those things are half-blind."

Doesn't matter much when we're all in the dark, Andre thought.

#

The team sat in the bus and watched the windows. The fog seemed to be growing thicker. *Maybe we'll wait until morning,* Andre thought, and that sounded good.

Easterling picked through his teeth with a ballpoint pen, dislodging the no-doubt unpleasant aftertaste of his MRE. He looked at Andre and said, "Command wants the sweep finished by dawn."

"How'd you know what I was thinking?" Andre shifted in his seat. His armor was coming loose again.

"I've known you too damn long," Easterling replied. "My curse."

"Assuming the fog doesn't let up," Bradford said, "We could try a baby drop. Bring them all to us."

"Problem is, we don't know how many of them there are," grunted Kessler.

"We didn't see anything on our end," offered Mink. "No trails, no nothing."

"Yeah, but they might be moving around inside the Mountain." Kessler sucked the last mouthful from a cup of applesauce. "You can never be sure whether you're dealing with smart ones or not. The ones who move in packs."

"Mobs, not packs," Easterling said. "Believe me, no matter how many there are, they're not organized. They follow each other for no good goddamn reason. Thinking the slime in front must have a lead on some prey. Next thing you know, you've got a cluster."

"I believe the scientific term is clusterfuck," Andre said.

"You'd know," the sergeant sighed.

Elrod turned in the driver's seat to face them. "I like the idea of a baby drop. We can use the low visibility to close the net. Worse comes to worst, we've got the bus. Snipe them from the roof."

"Mmm." Easterling seemed to be turning it over in his mind, then said, "All right. But we only use firepower if absolutely necessary. By which I mean a cluster…fuck."

Bradford stood and opened a compartment above her head. She handed out cudgels. The clubs were short and relatively light, made from the same polymer as the armor, but the rounded business end packed a serious punch when used right. BFT. Built for trouble.

"Who gets the crossbow?" Kessler asked. "I say we roll for it."

"It's my damn crossbow," Bradford said. "Get your old man to send you one."

Kessler whistled. "Down, girl."

"You're the one who oughta be on a leash," Easterling said. The team shared a laugh – not too loud, mind you, as the fog's undulating fingers continued to caress the Plexiglas windows. From the corner of his eye, Andre saw the movement, and couldn't help but tense up every time he did.

Equipped with night vision gear, he and Bradford slipped out the back of the bus. Bradford carried a small satchel, which she pulled open as they came around the front of the vehicle. All of the bus's exterior lights remained off, and the enhanced vision offered by the goggles was still hampered by fog. Andre kept his cudgel in hand, but his grip on the M4 was even tighter. He waited while Bradford emptied the satchel's contents onto the ground. She fiddled with the small object, then motioned for Andre to fall back. They rushed to the bus and clambered inside.

"Give me sound," Easterling told Elrod. The driver turned on a set of speakers, and the ambient hiss of night came in.

It was soon broken by a tiny, wretched cry. The wail of an infant.

The baby lure was designed for realistic movement that matched the intensity of its pre-recorded cries. It would lie out there in the dirt, squirming and mewling, for forty-five minutes.

That had to be more than enough time to draw out the slimes. They always responded to the cries of the young, the helpless.

Andre sat still and listened. As soon as they detected approaching footfalls, they'd be back out there with the cudgels (Bradford with her damned beautiful crossbow), and they would begin circling wide around the shambling dead. For all its trouble, the fog would provide great cover. And once the slimes had converged on the baby, they'd be in their very own little killbox and heads would fucking roll.

The team held their collective breath as that litany of pitiful cries pierced the night. Andre detected the creaking of metal from far away and raised a finger. Easterling nodded, whispering, "I hear it."

Kessler moved to the rear door and placed a gloved hand on the release handle. "Just say when."

"Let them get close," Easterling said. "Close enough for a head count." The fog was cloying as ever outside the windows, and they'd have to rely entirely on their ears. The bus had directional mics all over, providing something of a three-dimensional soundscape to those listening in, but Andre still wasn't digging the idea of using that alone to how many slimes. And where exactly they were.

Don't let them get too close.

#

Once they'd counted a half-dozen sets of footfalls, it became harder to identify new targets. The dead were closing in on the baby and their tired, muttered groans poured through the speakers into the bus. Easterling nodded to Kessler, who quietly opened the back door. All but the sarge and Elrod slipped out into the fog.

Easterling's voice was quiet and deliberate in the soldiers' headsets. "Keep your distance. Let's see just how many more come crawling out of the woodwork."

Andre pried his helmet up slightly so that he could listen to the sounds around him. The baby was still wailing. Suddenly, the wail escalated to a scream, and the groans within the mist grew louder. Even after the first slimes attacked the baby, it would continue crying to lure others out. With any luck, whoever grabbed the baby would drop it after realizing it wasn't real. The little guy could withstand a hell of a beating, but if some idiot slime decided to try and eat it, the skin would break eventually.

The groans moved away from Andre's position, as did the screaming. Damn. They were fighting over the frigging thing! Andre rushed forward, cudgel at the ready. He knew he'd be on top of the slimes in a matter of seconds. His goggles jostled atop his head and he steadied them with his free hand. "They're moving the baby," he hissed into his mic. "Gotta hit 'em now."

He didn't wait for a reply from the sarge – couldn't, because suddenly he was face-to-face with two wet, pale-skinned slimes. Neither had the baby. He registered that much before they lunged and he swung.

The cudgel caught the one on the right in the ear with a muffled clap. The dead man's head snapped to the side and he spun on his heels, arms flailing. The female beside him batted the arms out of her way and came at Andre with her filthy mouth yawning wide. He took one step back to plant himself, then threw an overhead swing that caught her square in the middle of her forehead. Her momentum carried her forward and she collided with Andre. Her thin arms wrapped around his waist. Panic seized him as he lost his footing and fell back with the woman atop him. She mashed her face against his chest plate, teeth scraping the plastic, then she looked up and their eyes met. One of hers was filled with black blood now, white in his night vision. The cudgel had split her head and loose skin hung from the wound. It looked like she was wearing a gruesome Halloween mask that had begun to fall apart.

She braced herself on one elbow and reached with her other hand for Andre's face. He grabbed her wrist but she slipped free. Goddamn, they were always slick with weeping sores and sloughing skin; she was probably shedding all over him as they struggled. Andre wanted to retch, but he steeled his gut and brought the cudgel down on her shoulder. No good. Not enough goddamn leverage to do anything, not even distract her; the slime's broken fingernails brushed his cheek and he screamed in spite of himself. He knew her fingers were going to enter his mouth. They were going to grab the root of his tongue and pull it out.

Then Kessler was straddling the dead woman, and he slammed his cudgel down on the back of her neck. She shuddered, eyes still locked on Andre, and he saw whatever was inside her shutting down and her face fell against his chest.

Kessler hauled her off. The male slime pawed at his back. He spun with an angry grunt and smashed the man's temple. Andre heard the slime's neck break.

He pushed the woman off of him. She rolled onto her back and stared lifelessly at the night sky. Kessler must have pulped her brainstem with that blow. As for the male, he lay paralyzed on the ground, still moaning, eyes dancing wildly.

Kessler asked Andre, "You good?"

"Clean. No bites. I'm fine."

"Did she scratch you? Get in your mouth?" Kessler looked concerned, but not for Andre's sake. Andre shook his head.

"Okay." Kessler sent his cudgel into the base of the male slime's skull. Another satisfying splintering sound. The moans ceased.

Andre sat up and fixed his helmet, then checked the straps on his chest plate. All the while his heart was hammering and he was looking from side to side for any movement. Fucking fog! He stood and stilled trembling hands.

"Two slimes down," Kessler said over the radio.

"Make it three," came Bradford's voice. "Where's the damn baby?"

Andre realized he could no longer hear the infant's artificial cries. They'd managed to break it. Now the soldiers were truly flying blind.

But so are they. And I'm faster, and I'm better. Let's make them deader.

He again tried to focus on the sounds around him. Kessler had disappeared into the fog. Faintly, he detected boots scraping the ground. Too rapid to be a slime. One of the other troops stalking their prey.

All right, come on. Use that adrenaline. Get yourself a few kills or you'll be the one cleaning that portable toilet on the bus. The only thing worse than slime is shit, my boy.

He hustled through the fog. Tendrils leapt at his face, then recoiled; he found himself swinging wildly at the ghosts and cursed into his mic. Then a deep groan straight ahead of him caught his attention.

Andre froze and waited. There was only silence and a curtain of mist.

He gritted his teeth and dropped into a defensive stance. Pursing his lips, Andre made a soft kissing sound. *Come and get it.*

A slime dressed like an honest-to-God cowboy came lurching forward. Andre sprang and hurled the cudgel into the man's jaw. The ten-gallon hat bounced atop the slime's head, and he threw his bloated arms out to catch his balance. His hands and forearms were covered in small, crescent-shaped welts. Looked like he'd been bitten by kids. Maybe entertaining at some children's hospital ward when they turned. Poor bastard. No time for pity now; the soul, if there was such a thing, had vacated the premises of Cowboy Steve a long time ago. Andre fell back, set his feet, and threw a crippling blow into the slime's neck. *Snap.*

The man sagged to his knees. Andre quickly followed up with a brutal shot to the temple. The slime's head rolled from one side to the other, and it was apparent that there was little keeping it attached at this point. The slime fell limp. The ten-gallon hat finally hit the dirt.

Andre consulted a compass on his wrist. The digital readout told him he was facing south, away from the Mountain. That'd put the bus somewhere to the southeast, assuming they stayed put. Things seemed to be solid. There hadn't been any radio chatter since Broadford's last statement. That was a good thing. If the shit had hit the fan, he'd have heard about it.

He said into his mic, "Another down."

"They're all over the place now that the baby's stopped," said Kessler. "I just got another one."

"Everybody in one piece?" Mink asked; he was the medic, and would be watching over all of them in the mandatory quarantine to follow once they returned home.

"Fine," Bradford said. "Maybe we ought to regroup and set another lure. Sarge?"

Radio silence. Andre stood in the swirling fog and waited. He thought he heard feet shuffling at his back and spun. Nothing there. Still radio silence. "Sarge," he breathed. "You hear Bradford? Come back."

"Fall back to the bus," Bradford said. Andre headed southeast.

He spotted the bus and made a beeline for the rear door. Mist parted and he saw it – the edge of the door, the open door, and something lying beneath it – and Andre dug his boot heels into the earth and traded the cudgel in his hand for the M4. He sidestepped around the back of the bus and saw what the thing on the ground was. A slime was crouched over something, tearing viciously with its teeth, grunting with the effort. The wisp-thin hairs on its head tossed about. Andre's heart dropped into his stomach like a runaway elevator, and an involuntary moan escaped his lips.

The slime didn't react. It pushed down on the body upon which it was feeding, and with the frenzied wrenching of its head, managed to tear a huge chunk away from Sergeant Easterling's face.

Andre stared into the bus. PFC Elrod was splayed out on the floor with another slime straddling him. Every surface was painted liquid black in Andre's night vision. He yanked the goggles off his head, knocking his helmet off, and black turned to rich flowing red. It poured and sputtered from places in the two fallen men, and neither of their killers had yet acknowledged Andre's presence. He reached up for his headset mic, to tell the others, and realized when it wasn't there that he'd lost the helmet.

Talk was cheap, he decided, in the part of his mind that could still form a thought over a storm of wordless screams. He lowered the M4's muzzle to the head of the dead man eating his sergeant. A burst of suppressed gunfire sent the fiend's quivering gray brains spraying all over Easterling. Andre put his boot on the slime's back and shoved it out of his path. He stepped onto the bus's bumper and took aim at the second creep.

"No!" Bradford cried at his back. He knew she was reacting to the sight of the fallen and didn't hesitate to fire. The second slime jerked up and back against the seats. It gawked at Andre. He put another generous burst through its mouth and watched the head collapse. Behind it, the windshield fractured and folded inward.

"Jesus!" Bradford pushed past Andre and climbed into the bus. "How? Why would he open – was the door secure? Kessler! Mink! *Where the fuck are you?"*

She stepped through the remains of the slime and dropped into the driver's seat. Andre slumped into the seat beside her and flipped on the headlamps. He felt numb as he went down the array of dashboard controls, throwing on the exterior lamps to help Kessler and Mink find them. Didn't matter if it tipped off any slimes. They were scrubbing this clusterfuck. The word made Andre think of Easterling. It was a weird random thought, him and Easterling grilling burgers in a mess tent outside Fort Wayne. Maybe it was the smell of blood in here. Andre's gorge rose, and he clenched his mouth shut.

"Watch our six," said Bradford as she started the engine. Andre looked back at the rear entrance. Nothing there, human or otherwise. No sounds either. Then Kessler lurched into view, slamming into the open door, which rebounded off its hinges and hit him back. Andre jumped in his seat. He felt his finger slipping across the M4's trigger and had to pull his whole hand away to keep from firing. He managed to croak, "Come on, Kessler!"

Kessler looked up at him with glassy eyes and said nothing. He just shook his head. As he turned from the doorway, Andre saw the wound in the back of Kessler's left shoulder. All of his back armor was gone. Long gashes raked over his shoulder blade and sank deep into his lower back. His left arm, similarly stripped of its armor, hung uselessly; a ragged strip of meat had been ripped from it, and his elbow was hanging out.

He must have been in severe shock, because he didn't so much as flinch when a slime came tearing through the fog and tackled him. Kessler dropped like a sack of potatoes. The world lurched and heaved beneath Andre. He thought he was about to lose consciousness, then realized it was due to the bus accelerating.

"Dump the bodies and get the door closed!" yelled Bradford.

"Mink!" Andre cried.

"He's on his own!" Bradford punched the steering wheel. "You know it, so just secure the damn bus!"

"We can get him—"

"NOW!" Bradford shouted. Andre fell from the seat and crawled along the wall to the rear. He grabbed a support bar and reached for Elrod's shoulder. He dragged the body to the doorway and, getting his arm under Elrod's shoulder, heaved him out. The man's legs flew up and out, and he was gone like the rest.

He snagged the dead slime by the arm and tossed the corpse. The door was rattling madly and swung out of reach every time he dared lean out the doorway. "Slow down!" he yelled, but Bradford probably didn't hear him.

The bus's wheels rose off the ground on the right. The door handle practically leapt into Andre's hand and he yanked it. The door locked into place even as the bus continued to tilt perilously. Metal screamed. So did Bradford. Andre looked out the front and saw they'd run up against Motor City Mountain. Its jagged slope was going to dump them over on their side. Bradford was pulling at the wheel, but it was clearly too late.

We're going to roll. We're done.

Andre was flung into the wall as his prediction came true. The last thing he saw before blacking out was the rear door popping open again.

That's just bad comedy.

This whole thing is.

A cosmic goof, and no one around with the cosmic stones to give us a laugh. Shame.

#

He must only have been out for a minute or so. Bradford was shaking him and, as soon as his eyes opened, she turned away and busied herself emptying the cabinets whose contents hadn't already spilled. She shoveled MREs and ammo clips into a backpack. "Andre, grab flares. Get yourself a helmet."

Andre sat up in the overturned bus and rubbed his head. "Where are we going?" he asked through an aching haze.

"High ground," Bradford said. "Come on, move your ass! They're going to come."

He did as he was told. Everything felt far away, even in his hands; it was as if all sensation had left his flesh. Or maybe he was just disconnected from feeling. Maybe he was just a thought, still ricocheting off the walls inside his head. Explained the nausea. Andre filled a pack and slung it over his shoulder. He and Bradford were both corporals, but she had seniority. He supposed she was his sergeant now. Hell of a way to get a promotion, but that was how it usually went.

He and Bradford knelt to exit through the sideways rear entrance. The fog swam in to greet them and Bradford swept angrily at it. "We're going up."

She leapt to grab the wheel well of a pickup that was sandwiched between two crumpled vans. "Don't think, just climb."

To the top of the Great Wall, then. As good a plan as any, for those lunatics who had a need to see tomorrow. Andre followed Bradford's lead and caught hold of the same truck. He lifted his feet off the ground hung there. When she'd said, "don't think" she must have meant, *don't think about the fact that you have neither the will nor the strength for this.* And she was right – thinking was what made a man hesitate before the dark when his steed was champing at the bit. Sometimes you just had to trust your horse.

Andre hauled himself up, getting a foothold on the van underneath the truck. He pulled himself past the pickup's bed and found an open window in the vehicle overhead. This one was slightly recessed and allowed him to plant his feet in the truck bed. Two levels up already. *Stop thinking about it.* He hauled his feet up and back into the open air.

Above him, Bradford grunted, "We're clearing the fog," and slung her arm around the roll cage of an upended four-by-four. The Mountain groaned around them. Andre held still until the wall's complaining subsided. As it did, he detected an alien hiss from below and chanced a glance over his shoulder.

The lights from the bus cast an eerie glow throughout the sea of fog. A trio of slimes were visible in silhouette, gathered at the base of the wall. They began beating their hands against the vehicles. They were trying to climb.

"Bradford—" Andre coughed, and he felt his hold weakening and grabbed in a panic at the nearest door handle. The door swung open, tearing free of his grip, and a black-eyed woman leaned out of the shadows beyond and snarled.

"Fuck!" Andre tried to swing himself out of her reach, but he couldn't manage it. From his knuckles to his elbow every joint was screaming. The noises from below rose to a cacophony of groans. They knew he was losing it. *No!* He was hanging from the wall by his right hand, and the M4 was slung over that shoulder. He slapped at the barrel with his left hand. "Bradford! Jesus!"

"Just hold on!" Bradford hollered. Andre kept his eyes on the female leering from the open door. She swiped at him with a mottled, bony arm. He was kicking his legs in fear, and it was only increasing the strain on his arm. He couldn't hold still with this undead bitch clawing at the air in front of his face! The slime let out a hissing growl. Her face – so feral, so hateful, more like a starving animal than a shambling automaton. She was naked, and the shriveled lumps of her breasts heaved with every hungry lunge. The gray, pockmarked skin of the woman's cheeks split like gills opening as she howled at him.

He looked up. Bradford had her crossbow in hand and was trying to line up a shot. It looked like the open car door was in her way. Andre looked back at the slime. *Just lean out here a little more. Give her a headshot.*

"Come on," he whispered at the slime, unable to muster anything resembling a war cry. "You want it so bad? I'm right here." His voice trembled in time with the muscles quivering in his arm. The slimes beneath him were pounding on the wall. They weren't rooting for the female. They wanted him to give up and drop.

"I'll let them take me," he snapped, and the woman almost seemed to understand. She made a mad lunge from the safety of the car, herself only hanging on by one hand; and a steel bolt struck through her collarbone with a THWOCK!

The woman hissed. She lost it. She tumbled from the car and down the Mountain.

Andre slung his left arm into the driver's seat the woman had vacated. He flailed and scrambled and caught hold of a seat belt. One foot found a tire and he steadied himself. God. He'd made it.

Andre craned his neck to give Bradford a nod of thanks. She returned the nod and shouldered the crossbow.

A half-rotted claw emerged from beneath a bumper at Bradford's left. Andre shouted her name, and she looked at him and then from side to side. The dead hand caught her hair in a vise grip.

Bradford let out a cry of shock. She fell away from the wall, but the hand held fast, and she was spun around by her hair. The crossbow slipped from her body and dropped into the fog. The strap of her M4 slid off her shoulder. She caught it blindly, unable to look down as the hand wrenching at her hair was joined by a second.

Fucking God, the Mountain's full of them! Andre began hauling himself into the car. He might be able to reach her hand if stood in the seat – she might have to drop but he'd catch her, there was no question, he had to.

He didn't.

Bradford had reached up to grab her hair and wrestle with the hands. Blood was running from her scalp into her eyes, and she'd begun kicking and screaming. Then she was falling. She passed Andre in a whirling blur of limbs and pleading cries.

He heard her hit the ground. He heard bone break.

Andre aimed his rifle down into the fog and squeezed off a burst at the shadowy trio of dead. He couldn't tell if he'd hit anything. That damnable fog seemed to close ranks around the slimes, and he could no longer see any shade of them.

Suppressed gunfire erupted down below. Bradford screamed again, this time in anger as much as fear. Andre could only sit there in that seat and stare down and listen and wait for something to end.

The firing stopped for a second. Then there was a final shot.

Andre looked up at the hands that had tried to take her. They were still sticking out into the air, both clutching clumps of red hair like consolation prizes.

A head with less of a face than a skull wormed its way out from that same space. Its soulless eyes fell upon Andre, and it opened its mouth, rivulets of slime streaming down. They spattered the windshield of Andre's car and he ducked inside.

There was now only the sound of the dead – grunting, tearing. Feeding on Bradford and clambering about inside the Mountain.

They were coming for him. He took his backpack and rummaged through it. He had maybe enough rounds to make a stand until dawn. Dawn, when surely someone would be sent to find what had become of the soldiers.

But they'd send a chopper, not ground forces. They might not touch down when they saw the bus and the dead around it. *Forget the Mountain,* they'd say. *Bomb it to Hell.*

Damn it all. They should have tried to raise someone on the radio before abandoning the bus. Even if the odds were slim, any odds were good in the face of this. The slimes at the base of the Mountain had begun scrabbling at it again. Steel creaked overhead. Andre threw the pack into the back of the car and followed it. Had to hunker down and wait out the dead. They'd forget what all the fuss was about before long. Maybe he'd be able to bug out before the wall was melted to slag.

The passenger side doors and windows were all blocked off. Through the rear windshield, Andre saw a mess of broken bricks and glass. There wouldn't be any getting into the trunk from outside. Might mean his safe haven. He switched on his light long enough to look for any levers atop the rear seats, something that would allow trunk access. He spied a grimy switch on the far left and killed the light. He pulled at the switch. It was stuck fast, probably jammed. He gritted his teeth and put his weight into it. "Come on, fucker."

That seemed to intimidate the switch, which popped loose, and Andre folded down the seatback and shone his light into the trunk.

Cramped, filthy. The smell of motor oil. A jack and a tire iron lay in a brown puddle. It was safe. He slung his pack inside, then turned and wormed his way backwards into the trunk.

Pulling the seatback into its original position, he silently prayed that he hadn't permanently broken the latch which secured it. There was a faint click as the seat settled into place, and he told himself that was good enough.

Lying on his side in a fetal crouch, M4 clutched to his chest, Andre panned his little light around the space. Satisfied there was nothing more to see, he switched it off. The only light now came from the readout on his wrist compass. He switched the display to show the time. Just after midnight. Christ. The minutes were going to feel like hours. Every second accompanied by the random creeping creaks from within the Mountain. He held still and listened.

At first, it was easy to separate the sounds of alien movement from the other ambient noise. He could hear a slime somewhere above him, maybe in another vehicle and trying to find a path down. The slimes at the bottom of the wall were still pushing and pulling at it, but their echoing struggles sounded weaker than before. He lay there, ignoring the stiffness in his back and his wheezy breathing, and in time, the movement overhead stopped.

That only meant the dead would lie inert until something caught their attention. He'd still have to deal with them when he got out. At least he might be able to catch them off guard. And maybe, just maybe, if there was anything such as mercy left in this world, the fog would be gone.

#

The brass should have just sent a full unit to begin with. This stupid preliminary sweep was only about procedure, crossing T's and dotting I's. Hell, it would have been just four men had Bradford and Mink not been added at the last minute. The two had a lot of field experience. Maybe Mink was even alive. He was a medic after all. The helmet Andre had taken from the bus lacked a headset and mic. Just as well. He didn't feel like talking. He just wanted to play dead.

A loud, metallic squeal made his legs jump, and he kicked the side of the trunk. He grimaced and forced himself to lie frozen. God, his back was really starting to hurt. There wasn't any room to stretch in here. He listened for any follow-up to the squeal and heard none. Some junker settling within the Mountain. The slimes themselves were probably used to that kind of noise. He could use that to his advantage when he escaped.

And then? Then he'd be on foot. Best to head into Detroit and find a real shelter. At that point, he'd be less worried about slimes than militias; more likely, less-organized raiders. They'd have a field day with a lone soldier loaded down with ammo.

His head resting against the trunk's dirty floor, Andre shut his eyes. Not to sleep – didn't want to chance that – but to go into a darkness that was his and his alone.

#

When he stirred, his first thought was: *I was asleep.*

Then: *What woke me?*

Something moved in the front of the car.

He turned on the light atop the M4 and aimed at the seatback. He could hear it clearly now – flesh slipping over upholstery, uncertain limbs shuffling in the dark. Andre looked at his wrist. It was 1:18 in the A.M. God, it had only been that long. It had only taken them that long.

The seat creaked. Andre held his breath and waited. If the slime just left, just moved on in its search, he could stay here. What slime would know how to open—?

And the seatback came down.

He saw a tiny, lithe figure, tatters of clothing hanging off its frame, its hair white and its eyes dead, the face peppered with bruises and mottles. It was a child, a child, and its pupils shrank in the light, and it raised its terrible little claws.

For half a second and nothing more, Andre was paralyzed with horror. A child. A little girl. This was the end of it. He couldn't do this anymore. He couldn't breathe, couldn't feel. Yet instinct took over and he felt the trigger beneath his finger.

But then—

The girl was alive.

She flinched away from his gun and shielded her face. Her hair was blonde, not white. Her skin was dirty but not cadaverous. When she showed her face again, he saw a reflection of his own terror.

Andre let out a soft moan and lowered the rifle. He'd nearly killed her.

"You can't be," he whispered, in spite of himself.

The girl's eyes were wet and pleading. Her mouth moved as if she were trying to form some response to what he'd said. Andre shook his head, dismissing his remark, and breathed, "Are you alone?"

The girl, who must have been just seven or eight years old, nodded.

"Are you okay…hurt?"

"Not bit," she said, baring her arms. She knew what he was really asking.

Andre sat up and whispered, "How did you know I was here?"

"I didn't," the girl said. The Mountain groaned and she drew into herself, eyes darting about. After a moment's pause, she said, "This is my place. I stuck the seat so it wouldn't open."

So that was why the seatback had been jammed. Whatever it was she'd done, she was smart. Andre wanted to ask how long she'd been here, but the more pressing question was how to get out to the Detroit side.

"We can get up top," she told him, "but then you'd have to climb down and it's not safe. They can get you."

Andre took a few clips and MREs from his pack, stuffing everything he could into the pockets of his uniform. "You'll be all right with me. Show me how you get up top."

"Promise?"

"Promise…?"

"It'll be okay?"

"I'll keep you safe," Andre told her. The words rang hollow in his head and he forced a grim smile.

The girl pointed upward, and Andre noticed for the first time that the car had a moon roof. That must have been where she came from. The girl began pulling herself up and Andre said, "I should go first."

"You don't know the way," she replied, her head and arms disappearing through the opening.

With no other reasonable option, Andre followed her up and into the dark.

The space above the car was pitch-black and tight as hell. Easy enough for the girl to navigate, but Andre found himself stuck halfway through the moon roof. He pushed the M4 across the top of the car and switched on its light.

The girl was crouched nearby. Above her, a trick lay on its side and she was reaching for the wheel well. "Turn it off!" she hissed.

Andre killed the light and they both sat motionless. If they hadn't seen the light, the slimes sure as hell could have heard her protest. Shit. Andre's legs dangled helplessly through the moon roof and fear began to set in again. He thought of the black-eyed woman and imagined her stripping his legs first of armor, then clothing, and finally meat.

He pulled himself along the top of the car. His back ached terribly, more so as he tried to angle his body so that he could bend and lift one leg through the moon roof. The only thing more claustrophobic than this cramped space was the darkness that filled it, enveloping and consuming him. His hands trembling violently, he fought to pull himself free of the car.

Hands seized his wrist. He almost cried out, but the girl said, "It's okay," and she tugged. Her strength wasn't much help. But the fact that she was trying, trying to save him, gave Andre a feeling of—hope?—and he worked one leg free, then the other, rolling onto his back atop the vehicle and panting.

"Up," said the girl. No rest for the damned.

#

The pair stood atop Motor City Mountain and surveyed the urban rot of Detroit.

There wasn't a great deal to see beneath the stars, just the outlines of skeletonized buildings, little more than steel frameworks jutting out from the earth like broken bones through flesh.

"I need to use my light for a second," Andre told the girl. He could see her uneasy frown in the night, but she nodded.

"My name's Andre," he told her.

"I'm Claire."

He nodded and switched on the light. He panned it over the cars around them, stepping to the edge of the wall. He spotted something standing nearby and moved toward it. It was a telephone pole. The lines were still connected to it, and they led out into the city. Andre squinted and tried to make out where exactly they went. It looked like they might pass over the roof of a small building about a hundred yards off.

He shut off the light, secured the pack and rifle on his back, then gestured to Claire. "I want you to get on my back and hold onto me."

"I don't want to climb down," she said. "They'll get us."

"We're not going down. We're going across." Andre gestured at the telephone lines.

"That's electric," Claire said.

"There's no power," Andre replied. "Trust me." *I'm saving one life tonight, even if it's not mine.*

Claire wrapped her arms around his neck. Andre crept to the very edge of the wall and reached for the pole. It was just beyond his grasp. "I have to step off the wall," he said. "It'll be okay. I'll grab the pole then we'll be off this thing. All right?"

"Okay," Claire said without a hint of confidence.

Andre swung his right foot out into space. He leaned forward, arms straining for the pole—gravity took hold of him and he lunged, Claire yelping on his back. He caught the top of the pole with both hands and slammed into it with enough force to knock the air out of his lungs.

"Did we make it? Did we make it?" Claire cried. Andre hung limp, waiting for his chest to relax so he could breathe again.

He wheezed, "Made it," and set about working his way around the pole. As soon as there was a line within reach, he grabbed it.

"Get your legs around my waist," he told the girl. She did, and the pressure on his windpipe eased up. He moved away from the pole and began moving hand over hand through the night. It took far less time than he'd imagined; he was concentrated on the girl's grip and making sure she didn't lose it. Once they were above the roof, he grunted, "Can you climb down my legs and hop off? Bit of a drop here."

Claire did so, pulling off most of his leg armor in the process. At least his pants stayed on. She dropped the last foot or so to the rooftop, and he followed suit, landing in the crouch that lasted maybe half a second before he folded, exhausted.

"It's okay," he said to the stars overhead. "Just need a minute."

Claire sat down beside him. She was shivering. He realized it wasn't from the temperature and patted her arm. She jumped at his touch.

"Whoa. Sorry, kiddo. We're safe now."

"I'm never going back," she said, hugging her arms to her chest.

"Of course not. We're going to get to somewhere safe."

Andre sat up and examined their surroundings. There didn't appear to be any way to access the inside of the building from here. But that meant no one could get to them either. There were taller buildings on either side of them, the windows all smashed out and dark. Seemed quiet. He walked around the perimeter and made sure there weren't any ladders. Then he sat back down and began picking up the armor plates he'd lost. "How long were you in there? What happened?"

"I don't know."

"Don't know which?"

"Either." Claire rocked gently back and forth, staring at her feet. She was wearing dirty socks that looked about ready to disintegrate. "I have trouble remembering when I...when it's bad."

"Okay. I get that." Andre replaced the armor on his legs. "I just don't know how you lasted on your own. You must be tough. Smart too. What grade are you in?"

"I don't go to school anymore," she said. "But I..." She looked as if she was struggling to recall. Andre sat quietly while she studied her feet. "I know how to read and stuff. I can do the times table."

"Pretty good for...eight?"

"Almost. Seven. My birthday is in winter." She looked up at him. "How old are you?"

"Twenty-something," he said. In truth, he was almost certain it was closer to thirty, but even before the shit hit the fan, he'd been fuzzy on things like time. A lot of gaps, missing days and nights and some things he was trying to forget. His trouble with remembering was that the worst shit stayed firmly fixed in his brain. Too much real estate upstairs belonged to...

When it's bad.

"Have you been a soldier for a long time?" Claire asked. He suspected she already knew the answer, but he shook his head. "Drafted. Just a few years now."

"What did you do before then?"

He smiled a little. "I told jokes."

Claire wrinkled her nose at him. "What?"

"I was a stand-up...I guess you're not old enough to know about stuff like that. I'd get up on a stage and tell jokes."

"Like what?"

"Nothing I can repeat," he said. "It was grown-up stuff."

She stared at him as if to say, *and what's this shit I've been going through?* But instead, she said, "You got paid?"

Andre laughed. Claire flinched at the volume and he caught himself mid-chortle. "Sorry. Yeah, I got paid sometimes. When I didn't walk the entire room. Used to get into it with the drunks. People drank at these things."

Claire's expression was blank. Andre said, "You know, beer."

She shook her head. "Don't know it."

"God bless you, child." Andre rested his chin on his folded hands. "They used to call me Dozens. I was pretty good at mixing it up. I wasn't a fighter, though."

"What was it like when it happened?"

Andre sighed. "You mean when people started changing?"

"Yeah."

"You know, funny thing...not funny really, just weird. For the longest time, we all acted like it wasn't going to happen to us. Like it was just something on the news, and the government was going to fix it and we'd all wake up tomorrow in the real world. But that didn't happen.

"The bugs...the nanos, you know, the little machines that change people?" Claire nodded at Andre, and he went on. "Well, they were everywhere. Inside people all over the place who didn't even know it. We never had a chance. It was always going to be this."

He gestured at the ruin around them. "It's in our nature, I think."

Claire said, "I heard other people with you. Are they dead?"

Andre had thought the conversation couldn't get any darker. He slowly nodded once.

"All of them?"

"I believe so. But you're safe. That's what matters."

"Because of them, too."

"Very much so, yes."

"What were their names?"

Andre closed his eyes. There was a thick clot of grief swelling in his chest, and he swallowed it down painfully. "Al Easterling. Rob Elrod. Scott Kessler. Chris Mink. Courtney Bradford."

"I'm sorry they died," Claire said. Then, "We should get away before they come back."

There was a faint snarl from the direction of the Mountain. Andre stood, M4 at the ready. He looked over the MCM's uneven silhouette. Something was atop it, kneeling.

"It's *her*," Claire breathed. "Kill her, please kill her."

Andre took aim. The shape atop the wall hissed and dropped out of sight. He could hear the thing scrambling about within the wall.

"Her?" he said from the corner of his mouth.

"The shrike."

Andre crouched beside Claire. "What's that?"

Claire shook her head. "She's going to come back. You have to get her."

"I can't see anything out there," Andre said. "Look, we're good up here until morning. I'll stay awake all night."

"Me too." Claire began shivering again. "The shrike is the worst one. She's fast."

"Why do you call her that?"

"A shrike's a bird," Claire said. "It catches grasshoppers and sticks them on things. Like barbed wire. It sticks them there and saves them for later."

When the connection dawned on Andre, he lowered the rifle and sat. "She...you've seen that?"

Thin lines of tears ran down Claire's cheeks. "Sometimes people come near. Sometimes they tried to get into the wall and help me. She got them."

Andre felt cold in his bones. He said, "Naked. Long hair and black eyes."

Claire nodded.

Andre put his arm around her shoulders and pulled her close. She didn't flinch away. She put her arms around him and shook with sobs. He rocked her, all the while his eyes fixed on the Mountain, and he continued rocking her when her breathing became soft and measured. He watched the Mountain, an amorphous thing of shadow, a monster in itself, until dawn.

TWO | SUMMER 2048: THE REAPER COMES AND CUTS THE ROWS

As evening fell, Claire walked down the main road which led past a security station and the MASH clinic. She heard sounds of small talk and, up ahead, barked orders from the other side of the creek. She'd be returning to the stables after dark to keep an eye on Emeli, one of two pregnant mares. Emeli was close. But for now, Claire wanted to find a perch atop the security wall to watch the sunset.

She crossed the bridge over the creek which separated the rest of the Field from the forward area restricted to military personnel. Andre had sweet-talked someone into giving her an anytime pass. He'd said it was necessary since she took care of the horses. Sometimes she came down here and trained soldiers to ride. Tried, anyway.

Andre and another man were outside the barracks working on a Jeep. The vehicle had been found here when the Field was established, and ever since, they'd been refurbishing it piece by piece. New parts didn't come in very often; required more wheeling and dealing on Andre's part to get those rare treasures sent out here to the ass-end of the world.

Claire didn't know what they were going to do with the Jeep without fuel. Maybe it was just something to do. "Progress" wasn't a word in the Fairfield lexicon. They were mostly sitting and waiting, waiting for Big Things to come down the pike and light a fire under their purpose. It was all about that dead power station on the mountainside. Andre told her that, as with the Jeep, the components necessary to turn the Army's dreams into reality came at an agonizing, indifferent trickle.

Andre waved to Claire as she approached. "You know B.D.?"

The other man, his balding head adorned with an eyepatch, gave her a nod. "Horse whisperer, right?"

Claire returned the nod. "You're a doctor."

"The one-eyed wonder doc," said Andre. "He's almost as good at emergency surgery as he is auto repair."

"Socket wrench, nurse," B.D. said, extending his hand to Andre.

"Ben here was just telling me," Andre said, handing B.D. the tool he'd requested, "about his cat. Thing lived seventeen years out there in the nothing."

"We were stationed in Nebraska," said B.D. "My C.O. hated that cat. Said it was a medical risk. But Paddy never so much as sniffed in the direction of the O.R. tent. Cats know death. They've got that sixth sense, you know."

"I just don't know how Paddy tolerated you given his sense of smell," Andre chimed in.

"You know, Dozens, the only thing more enjoyable than telling a story is *trying* to tell one." B.D. wiggled the socket wrench at him. "I'm gonna tighten your bolts one of these nights."

Andre grinned, but said nothing. Looked to Claire like he'd read between the lines of B.D.'s friendly old smile.

"I've seen cats weaving all nonchalant through hordes of slimes," B.D. continued. "They know the dead aren't people. We're still debating it."

"Well, the Church is," said Andre.

"The cults too," said Claire.

B.D. gave her an odd look, then shrugged. "I don't know about any of that cult business. But the Church, they're wasting their time on the sort of research they do. Still looking for the soul. I tell you, if there's a soul, slimes don't have it."

B.D. hunched over the open hood of the Jeep. Andre told Claire, "My mom had a cat. Cold little shit. Tried to kill me."

"Right," Claire said. "You're what they call a *provocateur*. I'm sure you had it coming."

"No, really. I was staying with my mom, and the minute she leaves to run errands, this thing starts leaping and turning around me like a weed whacker. Cut my arms and legs up good. I lock myself in the laundry room and he's still trying to get me." Andre thrust his arms out, gnarled like the claws of a demon, and made a heinous mewling sound. "Paws come under the door looking for me. Meanwhile, I'm trying to find paper towels and then…"

B.D. had risen and was listening now. Andre stood and paced a small circle.

"Then…?" Claire pressed.

"There was this show called *The X-Files*. Remember that, Ben? Remember the one about the guy who ate people's livers?"

B.D. let out a chortle. Evidently, he saw where this was going. Claire had never seen a working TV in her life and was still lost in suspense. "Then…?"

"This fucking—this cat somehow starts squeezing itself under the door," Andre said, eyes wide. "There's maybe an inch, and inch and a half of space. Linoleum floor. I swear this thing turned itself into Gak and started oozing into the room." He made the ominous mewling sound again and reached his imaginary claws toward Claire. "First its arms, then its head. Its face comes sliding under the door like it's being spat from a printer."

"A printer?" Claire asked.

"Not 3-D," Andre said. "Not the ones they use for armor and things. An ink printer that makes pictures. This flat, smeared face is oozing into the room. One eye, then the other." Andre made his eye bug out and cross. "The head's through. It reforms into a car shape. But for one second, I swear to you I saw its true form." He shivered.

Claire rolled her eyes, but she was grinning. She waved at him to go on.

"What'd you do, brave sir knight?" B.D. asked.

"Well, there's one thing I've always known about cats," Andre said. "If you put a shirt or a towel over them, they shut down. Like robots." Andre's arms and head fell limp. *"Mrrrrowww,"* he murmured.

"So I threw a bath towel over his head, and he stops. After a minute—the longest minute of my life, Claire—he begins to withdraw from the room. The towel goes flat."

Andre wiped his brow. "I lay there until Mom got back. The cat denied everything."

"And this really happened," said Claire.

"Would I lie?"

"It's not an old bit?"

Andre crossed his arms and gave Claire a stern look. "Reality is stranger than fiction, Clarissa."

"Like a printer," B.D. chuckled. "I can see it. That's good.

"Speaking of reality," he said, voice lowering lightly. "And printers. Don't suppose I ever told you how I became the one-eyed wonder doc."

Andre shook his head. "Figured it must have happened after the shit hit the fan."

"Right around there," B.D. said. He glanced at Claire. "Not for the squeamish."

She shrugged. "I've seen stuff."

B.D. cocked his head in deference and said, "So back then, right before everything went south, I got my new eye. Lost the old one to macular degeneration. It meant my career if I couldn't get a transplant pronto. Nerves and all."

Suddenly, Claire knew where the story was going, and in spite of her best efforts at steadying herself, her stomach turned.

3-D printing, industrial robots creating food, tools and even organs from raw materials—it had changed the world, they said. At first for the better. But nothing seemed to stay pretty very long in Man's hands.

With one's own cells, set in a sugar gel, they had been able to replicate healthy organs customized to the consumer. First ears, then livers, and before long, anything was possible. A severed and crushed hand could be printed—bones, tendons, veins, nerves, the whole enchilada—and successfully attached to the arm. With the use of stem cells, they had been able to restore sight to the blind and had given quadriplegics the use of their limbs.

Claire had been told many times about how it all came down. About some corporation based in China who'd been looking to the future—to the possibility of rolling one-size-fits-all organs off their assembly lines, "smart organs" that could function properly in anyone's system, regardless of blood type or anything else. They'd been doing research involving nanorobotics. The research was young. The bots weren't meant to be introduced into production yet.

Someone somewhere screwed up. A mislabeled lot, a tired worker, could have been any number of things. But it only had to happen once.

The organs had been implanted in people all over the western world before anyone realized. They only realized when people started dying.

The nanobots, assuming the task of biological maintenance, were attacked by the host's immune system. They had not been coded to cooperate with natural defenses. The bots fought back. They won. Despite the host's imminent death—or, perhaps because of it—the "bugs" replicated and set about adapting the entire body to run their way. They were able to resume basic brain function. But the person they'd killed was gone.

B.D. must have noticed Claire's expression, since he cleaned up the story's ending and didn't tell them how exactly he'd removed his new eye. "I was in a panic," he said. "No one knew which organs were infected and which weren't. If thine eye offends thee, right? I guess I was wrong, either that or I plucked it before the bugs spread. I don't know. We learned that bugs become inert and break down outside the body. No way to tell if the eye had been bad or not." He went back to working on the Jeep. That was that.

"Where you going to be camped out tonight?" Andre asked Claire.

"Probably on the wall by the reservoir," she said. "Then I have to get back to the stable."

"Best get a move on." Andre gave her a casual salute. "Be safe."

"Always," Claire told him, and headed back toward the bridge. The creek, which came in under the south wall and emptied into the reservoir at the north wall, was a muted blue-gray. It had been artificially created, branching off from a river some miles away and carved into a shallow slope in order to make it flow northward across the Field. The water rolled along at a leisurely pace. These moments at the end of the day were about as calm as one could ever hope for. Claire paused on the bridge and watched the water. She saw something floating toward her, a dark thing bobbing up and down. It looked like a large fruit. It seemed to pause in its progress. Was it caught on something beneath the surface?

The object began moving again. Something long and ragged-looking, like a piece of driftwood, appeared alongside it.

Then the round thing rose slightly, and it was close enough now that Claire could see that it was a head. It was—

"God. Slime!" Claire shouted. In her mind, she was already off the bridge and running down the main road. But her feet were fused to the planks, knees locked. She shook and stared as the dead thing floated toward her. The driftwood lifted and became an arm that grasped hungrily at the air.

"Claire!" Andre shouted from a world away. "This way! Come to me!"

She looked toward him and felt like she was looking at a miniature Andre, waving its stick arms and hopping up and down next to a toy Jeep. B.D. was holding a rifle. Andre started running.

A heavy thud jolted Claire, and she saw that the slime had hit the bridge and slung its arm over the side. It was a male with black, stringy hair plastered across its shredded face. It gargled at her.

She bolted from the bridge and collided with Andre. He pushed her toward B.D. "Son of a bitch!" he grunted. "How did it drift in under the wall? There's no room for a goddamned—"

There was a thunderclap accompanied by a bloom of orange light. Claire tumbled to the earth as a wave of heat struck her. Andre threw himself down beside her. The rising orange flower swelled and then became a terrible, angry black. Pieces of the bridge rained down through the smoke.

"Did it—what?" Claire sat up at the realization she couldn't hear herself. A tinny peal bounced back and forth between her ears. Andre leaned into her face and his lips moved. She shook her head. Behind him, the smoke seemed to multiply ad swim toward them. Claire had a sudden recollection of screams in fog and she seized Andre's arm hard.

"Hear me now?" Andre shouted. She nodded.

He started to say something else, but a metallic wail filled the air. A soldier had climbed onto the roof of the barracks and was cranking a hand-powered air raid siren.

Claire and Andre stood. B.D. joined them and aimed his rifle into the approaching haze. The smoke was thinning, but the creek was still obscured from sight.

"Don't bother!" Andre yelled. "Fucking thing is what blew up!"

B.D. stared at Andre. He said, "Slime was rigged? A bomb?"

Another explosion sounded to the south. Soldiers raced past Claire and the others. "We gotta roll!" B.D. said, and followed the troops.

"Stay in the barracks!" Andre told Claire.

"Bullshit!" she yelled. "My horses!"

"You can't swim across, Claire!" Andre pushed her toward the barracks. The siren rose to an ear-splitting crescendo. "Come on!" he said, eyes pleading. "I gotta go! I'll secure the stable! You stay!"

He stared hard into her eyes and she gave him a firm nod. He took off running.

Claire headed toward the barracks. She passed the entrance and skirted around the building in the direction of the forward command post. The armory was there.

#

The second explosion had been the south wall over the creek. Another slime in the water, it appeared. Andre still didn't understand how one of them could have squeezed under that wall while it was still standing. Would have become stuck in all the barbed wire and rocks planted there. Maybe the current had helped it through. And now…now there was a nice big smoking gap for any others to use.

Wired to explode. Probably had IEDs sewn into their body cavities. Went off after impacting something solid at just the right angle. It was the work of humans. Raiders. But why dare fuck with a fortified military installation, even one as remote as this?

There were screams from the direction of the mountain. The suburbs. At the wall, the creek was shallow enough to wade across. Andre and several others headed for the screaming.

He heard another explosion somewhere behind him. Goddamn! How could they have even gotten this close without being spotted by sentries? The slimes must have deposited in the creek miles off.

Another explosion, a big one. That one came from the north. Had another section of the wall been wiped out?

Maybe it wasn't raiders. Too coordinated. Too smart.

The red-streaked evening sky was beginning to darken with smoke. And before long, it would be darker still. No, this wasn't a raid for supplies or hostages. This was a hit. Someone was trying to bury the Field.

#

Claire stood in the shadow of the command post and watched soldiers race past her and into the ever-growing sea of smoke. Another memory of the MCM gripped her, and she found herself wanting not to retreat to the barracks, but to run. To run to the front gate, climb it, and race out into the middle of nowhere. She didn't feel safe in any place with a name or with people. *People bring the dead. They are the dead.*

She remembered a vagabond preacher saying that, "The namer of names does not name himself, for he does not wish to be known by Death." He'd gone by Father Nobody and sermonized to the huddled masses in exchange for food scraps. That had been many years ago. But maybe he was still alive. Perhaps more than most, Claire knew the value of anonymity, of fading into the gray. For all her nightmares about Detroit and being on her own, a part of her desperately yearned for that. To be the only one responsible for Claire. To be responsible for no one else.

But…Andre. Her horses. Just staying alive wasn't enough to make her feel alive anymore. She had to get across the creek. Several moments had passed since she'd seen anyone. Claire ducked into the command post.

#

How is this happening? So fast? From all sides?
The suburbs were ablaze.

The tents were going up like paper, fire leaping from one to the next. People raced in and out of the jumping flames like frenzied ants. Parents trying to save their children.

Andre began shouting at the top of his lungs. "This way! *Here!*" But it was no use over the chorus of screams. Now gunfire. He turned to see soldiers firing upon slimes that must have come in from the creek. But how had the dead gotten to the suburbs, at the back of the Field, without detection?

He saw his answer among the fire. A slime shrouded in blackened foliage shambled among the tents. Camouflage. Whoever had done this wasn't fucking human at all. *And they're out there, somewhere, watching. Waiting.*

Andre drew his sidearm. He took aim at the slime and popped it in the forehead. It slumped, tottered and fell onto its face. And exploded.

"No!" Andre cried. He ran along the perimeter of the suburb in an effort to find a way in. Had to lead those people to safety before more slimes went off. He felt as if he were slogging through oatmeal. Things were slowing down around him. Red-faced ghouls tore out from the burning tents and pushed past him. Some carried small smoking bundles. All of their faces were feral, teeth bared, eyes wide. Parents bearing their unconscious children out of the fire. And into a firefight.

Andre spotted a little boy at the mouth of a smoldering tent. He was pulling on an adult's arm, trying to get them out. Looked like a woman. As Andre drew closer, blinking away the ever-thickening smoke, fighting against the searing heat that was the air around him, he saw that the woman had been killed. Half her face was a red hole, either from an explosion or a stray bullet. Or maybe a suicide. The boy tugged desperately at her arm. "Hey!" Andre yelled. "Kid!"

The boy turned and yelped. He dropped the arm and began backing away. There was a roiling wall of fire creeping up behind him. Andre waved his arms. "It's okay! I'm a soldier! Come to me!"

At the boy's back, a hulking Roman candle disengaged itself from the rest of the flames. It moved stiffly on its roasting legs, arms swinging blindly in search of purchase.

"Kid! Boy!" Andre raised his pistol. The boy stared at him but didn't move.

The flaming slime caught hold of the boy's hair. Scarcely a scream escaped the child's lips before he was swept into the thing's lethal embrace. Andre screamed for him.

The slime erupted, and Andre was thrown back into darkness.

#

Claire waded into the creek at a point near the reservoir. She couldn't see anyone in the haze around her, but she heard cries and gunshots not too far off. Holding an M4 over her head, she walked into the cool water until it rose above her chest. Halfway across. On the other side, a storehouse and a security station. Beyond that, the stable.

A groan caught her attention, and she saw a slime in the water. It was floating toward her. Part of its head had been sheared away by a bullet; the remaining eye, yellow and buggy, fixed on her and the dead man began flailing his arms.

Claire lurched toward the shore. She got here, slung the rifle onto the ground and began pulling herself after it. Her wet hands slipped through the grass. She fell back. Smoke rolled along the earth's surface and into her face. Claire made another attempt, sinking her fingers into the ground.

The dead man grabbed her shoulder. Claire turned and threw her elbow into its eye. The slime held fast.

Claire focused, and she felt a calming warmth move through her body. The slime gawked at her for a moment, then its grip loosened and it drifted toward the reservoir. It cast one half-glance back, mouth still agape. Claire climbed onto the shore.

She took a quick look around. Still no one there. No one had seen her do what she'd done. Even now, with the world on fire, that was crucial. Especially in a panicked situation like this. No one could be allowed to see what they couldn't possibly understand. She barely did herself.

#

Andre felt a slap to the face and opened his eyes. Johnny Idaho hauled him to his feet. "Where's Claire?"

"Wh-what?"

"Claire!" Idaho shouted. "Man, we need to get those horses and bug out! The front gate's been breached! Slimes are everywhere!"

"Front gate…how do you know?" Andre tried to orient himself amongst waves of light and dark. Fire everywhere. Shots were being fired, but they were intermittent. He coughed up a wad of phlegm. "You got a working radio, John?"

"Had one," Idaho said. "Lost it after I heard about the gate." He stared intently into Andre's eyes. *Just believe me,* that look said. *We need to be gone yesterday.*

Murphy's Law in full effect—of course hardly anyone had a radio that worked, and the last scheduled shipment of long-life batteries had never shown up. Probably taken by highwaymen. Now Andre had to take the word of this coward or venture off alone into Armageddon.

"I mean it, man!" said Idaho. "Let's get to the stable!"

"Claire's up front," Andre said. "She's in the forward barracks, right at the gate."

Idaho's face blanched. "Oh God." So he was telling the truth about the front gate falling.

"Okay," Andre said. "Who's around? You seen anybody?"

Idaho swatted away smoke and flecks of ash. "I can't see shit!"

"Then let's just get to the stable."

#

Claire heard an explosion up ahead. She crouched at the corner of the security station. That had sounded real close. The stables were just a hundred yards ahead. She could see the fence. God, Emeli had probably gone into labor. Claire wouldn't be able to save the newborn. Maybe not Emeli either. Were they already being cooked alive inside the stable?

Claire bolted forward and cleared the fence. She saw the shadow of the stable. She saw slimes staggering around it.

Claire took aim at the nearest one. They hadn't noticed her yet. Time to announce herself.

"Don't!" a voice hissed.

B.D. grabbed the rifle's barrel and pushed it down. He spoke into Claire's ear. "They'll blow up if they fall. Just let them walk away."

He pulled her back through the smoke and they crouched, watching the dead.

"We've got to go now," Claire insisted.

"We go now, we don't make it," said B.D.

The slimes wandered past the stable. Claire's nerves were jumping within her legs. She wanted to move. B.D.'s hand stayed on her arm.

She heard the neighing of her kids as clear as day. The dead heard it too. They turned back to the stable.

"No, no," Claire mumbled. "Let me go, I can get them. Please."

B.D. tightened his grip on her arm. Claire relaxed her body, sagging against him—then jerked away, running not toward the stable but off toward the fence.

"Claire!" B.D. barked once, then silence. Only the crackling of flames. Claire hopped the fence and knelt. She was going to have to do her thing again. God willing, no one would take a shot at her.

Claire looked down at her arms and felt that calming warmth again. Her skin seemed to ripple, then grew paler. Gray. Mottled with what looked like old bruises. The blonde hair dangling around her face became white.

Her skin tightened. She stood and moved at a measured pace—as measured as she could manage, in her panic—along the fence. She took advantage of a thick wave of smoke and climbed the fence as it enveloped her. Now at the stable, she walked to the back door and removed her key from her pocket.

A slime stepped around the corner. It reached for her, then stopped. For a second, it seemed to look her over. Claire did not look back. She stared into space, swaying slightly.

The slime's arm dropped, and it shuffled past her. Claire waited until it was gone before opening the padlock. She rolled the door back just enough to ease herself through, the color returning to her skin as she did so.

Then tears rushed to her eyes, and her throat swelled with grief, keeping her from crying out.

Half of the horses lay dead. Emeli was there among them, and her newborn…it was there, unmoving, born into death.

Boy Blue tried to walk to Claire but stumbled and settled back. The heat was unbearable, the air swimming before Claire. She looked into Blue's eyes and saw nothing in them. They were milky, red-rimmed. He was blind. "Oh, Blue," she breathed. The horse lowered his head and let out a wheezing breath.

The front door rolled open. Andre and Johnny Idaho entered. "Oh Jesus," Andre exclaimed. "Claire!"

"Fuck…" said Idaho. "Are they all gonna die?"

Claire just stared at the floor. Andre rushed to her and pulled her toward the front entrance. "We've gotta find a way out. Come on."

"I won't—" she began.

"I'm not hearing it," Andre said, wrapping his arms around her. "You can hate me forever but you are going to live."

THREE | AND THAT'S HOW HADES' GARDEN GROWS

Claire was appointed in a flowing gown that moved like air across the floor. It covered her arms and rose to join a lace collar fastened about her neck. The gown was the color of wheat, but hardly plain, adorned with crimson trim that accented the golden-hued pearls Claire wore.

She stood in the vaulted entryway of a vast ballroom that seemed to swim with shadows. At first, she thought they were made of smoke, but the whirling forms began to solidify, resolving into dancing couples dressed in midnight black. Each was thin, graceful, and possessed by the rapture of their revelry. Watching them spin, moving in and out of one another, was dizzying. Claire placed a hand against the wall and tried not to swoon. She fought against the feeling because she knew, somehow, that they would pounce upon her if she were to fall.

If there was music, she didn't hear it. She felt like she was peering through a crack in time, staring into a world she wasn't supposed to know.

There was an elaborate framework erected in the center of the room. Minding every step as if it might be her last, Claire advanced, the dancers peeling past her without notice. She fixed her eyes on the framework. It looked like it was carved from obsidian. As she drew closer, she saw that it was, in fact, charred wood, the frame of a burned-out house. The dancers weaved effortlessly through its blackened struts. Claire felt violated with every turning pair who spun through the framework.

"Is this me?" she cried, although she didn't quite understand the words. Claire turned and shouted at the revelers. "Is this mine? Do I remember this?"

A lithe, white-skinned woman drew close to her. The woman whispered, *"Leave it."*

"No! I want to know!" Claire ran to the house-frame and slammed her fists against the wood. Ash rained down on her dress. The dress—it began to change. The color bled away and it became an ugly, moth-eaten thing of heavy gray cloth. Claire's upturned palms followed suit as she watched. Nails became black, hair white.

She turned and the woman was there. It was the shrike.

"Everything you are is *mine,*" snarled the thing, and the frills of its black dress began to elongate. They ran down toward the floor like melting taffy, then struck upward, tendrils ensnaring Claire. They coiled about her wrists and throat, and she wrenched uselessly against them. The shrike bared its broken teeth and howled.

Claire twisted away and found herself pressed against icy glass. She was thrust up against a window, and watched as a pickup truck tore across an open field toward her. Though it was dusk and the truck was some distance off, she knew Andre was behind the wheel.

The truck bounced out of the field and onto a road. Stars flew across the sky—no, not stars, but sparks from a fragmenting power line on the roadside. The flaming lines came down on the truck. Andre pulled the wheel hard to one side, struggled to correct the move. It was too late. The truck rolled.

"No! I'm here," Claire screamed. *"I'M RIGHT HERE!"* And the shrike's tentacles slipped around her mouth and into it.

The truck settled on its roof and sat in silence.

Claire could no longer speak. But she knew there was no truth in the spoken word, no more than in what her eyes saw or her ears heard.

Inside her mind, she said, *Daddy.*

Not Andre. Daddy.

The shrike pressed Claire's face against the glass. It began to web out with a thin cracking sound. Black tendrils covered Claire's eyes and all was nothing.

#

She woke, and Andre was there, as she'd known he would be, and she rolled into his embrace and sobbed. She wasn't sure why. The images of the nightmare were already fading from memory, but there remained a terrible, empty feeling that was as real as anything she'd ever felt.

#

They were seated among tall grass at the base of the mountain. To the southwest, columns of smoke rose to stain the cloud cover. The sun hung somewhere behind this curtain. Claire lay in the grass, her head propped on a backpack, and studied her hands for the umpteenth time.

"What are you looking for?" Andre asked. He wiped soot from his brow—he'd been doing so all day, and it wasn't helping.

Claire glanced around at the others inhabiting their pitiful little camp. They had a few bedrolls and some packs with, presumably, food. She assumed that since she hadn't heard anyone bring up the subject of how to eat. Johnny Idaho was there, and B.D., and an Asian woman Claire vaguely recognized. She thought the woman might have been a teacher for the kids. That made her think of the horses, and she shut her eyes against the vision that came. The last thing she remembered of Potter's Field was Andre dragging her from the barn as it began to burn. And she remembered seeing horses limping out of the building, with nowhere to go, blind and half-dead and unable to handle riders. Her mind had stopped working then, up until that dream. She thought that was a good thing. What she could recall was awful enough. The rest...

(Leave it)

Claire shuddered and looked at Andre. "Did I...when I was out, asleep...did I do anything?"

"You mean..." Understanding dawned on Andre's face, and he shook his head. "You didn't. I've never seen it happen when you were asleep."

"I had to do it while we were in there," she said. "Been a while."

"But it worked."

She nodded. "I guess. I'm alive. I guess."

Andre was the only one who knew. He'd helped her with it; not that there was any making sense of *why* she could do it, but he'd helped her figure out how to control it. It was about more than skin tone and hair color. The very texture of her flesh could change. And her eyes. She'd once spent an afternoon knelt over a pond, watching her reflection as she made her eyes go from green to blue to even purple, and then black. That last one had scared her.

The woman scooted over to Claire, being sure to stay beneath the grass line, and said, "I'm Ritter. You Claire?"

Claire nodded. "No one else made it?"

"We suppose some did," Ritter said, "but we haven't seen them. B.D. thought it would be smarter to make camp here rather than go running blind. In case…in case the people who did this are out hunting for survivors."

"And if we hadn't done that," Andre said, "we wouldn't have found this." He moved a blanket and upended a curved metal plate. It was emblazoned with intricate designs of shields borne by roaring lions.

"Is that armor?" Claire asked.

"Knight's armor," Andre muttered. "The Church's army. We found this on a guy outside the front gate. He'd taken a bullet to the brainpan, one of ours got him I guess. Guy was fully suited up. Religious undergarments and the like. Even had a little sword."

Claire sat up. "You think he was a real knight?"

Andre looked from Ritter to B.D. He said, "Yeah, we do."

"You think *they* attacked us?"

"Can't think of any other reason you'd have a knight happening by our little apocalypse while it was going on," Andre said. "And you know, they tried to make it look like raiders. Or maybe they were trying to frame one of those suicide cults, the ones who think we should all be dead. I don't know."

"There were those missionaries yesterday morning," said B.D. "Potter turned them away."

"Coincidence?" Ritter suggested. "I can't see them firebombing us just because we shut down some tent preachers."

"This had to have been planned long before that," B.D. said. "Maybe the missionaries were scouts. Meant to get a last look at our situation before the attack."

"The Church." Andre laughed bitterly. *"Why?"*

"They want to control every goddamned thing," spat Johnny Idaho. No one argued with that.

"We're rebuilders," said Ritter. "We've done more for the Church than any other faction. More for everyone."

"But we do it on our terms," Andre said.

Still, Claire thought, the cold brutality of the previous night's attack didn't resemble anything she'd known the Church to do. Their knights were dedicated to defending those who couldn't defend themselves. Of course, the Church was mostly out to save souls, if not lives, but surely the fall of Potter's Field hadn't accomplished either.

"We've got to get to the next camp," B.D. said. "West of here. I don't know how far, but if we head due west, we will find more of our people. Tell them what happened here."

"Unless the next camp's already been hit," said Idaho.

"You'd rather sit here, be my guest," said B.D. "You know there are slimes out there, and maybe more knights. I saw a little clutch of slimes just before dawn. Didn't dare approach them for fear they were rigged to blow. No sir, I say we head out at twilight and find the devil we know."

Claire tried to sit back and take stock of all that had happened over the last several hours. She felt numb; just the facts, no feelings. The Field was gone. Her horses were gone. And it had all been intentional. Sabotage. Mass slaughter directed, it seemed, by supposed men of God.

Then again, who was to blame for the bugs and the slimes? Was this anything new in her dead world?

Claire pulled off her boots and peeled the filthy socks from her feet. She massaged her aching soles, which awoke all the other unrest within her, and she felt knots forming in her shoulders and stomach. Someone asked if she was hungry. She shook her head. Didn't think she'd be hungry for a long while.

#

As it grew late, B.D. built a small fire and rested several flat stones atop it with which to cook up whatever they had. Mindful of the smoke rising from it, he continuously waved his hands over the rocks. "I know no one's hungry. But you will be once we're on the move, and there's no coffee break."

"God. Coffee." Ritter sighed. "Tell me we at least have enough water for the next couple days."

B.D. motioned to Andre, who pulled several plastic Thermoses from a pack. "Everybody gets one. Yours is yours, and that's it until we can find some fresh water."

"And boil it up," said Ritter. "You catch beaver fever, you'll end up leaving your own slime trail."

Claire smiled a little at that. Idaho wrinkled his nose and pushed away the Thermos Andre offered.

"How do you know that isn't contaminated?" Idaho snapped. "There were slimes in the creek!"

"This was bottled days ago," Andre said. "Besides, and I can't believe I have to say this, you know the bugs can't live outside the body. Water's fine."

"Says you. If we're such goddamn experts on this shit, why haven't we fixed it?"

Claire rolled her eyes. "Maybe it would help if people stopped spreading bullshit about the bugs. They don't work in water. They aren't in the rain. They aren't airborne. They don't infect animals."

Idaho smirked. "Right, that. Animals. It's not like I'm the only person worried about it. Have the top brass tested every species on Earth? I heard—"

"Oh, for God's sake," B.D. spat. "Do not start with the rumors." He sliced a brick of Spam, or Spam-like product, into several thin strips.

"Hey," said Idaho. "For real. I heard that the Chinese who made the smart organs tested them on apes. Apes are close to us."

"Closer to some than others," Claire said under her breath. Everyone heard it. Andre stifled a guffaw, if only to protect their position.

"Zombie apes running amok in southeast Asia," B.D. snorted. "Hope they don't learn to fly."

"You people with your goddamn jokes." Idaho sat back and shook his head.

"Sense of humor's a survival mechanism, hoss," Andre said. "Believe you me."

"I was a kid when everything happened," Idaho said. "I was in first fucking grade. There were kids in my school who…changed. I don't remember laughing about anything."

"Listen, John." Andre softened his tone. "We've all been there. If there's one thing we all have in common, it's that. Knowing the world that came before isn't necessarily a comfort."

"Damn straight." B.D. turned the sizzling meat atop the stones. "I had a house on the Cape. We were actually looking at boats. I was feeling real bold with the eye surgery coming up. Like a second lease on life. Exact opposite, as it turns out."

"Family?" Idaho asked.

"Lost them early on," B.D. said without looking up.

Idaho nodded. "Yeah. Me too. My folks sent me to be with my uncle. He was an Army guy, a prepper. I guess it was better that way. But I never heard from my folks again."

Claire offered him a sympathetic look. "Sorry, Johnny. I don't remember my parents at all. Everything's a blank."

"Lucky," Idaho said. He busied himself swatting at bugs in the grass.

"None of us are lucky," Ritter said. "We're all here."

"Where did you come from, Ritter?" Andre asked.

"Canada. When the border ceased to exist, I hooked up with a passing Army unit en route to their base. Told them I was a teacher. Which I almost was. Nearly had my certificate. Spoke three languages. Saved my hide."

"Come 'n' get it," B.D. said, handing out plastic knives. The company took turns stabbing at strips of meat. Claire finally gave up and scooped one into her hand. It wasn't too hot. Tasted vaguely of dirt. Didn't matter. As soon as it went down her gullet, she realized how grateful her body was the sustenance.

"Hrmph." B.D. smiled as he chewed. "Aliens."

"Come again?" said Ritter.

"When it first happened, there were people who thought it was aliens. Taking over other people. Or demons, I remember that one."

"I thought we weren't talking rumors," Idaho said with a pout.

"These are rumors long forgotten," B.D. said. "Don't hold an ounce of credibility no matter who you ask. Hah. Demons."

"I remember hearing something about some Amazonian fungus," Andre said. "They said it spread worldwide thanks to pot. Might have been my grandmother who came up with that one."

"The one that really caused trouble was the theory about the 666 chip," Ritter said. "That certain people had been microchipped by a global cabal in some eugenics conspiracy."

"Chipped to act crazy and eat other people?" Idaho sniffed.

"Sure. Just another government plot to turn the have-nots against each other." Ritter reached for a second strip of meat. "Either that or terrorists trying to kick-start the apocalypse. State-sponsored, of course, because how else could they have the technology? I remember countries at each other's throats threatening nuclear war."

"When we figured out it was these nanos," B.D. said, "it didn't help much. The province they came from had been wiped out, and the Chinese government was in total denial. We didn't know if these little robots could take to each other — could they control higher brain function? Strategize?" He took a big swig of water and choked it down. "We knew they were self-replicating and that was bad enough. A virus immune to modern medicine, and specifically targeting us. Hah. Franklin Ruehl suggested we find a way to transfer each person's consciousness to the Internet. But then he said scratch that, the nanos might evolve into a computer virus."

"There were times when almost all of those sounded like plausible ideas," Ritter said. "And I get people being concerned about animals and plants and the like, but there's just been no evidence of infection outside humans. If there was, we'd probably all be long dead."

Johnny Idaho shrugged. "All I know is, if I see a monkey I'm popping it."

"Speaking of guns, let's try and forget we have them, okay?" B.D. said. "Unless we run into a human threat, there's no need for them. We move under cover of darkness. Quiet. Quick. Avoid slimes."

Idaho nodded along. "Hey, I don't mind."

B.D. eyed the clouds overhead. "I just hope Mother Nature behaves herself. That looks like rain."

"Probably just looks that way because of the smoke," Andre said.

"Hmm." B.D. gestured to Andre. "Let's have a look in those trees up there. Just in case we do end up having to wait out a rain delay, I'd rather have some semblance of shelter. Hate to die of a cold after all this shit."

Andre nodded and, taking up an M4, he and B.D. duck-walked through the grass toward the treeline on the steep mountain slope.

Idaho looked at Claire. "You have any other friends back there?"

"What?"

"The Field. You have any other friends?"

Claire wanted to say, *Other than my twelve horses?* But she didn't. She said, "I didn't really know anyone. I mean, there were people I saw here and there. We talked. But I wouldn't say friends."

"Yeah, me neither," said Idaho. "You and Dozens are the only ones I ever hung around."

Claire wasn't sure what to say to that. She glanced at Ritter, who offered, "Well, you all made it out."

"You taught all those kids," Idaho said to her. "Jesus. You knew them and their parents. I'm sorry."

Ritter put up a strong front, but Claire could see the terrible ache behind her emotionless stare. Ritter took a drink and sat silent.

#

B.D. sat down at the base of a particularly full tree. He winced and rubbed his shoulder. "Glad the leaves haven't fallen yet."

"They will." Andre studied the colors in the canopy overhead. It wouldn't be long before the mountainside looked like it was littered with skeletons.

"Your shoulder okay?" he asked B.D.

The older man shrugged. "I tussled with a couple of slimes at the creek. Damn things were on fire. Thank God I got them off me before they blew up. But I think I got singed. Want to have a look?"

Andre nodded. B.D. unbuttoned his shirt and gingerly slipped it off his shoulder. Andre came around and saw a patch of red, welted flesh covering B.D.'s shoulder blade. In its center was a pair of long crimson furrows.

"Oh, hell," Andre muttered.

"Bad? Look infected?"

"You got clawed, Ben."

B.D. started and looked fearfully at Andre. "No." He reached over his shoulder and touched the wound. "It doesn't hurt like that. I don't even feel…" His fingers found the lacerations.

"It might be okay," said Andre. "It's definitely fingernails, not teeth. The slime would have to have had open cuts. And you were wearing your uniform, and the damn slime was on fire, so…"

"Yeah." B.D. sighed. "So."

Andre sat down next to him. "How are you feeling otherwise? Any nausea? Breathing okay?"

"I don't have any of the signs," B.D. said, but he didn't sound confident. Not at all.

"So we wait it out," Andre said. "I'll keep an eye on you."

"I ought to get away from you all," B.D. said. "I already…I handled the food. Fuck!" He threw his elbow back against the tree trunk. "God damn it all!"

"Easy," Andre said. "Look, I'm not letting you go off on your own. Doesn't make sense one way or the other."

B.D. said softly, "Right. It'd be better if you were there to do me when it happens."

"That's not what I meant," Andre said. "But I will do it. If it happens."

"I know." B.D. sighed. He wiped something from his one eye. "You know, what did I expect? Why did I keep going? Family's gone. Everything's gone."

"You're not a quitter," Andre said, quickly adding, "and they weren't either."

"You know what's rotten? I think they got off easy."

"Maybe."

"I'm stubborn is what I am," said B.D. "Made my wife help me pull that goddamned eye out of my head. One of the last things she experienced."

"Neither of you wanted to do it. But you had to. That's not stubborn, Ben, that's life."

"Yeah. Life sentence. What none of us asked for." B.D. kneaded his hands. "We'll tell the others?"

"We should. I think they can handle it."

"That Johnny Idaho's a little froggy."

"He'll listen to me. And then we'll wait it out."

#

The rain started coming down not long after. The five survivors relocated to the trees and wrapped themselves in bedrolls. B.D. sat apart from the others, staring into space.

After a time, he told them he was feeling queasy. He settled back against a tree and closed his eyes. Moaned.

"He's infected," Idaho whispered to Andre.

"I know," Andre said.

"Are you going to do it?"

"I will. But not yet. He'll fall unconscious. Then I'll do it."

"How?"

Andre pulled the bedroll tightly around himself. Couldn't risk a gunshot. Good old BFT, then. *You're only bashing your friend's skull in. You do it right it'll only take one hit. You've done it a thousand times before.*

Yeah. To monsters. Not B.D.

"I've got this," Andre told the others. "Trust me."

"Are you going to need any help?" Claire asked.

"No. All me."

Andre fished a cudgel from his pack and sat with it as rain pitter-pattered overhead, running lazily down the canopy of leaves and falling onto his hands. There was no more talk.

After a while, B.D. stopped making sounds. Andre shook off the bedroll and stood.

Claire lowered her head. Ritter covered her ears. Idaho looked like he was going to puke.

Andre walked quietly to B.D. He knelt and whispered the man's name. Once, twice. No response. B.D.'s head had lolled forward, and Andre had a clean shot at the brainstem. It made his stomach turn to see his friend that way. He wasn't a person anymore, just a bag of bones with a target on the back of his head.

That was how it had to be. *B.D.'s dead,* Andre told himself.

He heard fidgeting at his back. "Dozens?" Idaho breathed.

Andre raised a hand to halt Idaho's approach. Then he raised the cudgel.

Someone—Ritter, he thought—let out a soft, "Oh," when he brought the bludgeon down. B.D. shuddered and slid down to lie flat. Andre knew he had to land a second blow to be sure. He raised the cudgel again and heard Ritter begin to cry.

Tears in rain, right? Blade Runner. *Everything will be dry come tomorrow.*

Andre swung as hard as his quaking limbs would allow.

#

"You had to do it."

"I know."

Andre sat in the dark with Claire. The rain had subsided, but no one had made a peep about moving out. Ritter was asleep and Idaho, he was probably pretending to be.

"That this is the way the world works," Andre said, "the way it just is—that doesn't help. It means life is meaningless at best. At worst, it's cruel."

Claire put her arm around him. "I'm not going to cry," he said.

"So don't."

"Did you watch?"

Claire said, "Yes."

"Good."

"I know what you're going to say," Claire told him, "and there's no need. Yes. I will do it. If it happens."

Andre nodded. Neither spoke again until dawn.

FOUR | HOTEL 23

The best-laid schemes of mice and men often go oft awry, and those are the best-laid ones. They were four tired, dehydrated, soot-stained strays flying by the seat of their collective pants. They were headed out along the treeline under cover of dusk. They'd waited another day before venturing out. Creeping past the ruins of Potter's Field, Claire smelled flesh both cooked and uncooked festering beyond the crumbled stone walls. Meat, scattered, which once had dreams and images tattooed inside it. Names. And so Death had found them all on his list.

In so many ways, Claire felt like a no-name, a nothing. As she'd observed in the past, there was a surreal sense of comfort in that, but there was also that sadness. The definite feeling that she was supposed to be someone.

And who, then, should she be? Defining oneself by the few personal relationships one had was fruitless when upset and loss were a part of everyday life. The horses had been her world. She'd thought there was less chance of losing them badly, certainly not all at once. Life and death alike were full of surprises.

Then there was her knowledge that her own skin might not be what she thought it. The face she thought of as her own was what she wore in a resting state. It wasn't like the others she shaped from clay using her will. Yet—she was sure that when she'd first slipped her fair skin to pass herself off as a slime, it hadn't been a conscious design. She'd done it while writhing in the warped confines of the Motor City Mountain. It had simply happened. And those shadows around her which stirred and stammered had suddenly fallen still and silent. They'd withdrawn. They'd accepted what they saw without analysis.

And she'd done it without thinking. Soon after came the realization that she could choose to manipulate her flesh, but not that first time.

Andre had taught her about chameleons. "Sometimes they choose their color," he'd said. "But not always. After all, it's not a magic trick. It's their nature."

And what she knew about her nature, particularly where she'd come from, wouldn't fill a thimble. So was Claire, in her natural form, really Claire?

She was forced to suspend her musings when booms sounded in the distance. They'd left the mountain and were now moving due west. From straight ahead echoed those explosions. A haze that might have been confused for distant rain darkened and curled in on itself. Smoke.

"Shit." Andre motioned to the right. "Into the grass."

"I told you. They're wiping out all the camps." Idaho scrambled into the grass like a field mouse.

"You're a genius," Andre hissed. "Now shut up."

Claire crouch-walked through the tall grass as quickly as she could. Thin reeds slapped and scratched at her face, a few catching in her hair and tugging it. They felt like bony fingers, and she kept looking back to make sure they weren't.

The booms stopped after just a few minutes. Everyone slowed, kneeling, and exchanged glances through the grass.

"Are there any other camps out this way?" Ritter asked, barely audible. "To the north, I mean?"

"We'd have better luck going south," Andre whispered. "And I'd forget going back east, especially if it's the goddamn knights doing this. The Church is everywhere out there."

More explosions.

"Sounds like we're headed south," said Idaho.

"Right now," replied Andre, "let's just get away from those booms. We'll head north a bit. Just keep your head down. I know we're all stiff, but we gotta stay behind cover. We'll rest when we can."

Dusk gave way to night, and the sounds of war faded. Now a light wind rustled the grass, and Claire was more anxious than ever. The sounds of her own progress blended with the wind and, between that and the dark, she feared that a slime—or worse— could be on top of her before she detected it.

Andre had traded her his pistol for the rifle she'd pilfered. She felt more comfortable with a compact firearm close at her side. Idaho was behind her taking up the rear. He was murmuring something, but she couldn't make it out.

"Hold it!" Andre whispered. Everyone froze.

"Come up here," Andre said, his shadow barely visible as he waved the others forward. They joined him and saw they'd reached the end of the tall grass. Beyond sprawled an uneven, cracked expanse that looked like an old lava flow Claire had seen in a textbook. Andre snapped the light on his M4 on and off a few times, offering them all quick look at what they were facing.

"Highway," Ritter breathed. Andre popped the light on and off a few more times. The east-west strip of asphalt was riddled with webs of fractures, from which protruded weeds. Some entire chunks of road were gone. No sign of vehicles. Claire was glad for that. Enough bad memories for one week.

Idaho touched Andre's shoulder and pointed down the road. Barely visible beneath the stars, there was a hulking silhouette moving slowly back and forth on the highway some distance off.

"What I wouldn't give for night vision," Andre said through gritted teeth. He raised the M4 and snapped the light on and off, rapid-fire.

"Damn," he said, but Claire heard not dismay but wonder in his voice. He put the light on again and this time left it. "Look."

Claire had never seen a bear in real life before. But there it was, an honest-to-God brown bear standing on all fours in the road and glancing around. It stared at Andre's light.

"Thing must weigh a ton," Idaho said. He raised his rifle.

"Easy," said Andre. "It's a mama. Look close."

Claire saw a smaller creature moving about the bear's hind legs. Its head bobbed as it weaved about its mother, who lowered her snout to usher the cub back into her shadow.

"She doesn't want to mess with us. Just let them go," Andre said.

Ritter added, "They must have come down from the mountain. Probably scared to death."

"Dozens," Idaho whispered. "We could take them out."

"What, to eat? We're not starving yet. And we're sure as shit not shooting."

"Okay," Idaho said, and glanced in Claire's direction. "I'm just saying. We've gotta think about these things, right?"

Claire looked away. "I don't hate animals," Idaho insisted. "I had a dog. And fish."

"We've all had to eat our share of dog," Andre said. "It's fine. Just lay off that trigger, John."

"You've eaten dog?" Ritter's eyes widened.

"I didn't want to do it," Andre said sheepishly.

Ritter sat back and watched the bears milling about in the road. "I'd sooner eat shoe leather."

"Had that too," Andre said. "Boil it for a couple hours with some fresh leaves. It's not the worst."

"What's the worst, then?" Ritter said.

"Long pig, I'd think."

"You mean people."

"I've never eaten human," Andre said. "And while I'll bet it makes a plate of dog meat look like dog shit, I don't think I ever could. Grubs, okay. Velveeta I can choke down. Long as there's grubs."

"They're going," Claire said, motioning to the bears. The mother was leading her cub down the road and away from Andre's light. She looked back more than once, but her pace was relaxed and the cub toddled along after her without a care.

"Conversation aside, that was kind of amazing," said Ritter.

"What do you make of *that?*" Andre asked, pointing north. There was a flickering light on the horizon. It looked like it was high up off the ground.

"Torch?" Ritter wondered aloud.

"We don't do that," Idaho said. "Whose is it?"

"Your guess is as good as mine." Andre had switched off his light and they sat now in darkness. "I don't know if it was there before the bear. It might be in response to our light, and I'm not saying that's a good thing."

"Could anyone see our light from that far off?" Ritter said. "We're barely off the ground."

"If they have the right gear..." Andre trailed off. "But that could be anyone. Ours or theirs. Like John said, never seen a signal like that before. A single torch way up in the air."

"Maybe it's not fire," Claire suggested. "It just looks like it's flickering because it's so far off. Or maybe—maybe it's electric and they're using Morse."

"Huh." Andre weighed the idea. "Well, we can't be certain from here without binoculars. So let's see. We could continue north and try to figure out what the light is. Or we could turn and head south now, but we might run into knights."

"If we go west, we're going to run into that bear," Ritter said.

"There's nothing for us back east," Idaho grumbled.

Andre looked to Claire. "Feeling lucky?"

"As ever."

Andre smiled. "Let's try north. Slowly. Kissing the dirt. No lights." He slung his M4 onto his back.

"Got it, Corporal." Idaho flattened himself and began crawling onto the highway.

"I hope we run into a sergeant soon," Andre said. "I don't dig this leader shit."

#

Elbows raw, knees aching, the smell of cold earth in her nostrils, Claire wormed her way through thin brush and toward the flickering light.

It was a flame, all right, set atop a leaning telephone pole beside an interstate and just behind a road sign. *Exit 227 – Raylene – 2 mi.*

"Never heard of her," Andre said. "Must be a ghost town."

"Except someone's pointing us to it," said Ritter.

"Maybe." Andre propped himself on his elbows and sighed. "But now that we're here, and seeing that it *is* fire and not electric, I'm more worried than ever that it's a signal meant for the knights. Makes more sense."

"Or other survivors did it. Civilians," Ritter argued. "We don't all use the Army playbook."

"Let's say that. Civvies did it. Knowing full well that the people who burned the Field could see it just as well as anyone else." Andre shook his head. "Then they're idiots."

"We're all just trying to survive," Ritter said.

"Whatever. I don't like this. I'm not going to send you all into a trap—then again, if I ordered you not to go, that wouldn't mean a thing to you, would it?"

"Would to me," Idaho said. "I'm praying for it."

"Jesus," Claire said, louder than she'd meant. The others turned to her. "You know, we can lie here all night trying to guess what that is. Maybe it's nothing. Maybe lightning hit the damn pole when it was storming. Who knows?"

"So what are you saying?" Andre asked.

"Either we crawl away from the light, and hope we were right—or we go where it seems to be telling us, and hope we were right." Claire added, "Right about survivors, I mean."

"Who's in charge here?" Idaho grumbled.

"Everyone's got a right to speak," Andre said. "This ain't boot camp. Okay. Long as we're flying blind in any direction, I say we keep low and head toward Raylene. We'll see if we can get a read on things from the city limits."

#

The city, like most, was trash and steel. It was a great rusted skeleton whose yawning cavities had become home to dirt, debris and whatever thrived in that.

Though it was still dark, the darker silhouettes of the buildings gave definition to what smelled like one big landfill. *And it's just been raining, too,* thought Claire with a grimace. It'd be hard to breathe among all that moldy shit. She was all for turning back just based on the odor.

But Andre urged them forward, and they crept through hunks of crumbling concrete and fallen steel beams and made their way onto Main Street in the humble little city of Raylene. The sidewalks were eroded, and the street itself had sunk into the earth, likely as the sewer system underneath corroded—so that was the smell. Andre pointed his light down into the canyon. An unmoving, coagulated river of decades-old waste.

Claire tied a handkerchief around her nose and mouth and made her way along the sidewalk behind Andre. He snapped his light on and off, panning it over doors and windows. Those windows that hadn't been shattered by stress or vandalism were opaque. It was hard to tell if it was due to filth or some chemical reaction.

Andre said, "No signs of anyone having been here before us. Not in a long, long time. I'm more concerned about critters at this point."

"Like what?" Idaho cradled his rifle and looked from one direction to the other.

"Cats, snakes. Just stay sharp," Andre told him.

He led the group around a corner and down a narrow side street. On either side, hollowed-out office buildings creaked.

I'm worried about the dead, Claire thought. As if in answer, a slight wind kicked up. With the foul smell it carried, there came also a gentle moaning. *Just the buildings,* she told herself. *You know the difference by heart.*

Back onto another of the main thoroughfares, Andre stopped before a tall, very old-looking building and shone his light on a plague by the doors. *Historic 23rd Street.*

The glass that had been in the doors was long gone. He poked the light through the opening. "I think it's a hotel. Vestibule's barricaded. Looks undisturbed for some time."

They stepped through the doors into the vestibule. Now they faced a wall constructed from folding tables and shelves. Indeed, it looked undisturbed, thick layers of grime upon everything. Andre reached out and took hold of a sideways table. He tugged on it. "Stuck fast."

"This thing's probably deeper than it looks," Ritter said. "No getting through here."

"There have to be slimes in there," said Idaho.

"Old ones," Claire suggested.

"Let's go around the perimeter and see if there's any way in. If we find a smashed window or door, we may as well give up and move on." Andre eyeballed the barricade. "But I've got a feeling about this place. If it's secure, and we can get in, I'll bet we can clear a floor or two and hunker down for a bit."

"Think there's any chance of finding supplies?" Ritter asked.

Andre shrugged. "We'll see. Hotels have good stuff sometimes. Stuff that hasn't rotted away. Depends on how long it's been empty and how it got emptied."

"And *if* it's empty," Idaho reminded him.

"Thank you, sunshine." Andre turned to Claire. "Come with me. Ritter, if you don't mind, go with Idaho, and we'll sweep around either side of the building. Meet you in back."

They went back out into the night, moving from window to window; all of the first-floor windows, broken or not, had iron bars set firmly in place.

Claire tugged on a pair of bars and asked Andre, "If you want, I could go in first and look around."

"You mean, undercover?"

"Right. See if I stir anything up."

"Nah, I might as well be the one. Since we're trying to draw these hypothetical guests out of hiding anyway."

"Just saying…if I did it, I wouldn't have to worry about them attacking."

"Assuming they don't mistake you for a living human being in the dark. A living human being which, by the way, you are." Andre cocked his head at her. "Claire, you don't need to prove yourself. You're hardly dead weight. This is just a soldier's job."

Claire arched an eyebrow. "Someone once told me, 'We're all soldiers now.'"

Andre nodded. "Right. Potter. Well, Clarissa, we each have our own skillsets. Believe me, I can't do what you do."

"Don't call me Clarissa when you're actually patronizing me."

Andre leaned against the side of the hotel. "Claire. I'm not patronizing you. I know things are topsy-turvy right now. We're all running hot. Let's just try and do this by the numbers."

Claire gave him a curt nod. She started to turn and he gently caught her arm. "Hey," he said. Nothing came after that. It looked like he was searching for something to say. Or maybe just working up the nerve to say the right thing.

"I loved B.D.," he said at last.

"I couldn't do anything for them," Claire said. "They depended on me."

Andre nodded, letting go of her arm.

"Okay," she said, and they continued on.

The wind picked up steam, howling through the dead city. It was difficult to tell whether it was chasing something or running from it.

#

"Well, the good news is, that's a climb only a human could make."

The first floor of the building was secure – which was to say, unable to be breached. However, there was a fire escape running down the backside of the hotel. It terminated at the second floor, and the ladder, which allowed ground-level access, was missing.

"It won't be too tough," Andre said. He dropped to one knee and cupped his hands. "Claire. Have a boost?"

It didn't take long to get all four of them up onto the creaking second-floor platform. They surveyed the street below in all directions. Still clear.

"Okay." Andre shone his light through the nearest window. It still had glass, dark and smoky, although there was enough transparency to see that it was boarded up from the inside. Andre and Idaho used the armor on their forearms to smash the glass. Everyone winced at the sound, and waited for an answer from within, but there was none.

They pushed on the boards until they were loose enough to wiggle free without further commotion.

"Let's go in."

They found themselves in a modest-sized room containing a queen bed and a few tables. A grime-covered television sat opposite the bed, which itself was caked with dust. Thin sheets of cobwebs hung in every corner. As the wind entered through the window, the cobwebs fluttered and motes of dust danced in the beams of the survivors' lights.

Once he'd replaced the boards over the window and propped a table up against them, Andre removed the light from his M4 and handed it to Claire. "Here. Stay close."

The bathroom was empty, though its condition was awful. It looked like the pipes had backed up before they corroded. The door leaving the room was latched. It took prying with a combat knife for Idaho to free the latch, but with that, the door swung slowly inward.

They entered a black corridor. The carpet was spongy and smelled foul. A pair of carts sat at the end of the hall, empty of contents. Claire pushed them aside and rounded the corner with the light held by her face. Another barren corridor. All of the doors were closed. Her light caught the red lettering of an exit sign at the other end of the hall.

They moved quietly to the door beneath the sign. Andre eased it open, and Claire pointed the light into a cobwebbed stairwell. Her breath caught in her throat at the sight of the crumpled form on the landing below.

"Keep that light steady," Andre whispered. He drew his cudgel and crept down the stairs. Claire fixed the light on the still white form, something under what looked to be a bedsheet. Andre crouched on the last step and reached for the corner of the sheet. He raised the cudgel high, then yanked the sheet back.

The desiccated remains of a woman lay there, shriveled limbs pulled into a fetal position. Her toothless mouth hung agape beneath eyeless sockets.

Andre looked her over. "Broken neck. She wasn't one of them."

"Has she been fed on?" Claire asked.

"Doesn't look like. Come on."

They made their way down to the first floor and entered a vast, lightless lobby. There were overturned chairs and yellowed scraps of newspaper scattered about. Claire saw a shoe with something protruding from it. Stepping closer, she saw it was a severed foot.

In the middle of the lobby was a glass enclosure filled with plant growth. Claire stepped to the glass and pressed her cheek against it so that she could peer upward. "I see stars. It goes all the way up." Indeed, the atrium's vines had been hard at work, climbing up the balconies of the rooms that faced into the space, weaving themselves through railing in pursuit of the sun's nourishment. They had to be hearty buggers to have hacked it this long. The hotel was ten stories tall and the vines had nearly reached the roof.

Claire was watching the stars when something pushed through the foliage and hit the glass where her face was resting. She jerked back and shone her light into the black eyes of a haggard slime. It brought a thin, greasy hand down on the glass, but barely made an impact. The thing looked like it had little muscle left. Probably blind as well. It pressed its face into the glass and gnashed what teeth it had left.

"Good God," Ritter snapped.

"I don't think it can get out of there," Andree said. "John, walk around and make sure."

Idaho did, reporting that the entrance to the atrium was barricaded. "We should still kill it."

"Let's just hold off before we bring down any 'cades." Andre eyed the slime, which had stopped moving and was leaning motionless against the glass. "Claire," Andre said, "You keep an eye on it. Let's clear the rest of this floor, then we'll head back upstairs."

Claire pulled a tattered leather chair over to the atrium and sat down. She put the light on the slime's face and watched it. It was impossible to guess what gender the person had been. Outside, the wind pushed and pulled at the building and rustled the vines which stretched high above the slime's head.

#

Dining room, kitchen, and staff areas. Service door to a basement which contained the laundry. All clear. Andre returned from the basement to the ground floor and walked through what had been the business center. He had a small penlight, which was nothing like the one he'd given Claire, but it was more than enough to pierce the pitch black here. He passed between desks with open laptops and crumpled balls of paper. There was a small drugstore. The shelves were bare, save for a few keychains and other worthless souvenirs. *I died in the Historic 23rd Street Hotel and all I got was this lousy hat.*

He met Ritter in a ballroom filled with folding chairs. It had probably been used for business seminars. *Rebranding for the End Times – Getting Every Last Dollar. Includes complimentary lunch.*

They went to the front of the lobby and saw that, as Ritter had suggested, the main barricade was deep and formidable. The front desk and the office behind it yielded nothing of interest.

"I guess we're clear," Andre said. "I'm going to want to look at the kitchen and basement again for supplies."

Ritter nodded. "Want to do the upstairs first?"

"It can wait," Andre said, "So long as all the doors are secured and nothing can get down here."

In the kitchen, he found a set of tools as well as some decent knives. Downstairs, a supply room turned up some crumbled powder that may have once been soap. The idea of collecting rainwater and having a bath made Andre swoon. If only they could afford such luxuries. Maybe, maybe.

What else? Some thin, insect-eaten towels, a few pieces of cookware that'd come in handy later…matches! From under sheets of moldy cardboard, Andre unearthed a box containing dozens of matchbooks. He held his breath, plucked a match free, and struck it on his shoulder armor. Goddamn if it didn't flare right up. Jackpot.

There was a twelve pack of bottled water behind the matches. Son of a bitch. This must have been someone's personal hidey-hole. A two-pound box of noodles, too. He opened it and rummaged through the contents. Looked edible. Lastly, there were a few containers of seasoning. He pocketed those. What the hell, might make the noodles taste like food.

"Dozens," came a soft call. Andre returned to the stairs and saw Idaho at the top. The kid looked excited. "You're not gonna believe this."

He led Andre back to the office at the check-in desk. Idaho had opened an air vent and proudly displayed what he'd found. Two-liter bottles of Admiral golden rum.

"Never heard of Admiral," Andre said, taking one of the bottles. "Sealed."

"Both unopened." Idaho grinned. "I don't care if it's toilet booze, it's booze."

"All right, take it easy. You're not off the clock yet."

"But man…booze! Are you not happy right now? I'm happy as a pup with two peters."

"I don't drink," Andre said. Idaho looked crestfallen.

"I'm not going to stop you," Andre said, "but I am going to play bartender. These go in my pack."

"Yeah, okay," Idaho grumbled. "I'm no lush."

"I believe you," Andre said. He paused, then asked, "Did you say 'a pup with two peters?'"

"Yes, sir."

"Okay then."

#

The four rested for a bit, watching the slime in the atrium. It wasn't much of a show. Eventually, they headed upstairs to clear each floor.

The second floor was a breeze. There were a few bodies in rooms, but they looked like suicides – each tucked into a bed, pill bottles collecting dust beside them. Andre wondered what sort of people had become sequestered here. It seemed like it had been a fancy place. Rich folks. The dead lay dressed in exquisite suits and gowns. Where there was an open window, the room was covered in a layer of dirt, and the lack of footprints was reassuring. These people had been able to afford some semblance of security in their final days. They'd made this pocket of normalcy for themselves. Of course, they'd died regardless. But perhaps on their own terms.

On the third floor, there was a pair of elevator doors which were partway open. Claire shone her light into the gap and saw a body dangling in the shaft.

"Found another one," she sighed. It looked like the person had tied a noose made from linens to the elevator cable. It was a female with patches of gray hair still affixed to her skull. The woman had a thick, furrowed brow which made her look angry, but it was just skin that had sloughed off her forehead and collected over her eyes.

Open eyes. Black.

Blink.

Claire jumped back. The woman let out a throaty hiss and launched a bony arm through the doors. Her hand had three fingers and they strained for Claire.

"Jee-zus!" Idaho raised his rifle.

"No!" Andre drew his cudgel. He seized the woman's wrist and brought the bludgeon down on her elbow. With a snap, the forearm went limp and withdrew into the shaft.

"Fuck me raw," Andre growled. He grabbed the doors to pull them apart. The woman's other arm came through and swiped at his face. As he jerked back, the slime's jagged nails come within millimeters of his flesh.

Andre fell back beside the others. "You know what? Leave her. She can't get out. She can't do shit."

"She almost tore your and Claire's faces off," Idaho said.

"We can push the doors closed," Ritter said. "We won't have to get within her reach."

"Yeah. Good thinking." Andre let out a long sigh.

"You all right?" Ritter asked him.

"I feel great," Andre said. He stepped to the door on the right. "Give me a hand here."

The doors closed, shutting out the slime's snarling protests. "Okay, now we know there are infected up here," Andre said. "We stay together, sweep room to room."

"Let's just take a minute," Claire said. Andre looked at her and she added, "I need it."

"Okay." Andre leaned back against the wall.

The surprises didn't end there. In a maintenance closet, they found the body of a maid. She didn't look like she'd been infected, but there were deep punctures in her breast. Might have been done with a knife. Nothing there to explain why.

Another open shaft revealed a pile of bodies down at the bottom, lying atop a smashed elevator car. The dead, prone in a tangle of broken limbs, moaned when the survivors' lights hit their faces. The survivors closed the doors.

The fourth floor was uneventful. The fifth-floor stairwell was barricaded, and it took some effort to get through. Claire questioned whether they should even bother. After all, they had four floors.

"If we're staying, even for a day, we clear this shit," Andre said. There was the slightest tremor in his voice, one that wouldn't have been detected by anyone who hadn't known him half a lifetime. He was scared, and he was pissed.

"Okay," Claire said. "If that's what we have to do."

"It's the smart thing."

The fifth-floor corridor was filled with carts. Forks, spoons, and plates were everywhere.

"Oh, c'mon." Idaho nudged something with his boot. It was a dog, probably, though most of its bones had been stripped clean. There were still curls of white hair on its backside. Little toy dog, Ritter told Claire, the sort you didn't see anymore. An accessory for the wealthy. And a last meal, it seemed.

One of the rooms which looked out over the atrium had a wheelchair sitting on the balcony. There was a withered slime who'd been strapped into the chair with belts and sheets. It stared through the sliding glass door at Claire and gnashed its teeth. Looked like it had once been an old man. His suit had been nice, once, and little round-rimmed spectacles still sat on the dead man's face.

Andre split the frames in half when he bludgeoned the man.

Another room contained an undead boy in its bathroom. He was bound as well, lying in the tub in a thick layer of dried blood and excrement.

Ritter took the cudgel from Andre. "I'll do it. I need to do one."

"You're sure it has to be this one?" Andre asked her.

Ritter nodded. Claire left the room.

Andre joined her in the hall a moment later. "We're gonna be fine," he said. "This is just…it's bad. But it'll be over."

"I know. I'm right here."

There was a sharp crack from the room. Andre sighed. "You just kinda have to trick yourself. Enjoy the quiet moments."

Another crack from the room, and a choked sob from Ritter. Claire wanted to say, *We'll laugh again,* but right then that sort of platitude seemed not just insincere, but a lie. Maybe it would sound true later.

#

It was near dawn when they reached the tenth and final floor. It looked as if the elites' elites had made their last stand here. Unlike the previous floors, this had only six suites, each massive and boasting high, vaulted windows which looked over Raylene. Antique bathtubs with iron feet, faded paintings on every wall; despite the ruin of it all, it still stood in stark contrast to the absolute pit that was the rest of the city. Claire stood at a window in one of the expansive living rooms and scanned the rooftops below for any sign of life.

"More suicides," Idaho said as he entered. He held up a revolver. "Five of them. They passed this around the dinner table."

"And," Ritter said from behind Idaho, "there's roof access from in here." She pointed out the door and across the hall. "There's a ladder in there that reaches a service hatch."

"Let's check it out." Andre rose from the chair he'd been slumped in.

The roof was ringed by iron railings on all sides. The same barriers surrounded the atrium opening. In the early morning light, Claire leaned over the atrium and tried to spot the slime down in the foliage.

"Careful," Andre told her. "So what've we got here, a garden?"

"It was, once," Ritter said. Decaying plants in ceramic pots were upset and sprawled all over the rooftop, the withered lumps of their fruit squishing and squirting underfoot. Ritter knelt to examine the garden's remains. "Wonder what they used for fertilizer. Do you think…?"

"I'd bet on it," Andre said. Ritter wrinkled her nose in disgust.

"No difference between pig shit and what we put out," said Idaho.

"Maybe," Ritter said, "but I'd like to hold onto the misconception."

"Man, I could eat," Idaho. "What do you say, boss? It's been like a day and a half."

"Has it?" Andre stared out at the city. "Yeah. Just eat slow. Let your stomach tell you when it's done."

"I found some booze downstairs," Idaho told the others. He sat cross-legged on the roof. "Claire, you're what, twenty-two?"

"I don't drink," she said.

"I feel like I'm a school trip," Idaho snorted. He eyed Ritter and said, "Sorry."

"It didn't even occur to me," Ritter said. "I was just their teacher."

"Yeah, but I know you feel bad. I mean, you and that little slime downstairs…" Idaho let the statement hang there in the air. When Ritter didn't respond, he said, "I mean, that was a mercy kill, right? You wanted to do him. Because of the kids."

"I appreciate your prying," Ritter said, "and the pop psychology, but if I ever do want to talk about it, you'll know."

Idaho rummaged through his pack for food. "I'd never have kids. I don't know what people are thinking. I mean, okay, be optimistic, but bringing kids into this?"

"So I assume you got the snip," said Andre.

"Yep. Why not? Any soldier who does it gets the same perks, no matter your age or whatever." Idaho shrugged. "I know you didn't do it, Dozens. That's why you're still a corporal, man. Someday I might outrank your ass. Get clipped."

"I can help contain the surplus population without having my bag unzipped by some field surgeon," Andre said. "It's called self-control, little John."

Idaho smiled. "You should have been a chaplain."

"Your license to fuck is stamped all over your upper lip," Andre said. Idaho blanched, then turned beet-red as he covered his mouth.

"Oh, don't worry," Andre said, "you look clean right now. But you know stress brings on the herps. Keep an eye on it."

Idaho cast a miserable sideways glance at Claire. As if it made any difference to her. She stared hard into the atrium like she was searching for a needle in a haystack.

"Everybody's got 'em," Idaho muttered. "You know what, I'm not hungry."

"You're not getting a pull of that rum unless you eat," Andre said. Idaho flipped him off.

A loud metallic PING! sounded at Claire's left. She looked up and saw nothing but Andre, who was lunging at her in a blur. He tackled her into a mess of rotten leaves.

"Shooter!" he coughed. Idaho and Ritter hit the deck. Andre looked toward the railing off which the bullet had bounced. Idaho lay on his back, rifle in hand. Andre raised a hand to still him. "Wait," he mouthed.

"That wasn't meant for any of you," a man's voice called. "Just letting ourselves be known."

Andre looked furtively at the others. "Don't say a word."

"We can be friends," the voice said. "You Army?"

Andre shut his eyes and called, "We're rebuilders."

"Rebs," the voice said. "Must be on the lam from those knights, huh? I think they've moved on. I think."

"And who are you?" Andre shouted.

"I go by Max. We go by the Tribe."

"Raiders," Andre whispered. "All right. Here's what they want. They want our guns. They'll let us keep the food if we give them the rum. They're going to take the hotel."

"What do you mean, take it?" Idaho said.

"We don't know how many there are," Andre shot back. "But I'll bet they know we don't have anyone else."

"So we just let wave the white fuckin' flag?" Idaho snapped.

"Shut up," Claire growled. "Just shut up. You don't know what to do."

"I know this is my gun," Idaho said. "And this is our hotel."

"I'm ordering you to put that rifle down," said Andre.

"You done talking amongst yourselves?" called the man. "Why don't you stand up and relax? We're not out for blood, gents." The man sounded middle-aged, his voice thick and gravely, but still with that genial tone that was nothing but troubling.

"John. Drop it. Then we stand."

"This is shit," Idaho muttered. "Gonna bend over for these motherfuckers. I thought more of you, man."

"You're only thinking of yourself," said Andre. "You're not the only one here. Neither am I."

Andre got to his knees. "Lose the rifle, John." He rose to his feet.

Ritter and Claire followed suit. Claire left her pistol resting next to her foot. Idaho didn't move.

On the roof of the next building, a couple stories beneath them, a man with a gray beard and a bomber jacket stood with both hands open at his sides. He wasn't armed. But the ones behind him were. Crouched behind air conditioning units, men and women alike, all with rifles trained and unwavering.

"Where's the other guy?" asked the bearded man. "Don't tell me he went inside. That's not gonna be good."

Idaho stood. The M4 hung off his shoulder. Andre shot him a blistering glare.

"Why don't you do like your friends and set that down," called the man.

"Max, right?" Idaho called.

The man nodded.

"Yeah," Idaho said. "Fuck you, Max."

Andre tensed. He turned toward Idaho, who dropped the rifle into his hands. "Don't," he said.

Johnny Idaho's eyes had changed. Claire had never seen that intensity, that fever, in him before. He was a man who'd made a desperate decision and wasn't going back on it.

"Johnny," she said gently. "Not like this."

"Like what, then?" Idaho didn't look at her. He turned from Andre to face the man on the other building. "We all gotta get it sometime."

Andre let out a sigh, shoulders sagging. Suddenly, he was moving, steady and sharp as an arrow, slamming into Idaho's side and knocking him off his feet. The gun spat two rounds as the pair fell onto the roof.

Andre was on top of Idaho. They both had their hands on the barrel of the M4. Claire leapt forward and swung a boot into Idaho's shoulder. The soldier bellowed, but held fast to the rifle.

"Drop it, John!" Andre yelled. "Goddammit, you're going to get us all killed!"

"You are!" Idaho seized Andre by the neck. Claire gritted her teeth and stomped down on his forehead.

Idaho let out a grunt. His hands both fell free. He tried to roll away, but Andre stayed on him and tossed the gun to Claire.

Idaho grabbed his head and moaned. "What kinda— unnhh...*bitch!*"

"You got your dog leashed yet?" called Max.

Claire turned. "It's fine!"

"Put that rifle down, little lady, and it will be." The man smiled at her.

Claire slowly lowered the M4 and let it fall into a garden bed.

"Okay then," said Max. "Let's see all of you now."

Andre wrestled Idaho to his feet with the younger man's neck and arms locked in a vise-like hold.

Max looked from one face to another, seeming to appraise each of the four. Then he said, "Black guy. You in charge?"

Andre nodded, his expression hard.

"You sure?" Max asked. There were a few muffled laughs behind him.

"Just tell us what you want," Andre said.

"Let go of him," Max said. His smile was still there, but it wasn't real anymore. Claire glanced downward at the rifle. Her stomach was churning. Something bad was going to happen.

Andre released Idaho.

"Good," Max said.

Idaho rubbed his neck and shoulders. Claire was sure he was about to say something shitty when the first bullet tore through him.

He spun around and the second shot punched into his back. He hit the atrium railing and folded over it. Then he was gone.

No one hit the deck this time. Ritter didn't even move. Claire and Andre ran to the railing, panicked epithets spilling from their mouths. They saw Idaho three floors down. He'd caught a balcony railing—rather, it had caught him, and he dangled motionless with one shattered arm ensnared in the railing.

He looked dead. Claire called his name. It came out an indecipherable croak. But Johnny Idaho lifted his head and looked at her.

His arm, little more than a flesh sleeve filled with broken bone, slipped loose, and he dropped soundlessly, still looking up, until he was swallowed by the wretched greenery.

"Let's turn around and step to the edge of the roof," Max shouted. "We're good now. Come on."

Andre stared across the gap between the buildings. *"Good?"* he breathed.

Ritter's face was blank. Andre poked at her ankle with the toe of his boot. "Ritter. Listen. Just hear me." He spoke through lips that barely moved. "The hatch is right behind you. Two steps."

"So now let's talk terms," Max called. "We're coming over."

"They're going to take *us,*" Ritter moaned.

"Two steps back," Andre said. "Now. Now!"

"Are you paying attention?" Max yelled.

Andre shoved Ritter. In the same move, he bent to snatch up his M4, and he barked, "Claire, after her!" before opening fire through the railing.

Claire didn't see what happened next. She only saw the open hatch, Ritter slipping through it with her face still expressionless. Claire felt the impossible weight of her legs as she dragged them along. She heard the roaring of her own blood in her head. That and the way time seemed to slow to a crawl made her feel as if her blood had become a heavy sludge clogging her arms and legs. Then she was over the hatch, and falling through it, a distant sensation of burning as her hip struck the opening and her flesh on that side was raked raw all the way up to her armpit. Feet striking the rungs of a ladder, smacking her tailbone and head on said ladder, and finally flat on the floor. And glass shattering. It spun overhead and threw daggers of sunlight into her eyes. They were shooting through the windows.

Claire sat up. Ritter, in the doorway leading from the room, screamed at her to *get flat.* Claire was trying to process that when blood exploded from Ritter's stomach. Ritter turned but she didn't fall. She ran.

Claire flattened herself on the floor and pulled herself to the doorway. Into a hallway and the front door to the suite. She clawed at the hardwood and the plaster and kicked her way to the door. It was partially open—Ritter must have gone through it—Claire pulled it open and scrambled to her feet in the service corridor.

Her light was little use as she thundered down the stairs. The light's beam bounced and swung in her hand, and she was barely able to detect the debris littered ahead of her. Several times she stepped on something and skidded painfully to the next landing.

Knees and elbows crashed against walls. Her blood continued rocketing through her brain with a tsunami soundtrack. When she burst through the last door into the hotel lobby, Claire shouted for Ritter. There was no answer. The cacophony in her veins subsided somewhat. She didn't hear gunfire. The realization that they must have killed Andre fell upon her in a silence far more jarring than anything she'd ever heard.

She shined the light on the atrium. There was no sign of Johnny Idaho, but the glass was cracked in several places. Must have been from his impact. He must have bounced around in there before settling into the brush, before the blind slime's hands found him.

The slime emerged from the foliage and pressed its head against the glass. Claire stood motionless.

The slime's ragged, papery palms moved over the glass. It seemed to feel the cracks there, and rubbed back and forth over them. It rocked back and began pushing.

There was nothing anymore in this place but Claire and Death, and the latter was closing in on all sides. Claire willed herself to change. Her skin became dry and rough, her hair brittle. She willed her eyes black and empty. Glass fell inward and sprayed across the lobby. The slime entered.

Feigning a limp, Claire began moving away from the dead thing, dragging one foot behind her through the glass. The slime looked in her direction and started to follow. Claire quickened her pace. She didn't want to give herself away, but the stiff-legged cadaver was striding purposefully toward her—

Shit...it's blind. It can only hear me. My cover's no good.

She dropped the shambling routine and raced across the lobby as quietly as she could. The slime turned to follow. *Damn!*

No gun. No cudgel. No backup. Only Death. Claire vaulted over the check-in desk and landed on her ankle with a tearing pain. She suppressed a cry and made her way into the office, shutting the door behind her. Fire raced up her calf. Claire ignored it and pushed a desk up against the door.

What am I doing? She could wait out the slime's attention span, but the raiders would come. And they'd find her alone, and...

What would they decide to take?

Claire sat down in the dark and scooted underneath the desk. She cradled her throbbing ankle.

A light scratching began on the other side of the door. She wanted to scream as the damn thing to go away, to go fuck itself and be dead like it was supposed to. She could only bite down on her lip and concentrate on silence, on defying every instinct in her body.

She heard the sound of splitting wood. *No! It can't be that strong.* She braced herself beneath the desk. She'd hold it in place until she passed out. It felt like that moment might not be too far off.

Voices now. The Tribe. Thumping and dragging sounds. They must have shot the slime. So they knew where she was, and there wouldn't be any holding them back.

Claire crawled out from under the desk and pulled herself across the floor to the back of the room. She wedged herself as best she could behind a long file cabinet.

The door slowly opened, shoving the desk back, and silhouettes entered. One stepped forward. There was a snap, and a match appeared in the shadow's black claw.

"Holy—"

Claire gasped and hid her face behind her hands. "Don't!"

Her skin flushed and returned to its normal tone. The blotches and bruises she'd dreamed up faded in a second. She peered out between her fingers.

A scruffy young man held the match up against a small torch. As the torch flared to life, he stared in confusion at Claire.

"She won't bite," someone said behind him.

"No. It's just—I thought—forget it." The man held the torch toward Claire. "If you're bit, you tell us now. We're gonna find out anyway."

"Then why should I tell you?" Claire mumbled.

The man smiled a little. "It'll make all the difference when your time comes, I promise. Honesty's the only policy."

"I'm not bit," Claire said.

"Okay. Well, stand up and let's see."

Claire grabbed the side of the file cabinet and winced. "I can't. My foot."

The man turned to the others. "She wants a woman. Get Hina."

"A woman?" Claire frowned. "I don't know what you mean."

The man and his companions backed out through the door. A moment later, a woman scarcely older than Claire entered the room with a torch in one hand and what Claire recognized as a bowling pin in the other. Holding the pin like a club, the woman said, "Strip."

"What?"

"Come on. Bite check."

"Why? What do you want with me?"

"Listen," the woman said, sitting on the corner of the desk. "White boy had to go. You know that. Anyone could see he was trouble. But we're really not out for blood."

"That's why you killed everyone else?" Claire turned her face from the torchlight.

"Your man Andre is going to be fine," the woman said. "As long as he plays nice. He got winged but that's all. Where's the Chinese gal?"

"You. Killed. Her."

"Hell." The woman sighed. "Didn't mean to. That's not how we work. She upstairs?"

Claire shrugged.

"But you know she's dead."

"Gut-shot."

The woman stood. "Let me see this foot you're whining about."

"You can get fucked," Claire said. "Take our shit and leave us. Or dump us in a sewer. But don't think you're getting one inch closer."

"I'm a medic," the woman said. "Korn sent me in here to help you. And check for bites, of course. You want to refuse? Okay. I can tell you how that's going to turn out. See, either you come with us or you never leave."

"And who's Korn?"

"Max. You know Max."

The woman motioned at Claire's foot. "It's that one, right? Can you get the boot off?"

Claire didn't say anything. "Okay," the woman said, shrugging. She left the room, but the door stayed open. A man with a rifle stood there and watched Claire.

The woman returned with a man whose neck and head were bandaged. It was Andre. Claire gripped the cabinet and tried to raise herself on her good foot. It took effort, but she managed to sling one arm over the cabinet and steady herself.

"Sit," the woman told Andre, pushing him into an office chair. "Okay now, Claire. You're out of second chances. Andre's gonna sit here and you're going to get checked out. First, that boot."

The woman knelt and began untying the boot's laces. The gunman stood by in the doorway. "I'm Hina," the woman said. "I'm a registered nurse. Just do what I say."

Removing the laces entirely, Hina pried at the boot to loosen it. She pulled the tongue out and felt along Claire's calf. "Okay, this is coming off in one shot. Hold onto something."

She didn't wait for a response before pulling the boot free. Claire let herself cry out this time. "Sock," Hina said, rolling the cotton down over Claire's ankle. It felt like she was tearing Claire's foot off. Finally, the foot was bare, and Hina pulled a chair over for Claire to sit.

Hina gingerly looked the foot over. "Sprained it good. Running?"

"Does it matter?"

"Okay. Now I'll help you with your pants, but you take the rest off yourself."

Andre lowered his eyes and hid his face behind one hand. "Do you want him to leave?" Hina asked Claire.

"Andre or the guard?"

"Guard stays."

"Andre stays too."

There was a gunshot from somewhere in the building. Everyone paused and looked up. A yell echoed across the lobby: "We're clear!"

Hina reached to unbutton Claire's pants. Claire pushed her hands away. "I've got it."

"They need to come all the way off, over that ankle."

"I said I've got it."

The young man who'd first discovered Claire leaned into the room. "Found the Asian. She was too messed up to save."

That shot had been Ritter's death. Claire closed her eyes and tried to still her trembling form. She pushed her pants down to her knees.

"Caliban," Hina said to the young man. "Get lost."

"Huh? Oh. Right."

Claire managed to shake the pants off her injured foot without letting the agony show. Hina looked impressed. The medic stepped back. "Okay, the rest."

The guard turned halfway from Claire. It only pissed her off more that this "tribe" had some sort of moral code. That man Max had been cool as could be when his people gunned Idaho down.

"What did they do to you?" she asked Andre.

From behind his hand, he said, "Grazed me is all. Counting my blessings."

"You're a tough bunch," Hina said. She took Claire's shirt and bra from her, then lifted her arms and examined them in the torchlight. "That must be how you got away from the knights. Few did."

"How do you know about it?" Claire demanded.

"We know how to see without being seen." Hina lowered Claire's arms and stepped around the chair, pulling her hair away from her neck. "We didn't know, though, that you all were at war."

"Neither did we," muttered Andre.

"Figures." Hina pushed Claire forward in her seat so she could look at her back. "Want help with your underwear?"

"No," Claire said. "You honestly think a slime could have bitten my ass?"

"I've seen stranger. And worse," Hina replied.

Max Korn leaned into the room. "Let me know when you're done. Want to talk to the girl."

Claire covered her breasts and shot him a glare. "Didn't mean it, little lady," Max said, then disappeared.

"What would he want to talk to me about?" Claire murmured.

"I don't know," Hina said. "Whatever it is, just tell him the truth."

#

With her ankle wrapped a clean (less filthy) set of clothes from down in the laundry, Claire sat alone in the office. Max and the young man, Caliban, walked in.

"All right," said Max. "Right to it, short and sweet. My friend here is damned sure that he saw something, something that doesn't make a lot of sense. But it wouldn't be the first time I've heard of it."

Claire's heart sank. This couldn't be. God, why hadn't she changed back right when she got away from the slime? She wanted Andre. She needed him to help her explain, to make them see.

"You looked like you were dead," Caliban said. "I mean the whole number. You looked rotten. Then you waved your hands and poof, you're normal."

"See," Max told Claire, "there are all sorts of tales people tell out there. You live long enough, travel enough, you hear all the best ones. You hear about people who've evolved. Who can play dead."

Claire shook her head at Caliban. "I don't know what you think you saw, but you looked just as scared as me. Probably expected another slime."

"Girl, you need to be straight with us." Max knelt next to her chair. "Some people think it's the other way around, you see. That people like you are slimes who play alive."

"I am alive," Claire said. "I have a pulse. I have a mind. Ask Andre. He's known me fifteen years."

"We will," Max said. "Provided you do the next thing I ask of you. Okay?"

Claire shivered at his friendly expression. "Wh-what?"

"Turn your hair red."

Claire stared at the space between the two men. Max stood back up. "Or I feed your friend to my dogs. I'm nice, Claire. But I can be mean if I'm pushed."

She wondered if he meant literal dogs or something else. She didn't want to know. She certainly didn't want Andre to. Claire closed her eyes and asked, "Are you going to kill me?"

"Of course not."

"You'll sell me then."

"The way I see it, Claire, you're too valuable to let go. And that's good, very good, for you. And Andre. Provided you are what I think you are."

"I'm a person. I'm just a person," Claire insisted, her voice breaking.

"You're a special person," Max said softly. "You had to know this day would come. Let me see now. Dark red."

Claire let her head fall. She said nothing as her hair rippled and darkened, as if each strand were a vein filling with blood.

"Can you make it longer?" Max asked, his voice an awed whisper.

"No."

She willed the tendrils of her now-crimson locks tightly together, drawing moisture from them as well as her scalp, giving herself the appearance of a shorter, thinner style. She turned her hair raven black and looked up. "I can do that."

"And your skin. You can make yourself black, yellow, anything you need. I'll bet you can reshape your eyes." Max's own eyes were alight with excitement. Claire felt like an animal in a cage.

"Can you make yourself tall, or fat, or..." Caliban looked at Max, who silenced him with a grimace.

"Just texture and pigment," Max said. "Still, incredible."

"You're a scientist," Claire said. "Aren't you."

"Just an enthusiast, Claire. I owned a bowling alley." Max patted Caliban on the shoulder. "Thank you. Go take care of your arrangements. And let's be discreet about this."

Caliban left the office. Max told Claire, "You have nothing to worry about." He picked up his torch from where it was propped in a desk drawer and said, "Let's get you up and moving around. Better for the ankle."

As he walked out of the office, calling across the lobby to someone, his bomber jacket hitched up slightly. Claire only saw what she saw for a second—and, just like Caliban had been, she was damn sure of what she'd seen.

Metal armor.

FIVE | MEET THE ROYALS

Eli Joleni shook a few last drops of piss from his member and stepped away from the hole in the floor. He'd commissioned ceramic faux-toilets to at least offer the illusion of civilized comfort, but as always, progress tended to move more quickly when achieved through destruction rather than creation. There wasn't a great deal left to destroy around here. Eli walked to sink where, in lieu of running water, there was a bowl of vinegar scented with flower petals. He dipped his hands once, shook off the excess, and then wiped on his robe.

Stepping out of the restroom, he took a moment to enjoy the morning warmth streaming through the windows. The hallway was appointed with several fake plants whose vines framed each glassless opening. Very Old World. Or Old-Old World, he supposed, smoothing his robe and fastening the buttons about his collar.

"House-Major?"

Eli turned toward the voice and saw one of the high servants, Hansom Fete, walking briskly down the hall. He had some parchment in his hand. Eli rolled his eyes and asked, "What is this now? I've scarcely eaten."

"It's the last bit of paperwork for the demo order," Fete said, holding out the parchment. Fete was in his thirties, probably Eli's age, but his finely trimmed beard was white as snow, as were his thinning sideburns. He was worked hard, but the results spoke for themselves. Eli snatched the parchment and unfolded it, reading over the hand-written document.

He snapped his hand and Fete gave him a fountain pen, then turned dutifully to offer his back as a writing surface. Eli signed the parchment. "I like this ink," he said.

"It's made from insect dye," Fete said. "You requested a full set last month, I believe. They should arrive any day."

"I'm sure."

"House-Major, with all due respect…"

"I've never heard that phrase followed by anything worthy of it, Fete."

"The Arches generally prefer to be consulted on projects such as this demolition you've ordered. Anything regarding aesthetics, really—outside of your personal estate, of course."

Eli stepped back and folded the parchment. Fete took it and looked to Eli for a reply. Joleni let the silence hang there for one second, then two, until Fete looked away in discomfort.

"It's a water fountain," Eli said. "And it's ugly, and it's wasteful, and it's filled with bacteria. Do you really think the Arches need to be bothered with such things?"

Fete nodded. "I'm only looking out for this house."

"You mean me." Eli smiled. "I am the house, remember."

"Of course, yes."

"We're done then." Eli began striding toward his office. He stopped and spun sharply on his heels. "Wait."

Fete, who was heading in the opposite direction as quickly as possible without breaking into a run, stumbled and froze.

"The Twenty-Fifty irrigation plans," Eli said. "I still haven't seen them."

"Oh." Fete faced him and offered a sheepish expression of remorse. "Neither have I, sir. I don't know what the delay is."

"Is there someone," asked Eli, tapping one finger against the side of his jaw, "whose job it might be to deal with such matters?"

Fete began to speak and Eli cut him off. "I would think that such inefficiency ought to be rectified before any echo of it reached the House-Major's office. Wouldn't you?"

Fete didn't speak. The parchment in his hand was rattling as he shook. Good. It was good for him to know that, even after all this time, he was not above reproach, nor punishment.

Eli told him, "Were I of a certain mood, I might want to have this person brought to me for a personal reprimand. As it is, though, I'm quite busy. You know that. No time for play."

Fete gave a shaky nod.

"So then," Joleni said, "I'm going to hand this off to my most trusted servant, Hansom Fete. I know that he will prevent such...what's the word...cocked-up bullshit from entering my sphere of awareness ever again."

"I'll fetch the plans," Fete said, and this time, he ran.

Eli pushed open the office doors and found a maid dusting the end tables. When she glanced up, a wet shimmer crossed her blue gaze. "I'll come back," she stammered, leaving through the door on the other side of the room.

Eli unbuttoned his robe and collar and tossed them over the back of a chair. He rounded the long desk at the center of the room, took off his dress jacket, and seated himself. Rolling up a shirt sleeve, he removed a key from his breast pocket and unlocked the bottom drawer of the desk. As he pulled out the drawer, he observed the bruised welt on his inner arm. It no longer hurt but it was painful to look at. He'd apply some honey balm and use the other arm next time.

On a small serving tray, he placed the syringe and the little black vial from the drawer. Humming a nameless tune from his childhood, he sat back and began tying his arm off with a length of lace.

The main doors rattled. Eli snarled and jerked the knot from the lace. He swept the tray and its contents into the open drawer, followed by the lace. He was unable to pull down his sleeve before the doors swung inward.

"Good morning, Eli," said the House-Lady.

"Miranda," Eli grunted. He left his sleeve rolled up and leaned on his elbow to glower at her.

"Getting an early start?" Miranda asked, pursing her lips and offering her most condescending smile.

Eli closed his fist and listened to the cracking of his knuckles. He said, eyes closed, "Actually, dear, I came in this morning expecting to find the Twenty-Fifty irrigation plans on my desk. Would you believe they aren't here?"

"Well, Eli," Miranda replied, "in all fairness, I don't think anyone anticipated your sudden lust for paperwork."

"I designed those canals myself," Eli said. "I am overseeing every aspect of this project. I'm sure my attentions would be appreciated by a better class of people."

"No doubt the Arches will be impressed."

"This isn't about politics. I'm doing it because it needs doing. There are seven houses in the province, and we're the only one that can't raise our own food."

"That does bother you in a particular way, doesn't it?" Miranda lifted his robe from the chair where he'd placed it and dropped it unceremoniously to the floor. Sitting in her long dress, Miranda added, "You've always found a way to eat."

Eli realized his fist was closed so tightly that his nails were biting into his palm. He opened his hand with a grimace. "My predecessor wasn't as concerned with living well as he was dying brilliantly."

Miranda's stare darkened. Even amongst the thicket of calligraphy she tattooed on her face every day—stenciling made from the same bug dye as those pens—he saw her reaction and drank it in. Even the most painful truth needed a little extra edge to it. The fact was that Eli's predecessor, the House-Lady's late husband, had been born into the role of leader, and most certainly behaved like it. Eli had been working eight years now to restore the dignity of this estate and there was still much to be done.

He had to learn, he told himself, to live from one day to the next, as he had in the past, and to appreciate the little things. Seeing Miranda's façade crack behind the veneer of her makeup and the accoutrements of her station was nice. It wasn't the sweet sting of the needle, but it was bitterly pleasant. Like watching a spent bee writhe while its tiny guts throbbed on the end of the stinger it had planted in one's flesh.

But she recovered quickly. A formidable sparring partner if ever he'd had one. Miranda straightened in the chair and said, "You'll want to know that your pens are downstairs. They look lovely. I'm sure they'll get a workout."

Eli cocked his head and rested it on his hand. "Miranda, do you hate me?"

"You know I do," she cooed.

"*You* know I have never tried to take Iain's place in your life. Only his seat." Eli stuck out his lower lip in a pout. "I wish we could work together. Or is that it? Do you feel I took *your* seat?"

Miranda stood. "I have meetings."

"Sounds exciting," said Eli. "Do keep me apprised of anything important."

He watched her go and rolled down his shirt sleeve. He felt much better now. He donned his jacket and fetched the robe and collar from the floor.

The pens were lovely indeed. He'd ordered one in every available color and there were seventeen in all. All for his personal collection. He tried not to hop and skip as he mounted the stairs back to his office. This time, he locked the doors.

He returned to his desk and got everything he needed out. Syringe, lace. No need for the vial. He unscrewed the first pen, taking note of the exquisite work that had done on the polished wood casing. He removed the plastic cylinder containing what looked like ink and stabbed the syringe into the top.

It had been worth the wait. This was far purer than the street grade he usually imported. He silently congratulated himself on the pen ruse. Miranda had been out to cut off his supply ever since she'd first seen him high—which was to say, happy—and he'd had to become especially creative to get around her little spies.

As she'd noted, he always found a way to eat.

He found his vein and sank the syringe into his arm. Mere seconds passed before warmth and light flooded through him. He pulled off the lace tie and leaned back. Calming tingles swam up through his spine and into his brain. He watched the world drift away.

He thought of things, of colors and sounds. He imagined tastes and textures and they came to life, pouring over his skin and into him. He thought of soft alabaster flesh. Soft alabaster breasts, all too yielding in his hot palms. Skin peeling from muscle peeling from bone. Copper, rich and purifying. The odor had once made him sick but now he sucked it deep into his nostrils. Hips, smooth and wide, bucking against him. Thighs spread, quivering, hungering. Silk sheets and rope. A thick, downy pillow molding to the screaming skull of Iain DiPontiac. Those final heaving, choking struggles. Official cause of death: cardiac arrest. No, no. Murder weapon: pillow. That made Eli laugh, and his laughter felt like champagne bubbles that emerged from his lips and filled the air, ensnaring the light and sending a cascade of colors raining down on Eli. He reached his hands up and stuck out his tongue to catch the bits of spectrum, like snowflakes. He hadn't seen snow in so long. The thought of crystal flakes on his cheeks made him think of Miranda Sortho's miserable tears as they buried Iain. Iain was in a cold, dark hole without color or sound. Iain was in Hell. He probably couldn't tell the difference, the uncultured plebe. Eli had lived in the dark for a long time. But he'd learned to reveal and see and taste the color hidden in it. He lived brilliantly. He said, let there be light, and then he *was.*

He made a half-hearted effort at sweeping his contraband into the drawer, then lay on the floor behind his desk and drew lines in the air above him.

Some time later, he awoke from a deep sleep. Eli tried to catch the fragments of dreaming that still lingered, but they were as smoke and slipped through his fingers. He rested his head on the carpet and tracked beads of sweat as they climbed down his brow and neck.

Miranda had planted a tree where Iain was interred. It produced some noxious little white flower whose scent made Eli's head hurt. He thought maybe he'd tear the whole thing up and plant an apple tree there. Or an orange tree. The thought of the juice running down his chin made him salivate.

#

Miranda sat atop the roof of her wing of the mansion, reclining in a chaise with a wide-brimmed hat shielding her eyes from the sun. She could see Iain's grave from here, but she stared through it at nothing. Her thoughts of Eli—not even thoughts, just raw emotions—consumed all her senses and left her feeling numb on the outside.

"I've said it before, why not poison the devilspit?" The man standing behind her rested a hand on the back of the chaise and brushed his fingertips against her dark locks. Miranda turned her head to rest her cheek against his hand.

"He's the Senior's prodigal son," Miranda said. "He stole that from Iain too. Eli is beloved. It's well-known that he uses devilspit—even if it looked like an overdose, they'd run tests."

Arch-Major Salt was quiet for a bit. Miranda listened to his breathing, slightly labored but rhythmic. He was twenty years older than her, and bore signs of his age, but they were subtle. His mind was fiercely sharp as ever. The way his bushy eyebrows met when he glared in deep thought was oddly handsome. It was comforting, at the least.

Salt spoke. "Our red-*handed* stepchild. Seems everyone but the senior knows all about Eli's tastes. And his guilt."

"The Senior knows," Miranda said, clicking her teeth. "He didn't really care for Iain. I think he prefers Eli as a successor. Perhaps even more so for killing Iain."

Salt harrumphed. "But would he favor me if I killed Eli? No. Eli is held to different standards because of his lack of sophistication. It's obscene."

The Arches and the House-Majors were no less than the former captains of industry and government. It was only because of this that they'd been able to fortify themselves so well—and quickly—against the undead threat, and to preserve a semblance of modernity. Most of the region they held had been fortified long before the outbreaks. The province and its houses sat atop mazes of nuclear bunkers and power stations. Eli, it was said, had come from some family fallout shelter on the outside, surviving for years on his own. He was a savage. And it seemed the Senior Arch-Major admired that more than he had his own son, Iain, who had only lived by the values his father handed down.

No, felling Eli would take more than a vial of poison. To bring him down would mean bringing down those who supported him. It meant treason. It meant a new war, a secret war, and it was already underway.

SIX | THE STRANGE DEAD

Eli walked down a dimly lit tunnel of stone, his shoes clapping on the uneven floor. He was flanked by four armed guards. Hansom Fete hurried along behind him.

"Sir," Fete called. "A reminder—the Church's representatives are set to arrive tomorrow afternoon. It would be best if all this was done by then."

"It'll be done tonight," Eli said. "On my end, anyway. You'll take care of distributing product. Are you sure none of the Church people would care to indulge?"

"I really don't think so, sir."

The tunnel widened, and with it came more light. Torches were set into the walls every few feet. A group of disheveled men waited there, hunting rifles on their shoulders and knives in their boots.

Eli offered a cordial smile. "Let's see, then."

The men parted. Behind them was a large tarp weighed down by chains. The tarp stirred and the lumps beneath it undulated. Then it began to heave.

One of the men motioned to another, who grabbed the chains and peeled the tarp back. A half-dozen manacled slimes rose. They immediately lurched forward, but they were each chained to the rest and the little horde only succeeded in spilling itself onto the floor.

"Three male, three female," said one of the men. "All adults. Two white, four Latin. As per his request."

"Good. And the extra bit?"

The man stepped on the back of a slime's neck and knelt to draw his knife. The slime snarled and wriggled as the man slit open the back of its moldy shirt. He pried at lengths of duct tape and finally tore them loose, taking some skin as well. The tape held several packets of dark powder.

The man tossed a packet to Eli. Eli caught the bag and tossed it aside. "I'll choose," he said, coming forward. He peeled another packet away from the tape. "Knife?"

The man scowled, but handed over his blade. Eli made a tiny hole in the package. He licked his pinky and dipped it into the powder. It was thin and grainy. The liquid form would probably be gritty also. Nothing like what he'd gotten with his pen collection. Still, it was plenty good enough for the common user. Eli licked his finger clean and closed his eyes to concentrate on the buzz. A little lift, some color, nothing special. But it was street grade and that was what he'd ordered.

"All right," he said, taking the tangle of duct tape from the man. He handed it over to Fete. "Sort it. Cut it. Sell it."

To the man, Eli said, "Two foals and a calf. They'll be upstairs."

"No, no," the man said. "Two calves and one foal."

"Your payment is upstairs," Eli said, and turned to leave. The man caught his arm.

Eli turned back with a look of genuine curiosity. There must have been something else in that look, too, because the man let go of him.

"One calf wasn't the deal," the man said, his tone far less assertive.

Eli nodded. "And you spoke to whom…?"

"It wasn't me. One of my guys met with one of yours on the outside. The whole thing was settled. Square. We wanted two calves."

"Well, I'm terribly sorry," Eli said. "But you're getting two foals. That's what I heard on my end. That's what you're taking. Remember, your original deal with the Maestro would have given you zero calves."

"We don't deal with the Maestro." The man was red-faced. His companions were stock-still, as if awaiting some order. "We deal with you."

Eli leaned in, close enough to smell the foulness of the man's breath. He waited until the man stopped breathing in dreadful anticipation.

"Then deal with *it,*" Eli said.

He yawned. "I can always find other suppliers."

"The other suppliers know better," the man said. What a petulant little thing. "This is our route. This is our gig."

"As long as you're alive, sure," Eli said. "Let me be crystal fucking clear with you, gents. You are pig shit. You are nothing if not replaceable. You," he said to the lead man, stabbing a long finger in his face, "are. Pig. Shit."

The man's skin was practically boiling with anger and embarrassment. He stared hard at Eli, who answered the look with something not unlike complete indifference.

The guards behind Eli had not moved in all this time. When he snapped his fingers, they trained their automatics on the others.

"What's your name?" Eli asked the man.

"Wh-why?"

"Your name is Why?" Eli frowned. "I don't think so."

"Kelvin."

"Try again."

The man shook his head. "That's my name."

"No. I told you. Say it back to me." Eli was in the man's face again. "Say it."

Then the man understood, and his face went from red to purple. He shook. Eli smiled broadly. "Go ahead."

The man cast a look back at his group. On the tunnel floor, the slimes squirmed and grumbled.

The man looked back at Eli. Barely above a whisper, he said, "It's Pig."

"I didn't hear you. Actually, *they* didn't. Turn around and tell them."

The man bared his teeth. Eli grabbed him by the shoulder and spun him around. "Come on. You've already lost the calf. Want your foals?"

"What?" the man exclaimed. One of Eli's guards stepped around him and pressed a muzzle into his ribs.

"For two foals," Eli said into the man's ear. "Tell them."

"P-Pig."

"What's Pig? What do you mean?"

"My name." The man seemed to have shrunk a good five inches. With Eli's hand resting on his shoulder, he said, "My name is Pig."

"Pig what?"

Dead silence in the tunnel. It didn't sound like anyone was breathing now. Just a bunch of dead people standing around.

"My name is Pig Shit."

"Pig Shit," Eli said, "you and your men are free to go. Your *foal* will be upstairs at the gate. We appreciate you."

The man did not look back at Eli, nor did he say anything else. He walked to his men, and they turned to follow him past the chained slimes and into the dark.

#

There were two large, caged service elevators at the other end of the tunnel. The slimes were herded into one by the guards, and the car descended; Eli took the second down by himself.

At the bottom, Eli's cage opened onto a black corridor with a low ceiling. The air was ice. Cooling units hummed in the shadows.

Eli stepped out. The other elevator remained closed, and the things within thrashed. Eli called down the corridor. "New flesh!"

A little old man hastened into the light of the elevators, fast as his tiny bow legs would allow. He straightened a pair of spectacles and peered into the closed car. "Six, then?"

"It's whatever he ordered."

The man clapped his hands once. Two larger men with plastic bite armor and long poles approached. The poles were affixed with dull hooks to snag the slimes' chains. The pair opened the cage manually and stabbed the poles into the mass of struggling flesh.

Eli followed them at a safe distance as they wrestled the slimes through the darkness. There was a light ahead. And music. Tinny, warbling music, something slow and trance-like. Eli had worked in this house for eight years, running it the last five. He'd been down here a hundred times. Yet it never felt right. It reminded him, deep in his bones, of old, bad places.

Entering the lit area, he realized the little old man was gone. Eli searched the shadows at his back, but saw nothing. One of the larger men called to him. "He'll receive you now."

The light came from a lamp hanging in an alcove. There was a doorway beneath it. The two large men pulled the slimes further down the corridor, leaving Eli to stare at the little doorway. He steeled himself and stepped through.

The light in the next room was tinged red. Every lamp and lantern had a shade over it that turned the room and its contents into an indistinct wash of muted crimson.

A dark red figure disentangled from its surroundings and approached him. The figure moved to the nearest lamp and removed the shade. Bright halogen light made Eli flinch away. The man did not speak until he had turned back.

"Brother Eli," said the Maestro. "Thank you as always. Come in, come in!"

The man turned with a flourish, the surgical gown he wore twirling about his legs. He strode to the rear of the room and pulled back a sliding steel door. Blue light poured through. "Come!" the Maestro repeated, in that strange dwarf-like falsetto.

Eli went to him. The Maestro's smile, the only part of his face visible other than his eyes, was wide with delight. He was wearing a gold mask today, a thin papery mask with subtle curlicues tracing across the surface. A string woven through his matted black hair held it in place. He looked like a doctor who was late for a masquerade ball. He was neither of those things.

The air was as dry as it was cold and it upset Eli's lungs. He coughed into his fist.

"You'll get used to it. You always do." The Maestro entered the blue room. It held a cart piled high with surgical instruments and other tools. Half-open drawers revealed loops of twine and barbed wire, along with things Eli couldn't discern. Opposite that was a table with a phonograph atop it. The music came from this machine, now a thrumming, haunting tune that filled the small space of the blue room. Along the back wall hung a curtain. Eli already knew what lay behind it.

"Fever Ray," the Maestro said as he consulted his toys.

"What?"

"The music. Fever Ray, 'If I Had a Heart.' I used it for the Valentine show. Closing number." He looked up and tapped his Adam's apple. "Unrelated. Frogs. Plague of frogs? Someone write that down!" His call echoed out into the red room, unanswered.

The Maestro affixed a surgical mask over his mouth, then pulled on latex gloves. "You know how to keep a secret, don't you, Brother Eli?"

Eli nodded. "I'm afraid I'm in a rush."

"Oh, I have to get your reaction," the Maestro insisted. "It'll take but a second. The new pieces are nearly finished. No one else has seen them outside of my staff. Ready?" Without waiting for an answer, the Maestro tore the curtain back and threw his arms wide.

There stood three slimes chained to a stone wall. If one could even call them that—these things weren't just dead, they were purely *inhuman.*

The first was a bloated woman, her pallor cast in azure by the light. An eyeless steel hood was clamped over her lolling head. Most of the meat below her sagging breasts had been cut away, guts scooped out, leaving an open cavity within blood-caked ribs. The cavity was encased in glass, creating a sort of terrarium. Hive, rather, Eli thought, correcting himself as buzzing rose in his ears.

The woman's abdomen was teeming with bees. They had constructed networks of honeycomb inside the ribcage and down the spine. Workers were scrambling busily over one another, oblivious to their nightmare world.

"The bees have been very well-behaved." The Maestro went to the phonograph and picked up the needle. The silence was jarring, but the song of the hive quickly filled it. The Maestro removed the record and slipped it into a paper sleeve, placing it atop a stack of other music. "'Warning.' *Morning View,"* he said to himself. "There was a time when vinyl was considered a relic, Brother Eli."

Eli hated that, the *Brother* thing. What didn't he hate about this abattoir? He watched as the Maestro found the record he wanted: Incubus, *Morning View.* "This is so I don't forget the frog thing," the Maestro said, as if that made any sense. "I need a water tank anyway. I can do a frog piece before I do the piranhas. You know, the common Suriname toad emerges fully developed from a pouch in Mother's back? Popular pets here in the States. Wouldn't be hard to find. Just imagine, though, a soft gray man tethered by algae at the bottom of the tank. See it? See the frogs emerging from *him.* "

The mental image of a corpse riddled with tiny holes—holes straining, then splitting wide as frogs broke free—made Eli nauseous. Looking back at the walls of hexagonal cells inside the ruin of the dead woman caused his gorge to rise. He looked to the second restrained slime. A black male, he stood in a metal box that rose to his waistline and was fastened tight around it. The dead man actually looked relatively unharmed, save for the stitching on his head. Eyes, nose, and mouth had all been threaded closed. His ears were pinned shut as well. Stepping closer, Eli detected movement in the throat.

"Christ," he uttered. The Maestro was suddenly at his side.

"Yes? I can tell your viscera is in rebellion, Brother. If you must, use the bucket just inside the red light. Just remember," said the Maestro, approaching the third slime, "that this isn't for shock's sake. You'll see it all in context when you see the full production. I can count on you to attend?"

Eli pressed a fist against his wet lips and swallowed. "If I can. We're doing a lot of work on the house."

"The mansion or the entire community?"

"The community," Eli said. The Maestro lifted a conductor's wand, and a bright point of light bloomed at its tip. The third slime's eyes drifted to the wand. The Maestro moved the light back and forth a few times, the slime's eyes following. Seemingly satisfied, the Maestro went to his instrument cart and traded the wand for a scalpel.

This third "piece" was sexless from head to toe, the body so graphically scarred that it was almost hard to see the thing as *H. sapien.* Its arms were gone, its legs sewn together from the ankles up. The Maestro had inserted some sort of curved rods into the flesh of the torso, creating the look of a ribbed body. A worm? Clearly there was an insect theme here. Were worms insects? Eli thought the better question might be, *Why am I down in this hole asking myself this shit?*

The worm's lips were pinned back. Some sort of mouthpiece stretched and shaped the maw into a gaping circle. The slime's eyes suddenly fixed on Eli. It was unable to work its jaw, but a thin moan came from its throat.

"Easy," said the Maestro. He stepped in front of the slime and took its attention from Eli. The scalpel wavered in the air in front of the worm's face.

"No, piranhas ought not be hard to find either," he said. "So many waterways clogged with forgotten creatures from zoos and the like. Crocs and pythons and eels, and they've acclimated to the ecosystem. They are the ecosystem. True survivors. You can appreciate that."

Was he speaking to the slime or Eli? The question fell by the wayside as the Maestro caught the worm by the neck and began sawing into the bridge of its nose.

"I was just going to flatten it," he said as he worked, "maybe melt it with acid, but it occurs to me that if I just cut the damn thing off, I can expand the mouth."

"I really have to go," Eli said.

"Always nice to visit with you. Please make a note about the frogs and piranhas, if you would."

The Maestro grabbed the severed nose and yanked at it. With a snap, if tore free, and he turned it in his palm. He looked transfixed. Eli seized the moment and backed out of the blue room.

#

Another day, another dose. Eli sat in silent bliss behind his desk.

Someone knocked, then entered. He groaned. Had to remember that lock those damn doors.

"What's this meeting you're having with the *Botar-Elite?*" a gruff voice snapped.

"The what?"

"The Church," Arch-Major Salt yelled. "Are you on that junk?"

"You wouldn't call it junk if you were on it," Eli said. He shifted himself into an upright position and rested his arms on the desk. "Yeah, they're coming later today."

"And for *what?*" Salt placed his hands on the other side of the desk and leered at Eli. "I'm not asking for myself."

"Who then, Miranda?"

"Senior A-M DiPontiac."

"Mmm." Eli reclined again. "Just a diplomatic gesture, nothing else. Little glad-handing. I might let them have a chapel here."

"Now, Eli," Salt said, his tone becoming that of the scolding schoolteacher, "we work support the Church the same way we support the military. From a polite distance. We're not in bed with them."

"Who *are* you in bed with?" Eli grinned, then laughed. "Don't, don't tell me. I can't take it."

"I don't know how this place is still standing," Salt growled.

Eli was suddenly on his feet. Bloodshot eyes bored into Salt until the old man's furrowed brow began to sweat.

"And yet it is standing. And growing. And the Senior is pleased." Eli stuck his index finger in Salt's sternum. "I'm given a certain degree of latitude in how I run things. This has never been a conventional house. When's the last time you visited that dungeon in the basement? Any problem with that freak show?"

"You're talking about the Senior's son," Salt said, pushed Eli's hand away. "His *surviving* son."

"Yes. Another purebred son, and just as competent as Iain. That's the point. The Senior has entrusted me with this house. Me. He didn't send you here. You'll have to do better, Arch-Major."

Eli chortled. "Hell, DiPontiac trusts the Maestro with a stable of slimes. Even *he* could pull rank on you, Salt. No one cares who you were in the old world. Take all your play money and flush it."

"I was Secretary of the Interior—"

"What part of *I don't give a shit* isn't translating? New world. New rules. New rulers." And Eli sent an open hand rocketing into Salt's face. The resounding crack sent tingles up Eli's arm.

Salt's head jerked sideways, his entire body teetering for a moment, then his hands were at Eli's neck.

"Go for it," Eli spat, smiling ear-to-ear. Tears ran from Salt's eye where he'd been struck. There was a nice handprint taking shape on that side.

"I want to do it," Salt snarled, heat coming off his face. "I want you dead. We want you dead."

"Everybody dies," Eli said. Salt's hands were still around his windpipe, but the man had never taken firm hold. Eli's smiling eyes dared him to try.

Salt let go. He cleared his throat and smoothed his robe.

"So yes, the *Botar-Elite* will be here around three or so." Eli sank into his chair. "Did you need anything else?"

Salt walked to the doors. He paused there, hands on the knobs, but did not turn. Eli clicked his tongue. Salt exited.

Eli left, too, into dreams and remembering.

BEFORE | SPRING 2031: BUNKER

He'd been sixteen when he watched his grandfather strangle his father. The boy had pretended to sleep, even when his dad had cried his name with his final gasping breaths.

Eben was Eli's maternal grandfather, and the bunker was his. Mom had been a doctor and had, until the very end, been working in triage camps. They hadn't been able to reach her before the dead did. It couldn't have turned out any other way. Sometimes Eli thought she'd wanted it. Like a lone soldier, or better yet a faith healer—a martyr spinning her wheels and waiting for martyrdom. Martyr, mother. She'd chosen herself over her son. Now Dad, he was loyal to a fault, but in the same way as a beaten dog. Eli had always known the man was weak. He'd recognized the contempt in his grandfather's eyes, the irritation at having to give his daughter away to this mewling grub. And now, in the bunker, he was giving away space and supplies. He was forced to breathe the same air as Eli's Dad. The tipping point had come quickly.

Eli's grandmother Ursula had sat muttering some Gypsy lyric in a dark corner while Eben did the deed. When Dad stopped making sounds, Eli rolled over and rubbed pretend sleep from his eyes.

"Your father's gone, boy," Eben wheezed, sitting back and crossing his legs on the floor. He wiped his face with his sleeves and fingers fumbled about on the floor until he located his glasses. Eben Cromartie's face was weathered, scarred, a tapestry of myth. He'd regaled Eli with many stories of his life as a world traveler, a missionary and an alchemist of traditions that had come before Man. He was a man who had truly lived, and deserved every breath he took. Eli lay there and looked at his father's body. It seemed gray and faded. There was no man there. In truth, there hadn't been much to begin with. Eli thought he would miss Dad more than Mom, but again, it was like seeing a dog put down after years of quiet misery.

The bunker had three rooms: the main room, where food and medical supplies were kept, and where a ladder led to the secured hatch; a toilet and shower; and an empty room where Eli or his grandmother sometimes slept. The walls were a bluish stone, the lights in the ceiling harsh yellow. It was an altogether unpleasant space that offended every sense. But the world above was worse, of that Eli was certain. Down here, there were rules. Things made sense. His father's corpse, being dragged by Eben into the third room, made sense. It was easy to accept. The grunting and chopping sounds that followed meant little to Eli, although he was somewhat curious. With Ursula still rocking and muttering, Eli stole to the curtain which divided the main room from the third and peered through.

"Come," Eben said, shaking blood from his hands. "You help."

Eli did as he was told. He pushed through the curtain and stared at the remains of his dad. The arms had been severed and were lying side-by-side in the corner. Eben was working on the legs now, using a hatchet to cleave through the meat of the thighs. He handed the tool to Eli. "I need to sit."

Eben motioned for Eli to take up where he'd left off. Eli studied the open wounds for a moment. Blood glistened amongst the blossoming folds of slashed meat. He pressed the hatchet blade into one of the wounds and began sawing.

"No, no," Eben scolded. "Chop, boy. That's bone there. Come on."

Eli lifted the hatchet in both hands and brought it down. He missed the thigh and planted the blade in Dad's groin. Blood brimmed around the blade and he released the handle. Eli gritted his teeth in embarrassment.

"Let me see." Eben leaned forward and pulled the hatchet free with a sucking sound. He turned it so that he wielded the flat back end of the blade. "Use it like this instead. Break the bone up nice and good. Then you'll chop."

It took several practice blows, but before long, Eli heard the satisfying cracking of bone and applied himself to the task with enthusiasm. Eben told him when to begin chopping, and the first leg came away easily. The teen went right to work on the second.

"Are we going to put it outside?" he asked.

Eben shook his head. "Wasteful. And it would attract those ghouls anyhow. Eli, do you see what's before you?"

Eli nodded. Eben looked expectantly at him and he said, "It's my dad."

Eben wagged a finger at him. *"He* was your father. What is *it?"*

Eli looked hard at the remains, hoping the answer would reveal itself before Eben grew disappointed. Suddenly, his eyes lit up and he said, "Meat." Then his gaze fell.

"That's right, boy. Now you look around. We live in a hole. Water has already grown scarce. We'll be eating handfuls of powdered milk before long. And the generator, it'll eventually quit no matter how hard we crank it. It's going to get cold, and dark. We'll hunger. Your belly will turn into a fist and squeeze until you can't see straight. This will happen. But not so soon."

Eben pulled on the second leg. It snapped free. He stripped off the pant leg and sock. "It's true that we aren't just simple animals, Eli. But we are all cannibals." Pulling a straight razor from his trouser pocket, Eben unfolded the blade and began drawing it across the leg. He was shaving it. Eli swayed and dropped the hatchet.

"There comes a time when survival is no longer about cooperation," Eben continued. "It's no longer about prolonging the species. It's about you. This is true for all life at the end. Only a born-and-bred survivor knows when the time has come."

He told Eli, "Go get the little stove from next to my bed."

The boy went and returned in seconds. Eben continued speaking. "The survivor—you're the one the others look to when things go bad. And you may lead them, for a time, and you may even succeed in putting off the inevitable. But not forever. You will know when the human family has reached its end. And you will have to eat."

Eben pointed the razor at his grandson. "I see a survivor in you, boy. There's a voice in you telling you right now that this is unforgivable, this thing we will do. But who is there to forgive us? To whom are we to apologize? God? The dead?"

"Of course it's unforgivable," he concluded. He sliced into the ankle he held.

#

"Expect nothing of the first taste," Eli's grandfather said. He passed Eli a paper plate with several cooked strips.

Ursula didn't hesitate to eat. She seemed to be in better spirits now. Eli lifted a piece of meat to his lips. It smelled good. He popped it into his mouth. It saltier than he expected, a little tangy. Eli chewed, swallowed, and the feeling of meat in his stomach warmed him.

Eben turned on the radio. Someone calling himself "Bert the Flirt" had hijacked the frequency that used to carry emergency broadcasts. He was pretty funny. He even put on an old record that Eli's grandparents recognized, and they sang along while Eli ate.

#

Ursula caught a cold a week later. Eben said was more than that and sequestered her in the third room. He told Eli that it sounded like a lung infection. There had no medicine for it. She passed one night after a hideous, bloody coughing fit.

They didn't eat all of her. The lungs were set aside. Eben did the same with the heart. He said it was in her honor. The organs were burned to ash on the stove. Eli wondered if he would ever know love like that.

#

It was a couple more months before Eben began shutting down. He spent that time telling Eli his life, every story and every lesson learned. Eli knew his grandfather was preparing him. When Eben took ill, he said to the teen, "You'll survive, boy." He did not speak again after that. He'd chosen his last words and that was that until he died.

Eli carved, seasoned and cooked Eben as he'd been directed. He took his time, chewing each bite slowly and sending it down his gullet before picking another. With each bite, he thought of the things he'd been told. He took those lessons into himself.

The hatch was plastered with sod to camouflage it among the rest of Eben's sprawling farm. Roots had sewn the land together, and it was a bit of a struggle to get out of the bunker. Eli emerged on a rainy morning and walked through the birches to the house.

Eben had told him the combination to the safe in the third room. Eli had two revolvers and a satchel of ammunition. When he heard yelling from the house, he drew both guns and stalked forward.

Sure enough, a pack of filthy squatters were rampaging through the place. He went in through the back door and listened to the hail of shattering glass from upstairs. Eli walked up the stairs and, at the landing between floors, came face-to-face with a fat man in ragged fatigues.

"Who the fuck are you?" the man exclaimed.

"This is my house," Eli said, and shot him twice through the gut.

The shouting from the second floor stopped. Panicked whispers. Floorboards creaked. Eli just stood over the sobbing fat man and waited.

A man and woman crawled into view, guns in hand. Eli unloaded the revolvers into their heads. Smoke and splinters rocketed up from the floor. Eli knelt to reload, listening intently as he did so. He thought he'd killed them both but neither was visible anymore.

A whining moan grew to a scream. The woman was alive. Eli ascended to the second floor, stepped over her boyfriend's pulped skull and trained his guns on her.

She lay on her back. One eye was gone, and a bullet had slashed her cheek open. Her feet kicked at the carpet as she wailed.

He put a final bullet through her other eye and searched the rest of the house. Satisfied that it was once again his, Eli set upon the bodies with the hatchet.

The place had been ruined. He wouldn't stay long. He'd eat what he could, then pack as much as the leftovers as he could in salt and foil. He wished he had time to tan the fat man's gut and make a new satchel.

#

What Eben had not been able to teach him he would learn. Eli sat on the roof and watched the undead meander through the trees toward him. They'd fill the house, and the next people who tried to take it would have a real fight on their hands. These dead people—

they were survivors in their own right. Each looked out for his or herself. Each acted without hesitation. That little voice which shamed certain necessary acts as *unforgivable* was wholly foreign to these people.

And boy, did they eat. He rolled the remains of the fat man off the edge of the roof and watched the horde feast. Good dogs.

SEVEN | SUMMER 2048: THE GREATER GOOD

Wormham, the Church's *Botar-Elite,* was accompanied by a pair of knights and a woman scribe. The pomposity of his adornments outdid even that of the Senior Arch-Major. He wore no less than three flowing robes and seven rings. Eli supposed he'd have to sit and listen while the symbolic importance of each was explained. Wormham's bald head was capped with a ridiculous little pyramid sort of hat. The knights probably spent more time trying to keep that thing from falling off than they did protecting him. Eli wished he could have shot up right before they arrived.

He welcomed his guests into the office. Miranda was there, much to Eli's chagrin. She bowed before Wormham and led him to the best seat in the room, Eli's. Wormham reached to kiss her hand and said, "The Lady of House Salome, I presume?"

"Yes," Eli interjected, "and thank you, Madame Sortho. We'll be good from here."

Miranda gave him a look that said, *I know what you're up to.* It wasn't the glint in her eyes so much as the little smirk that bothered him. She excused herself and Eli locked the doors.

"I take it she's not privy to the matters at hand," Wormham said, rising from Eli's chair. "A shame when you can't trust your own woman."

"She's not mine," Eli said, taking the seat that was his as Wormham pulled over another chair. "And no, she isn't privy. Only my most trusted aides have any knowledge of it, and none of them know everything." Eli glanced at Wormham's entourage. "Knights and a stenographer. Lovely."

"Everyone here is safe," Wormham said. He rummaged through his robes for one leg in order to cross it over the other. The pyramid atop his head wobbled. Eli swallowed a grin.

"On my side of this operation," Wormham went on, "there's a great deal more work involved, and more hands required. I have full faith in these people."

"Including the Tribe?"

"They make proper knights," Wormham said. "The thing I like about using these—outside contractors—is that they don't have any emotional stake in this. They're happy to suit up and carry on as directed."

"So. Progress?"

"Seven rebuilder camps have fallen," Wormham said. "Few survivors, but enough to spread the word."

To spread the word that the Church was waging war against the rebs. To plant seeds that would quickly and violently bear fruit. Eli had to give Wormham credit for suggesting they enlist raiders to play the role of the knights. It meant involving fewer of the actual High Holy Guard, men blinded by faith in an invisible king and the old man who claimed to have said king's invisible ear.

Still, Eli didn't like having *any* knights involved, no matter how loyal they were to Wormham. Didn't care for a two-knight escort and a damned scribe. Glancing at the woman now, Eli saw she hadn't written a word. She batted her eyes and gave him a decidedly un-Christ-like smile.

Fine then. He supposed the entourage was necessary in order for the *Botar-Elite* to keep up appearances. One had to act like a team player if one wanted to get close enough to hobble the quarterback.

Wormham oversaw the softer side of God's army, the missionary *feders*. Unlike his sword-bearing counterpart, he was a shameless pitchman for the Lord. A politician's politician. He would be a strong ally in the future, so long as he didn't begin buying into his own con.

"Your council of Arches is still in the dark?" Wormham asked.

"Reports of violence haven't even made it this far east," Eli told him. "When they do, the Arches will believe the same thing as the rebs. Church gone mad."

"On that point—our meeting today hasn't raised any eyebrows?"

"A couple. But nothing to worry about."

Wormham nodded. "I'd much prefer to have all this out in the open, with full cooperation. As, I'm sure, would you. Too often, progress means having to break away from the pack."

"Too true," replied Eli. He knew that Wormham's boss, the Church's *Goni* Leber, was as clueless as the Arches. Wormham, without question, was eyeing the *Goni's* seat. Eli would decide later whether or not to allow it.

"Let me ask one more thing," Eli said. "Your fortune tellers. Have they made any noise about this?"

"The Illuma Consul? No, they have no idea."

Eli shook his head in mock disappointment. "They're not doing a very good job."

Wormham laughed. "The time of the prophets is over. You and I will forge our own destiny. Yes?"

"Of course," Eli replied.

"And these rebuilders will learn to live that path. We can't have a kingdom to every man." Meaning the rebs needed to stop dreaming of a life without reliance on a higher power. And Eli was happy to be that power. This world had potential yet. Of course, if the time came that such potential was exhausted, he and he alone would know.

#

He was having dinner in his office when the Senior Arch-Major entered. Eli masked his dismay by inhaling a mouthful of pork. "Mm-hrmm hrr."

DiPontiac surveyed the office. "No books, Eli?"

"I do my reading in my chamber," Eli said. He took a swig of wine to wash the meat down. "This vintage is sublime. My compliments."

DiPontiac sat across from him. "I suspect you'll have your own vineyard soon enough. How is the irrigation project coming along?"

"Good, good," Eli said. He still hadn't seen the plans yet. He made a mental note to strangle Hansom Fete a little bit.

DiPontiac smoothed his beard and folded his hands over his prodigious belly. "And I hear you're undertaking a beautification project as well. The fountain is being gutted."

Uh oh. At least he hadn't come about the Church meeting. Eli swept some gravy and peas around his plate and made himself look busy. "Yes. More of a sanitation issue."

"I wouldn't mind if you ran something like that by me," said DiPontiac. "That fountain had been in our family for four generations."

"Oh. Well, I meant no harm. It's simply swimming with bacteria. I don't want and of that getting into the new water system."

"Just the same," DiPontiac said. "You know dinosaurs like me. We grow sentimental."

Eli set his fork down. "Dinosaurs are feared, not pitied, in my book."

"How is my son?" DiPontiac asked.

Eli was caught off-guard. He stared at DiPontiac for a moment, then exclaimed, "The Maestro! I visited with him yesterday. New show's coming along. Looks brilliant."

"That it may be." DiPontiac sighed. He was feeling sentimental all right. Eli steeled himself for a long conversation.

"He's a good boy," DiPontiac said. "He was a dedicated student once. And a soldier. He enlisted under his mother's maiden name. Didn't want special treatment as a DiPontiac. He's always been humble."

"His art is transformative," said Eli. "It's something we need in our time. Many don't think of art as the precious resource it is."

"That's kind of you." DiPontiac drummed his fingertips on his gut. "When I sit in my box and I watch him perform, I fear for him. I fear he'll be killed. I dread that scream that comes with the bite. Sometimes I dread the applause even more.

"Eli, watch him closely. Your eyes are much sharper than mine." DiPontiac plucked a hand-rolled cigar from his robe. "You don't mind?"

"Go ahead," Eli said. He fetched a second wineglass from a nearby shelf and poured out some red for the Senior. Truth be told, the sweet cigar smoke made him ill, but he was willing to make a small sacrifice for the old man.

There was some affection there, he knew. He liked DiPontiac. Yes, he was a dinosaur, and feared by few who knew him, but Eli remembered a different time. After years in the wastelands, running with raiders, robbing couriers and making war with vagabonds, Eli had been captured by a group of slavers. They'd identified themselves as such. "You're going to serve the royals, boys," the slavemaster had declared after separating the males from the females. The women would likely be sold into prostitution. Perhaps some of the men too.

"Believe me when I say this," the slavemaster told them. Eli, twenty-three, knelt and listened while his fingers explored the cuffs binding him.

"Believe me, and listen well because I won't say it again. Anyone who engages in fuckery after this speech will get an arrow to the head." The slavemaster, lanky and dark, his face a patchwork of old and fresh cuts, looked at each man in turn as he spoke. "Your lives are about to improve dramatically. I don't want to hear a goddamned thing about living free in this cesspool. One peep like that, arrow to the head.

"You're going to live in a house. You're going to have food, good food, and clean water. Clean clothes. You won't simply live among a higher class of people—you will join them." The man pulled a crumpled bit of paper from his pocket and unfolded it. "Does anyone know what this is? Don't be afraid to speak up."

"A dollar," Eli said.

"Good!" The slavemaster pointed to him. "It's a dollar. And what is it worth?" He scanned the line of men, but his eyes stopped on Eli.

"Nothing," Eli said.

The slavemaster gave him a toothy smile. "Now see here. Once the royals have set things back to how they used to be, this is going to be worth something again. More than it ever was. And when that happens, your pockets will be filled with the stuff. You'll be employees, not slaves. And you'll know what freedom is."

He grabbed Eli's arm and hauled him to his feet. "You're a means to an end, to be sure. But unlike the world out here, with the royals you will benefit from that end." He patted Eli on the shoulder. "So that's it. Speech over. Anyone fucks around from this point on, arrow."

He hadn't been kidding. As they'd traveled east, Eli had seen many a boy and girl take an arrow to the head. Always one clean shot. The slavemaster was well-practiced.

Eli had started out cleaning the stables at House Gotha. When one of the other stable hands discovered a small hole in the perimeter wall, Eli had sat up long nights with the other man plotting their escape. Then, while brushing her favorite steed and making small talk, he'd told the House-Lady.

He'd been taken before DiPontiac to bear witness against seven terrified young men. He'd looked each in the eye as his tongue tied their nooses. DiPontiac had watched with cold fascination, then sent the seven away to hang. And Eli?

He'd survived.

EIGHT | THE STRANGE DEAD, II

The Maestro sent out an announcement that his newest show, "The Long Eye," was ready. Eli sent a woozy Hansom Fete to the performance hall to supervise preparations.

DiPontiac had invited Eli to join him in his box for the show. At least he wouldn't have to sit with Miranda this time. Maybe that would help with the nausea.

#

Miranda asked Salt to join her in Eli's seat. Third row, center; she didn't like being so close to the stage, but she knew she was expected to be an enthusiastic supporter of DiPontiac's son and Iain's brother. The hall, seating five hundred and usually near capacity, was festooned floor-to-ceiling with red curtains and gilded railings. It reminded Miranda of the Muppets' theater from her youth. The box where those two heckling codgers sat would be occupied tonight by DiPontiac and Eli. She promised herself she wouldn't look up there during the performance. Best to stare forward and unfocus her eyes. Hopefully, the music would be the kind that would lull her into a fugue where she could sit calm in space and think about her plans.

The hall filled quickly. Canned laughter and compliments filled the air. Miranda squirmed in her dress. It was a heavy material and she hated it. She'd pull out an old set of silk pajamas when she got home. Whenever that was—the length of the Maestro's pieces was as unpredictable as the content. The only thing she knew was that it was going to be bloody.

The last show she'd attended, the Valentine's Day show, had been the most ambitious and gut-wrenching yet. It had opened with a piano piece that sounded like a horror movie theme. That was segued into The National's "Graceless." All of the Maestro's music was on vinyl, and most of it was from the modern pop era. Miranda didn't know whether that was meant to stand in contrast to the visuals or to complement them. The sight of several slimes being lowered from the rafters did nothing to settle the question.

Their torso and limbs bound in rope, the slimes had stared blankly out at the audience. Their legs were made to move as if they were walking on the air. Then they began to turn, end over end, puppeteered by the Maestro's assistants. The dead spun and groaned. Laughter. The dead settled into lazy revolutions, moving about one another now, celestial bodies in a hellish universe.

A platform began to descend in the center of this madness. The Maestro stood upon it, secure in a harness and sporting a belt with all of his gruesome tools. Applause. The Maestro reached out with a heavy glove and caught the nearest slime, a woman, and pulled her into an embrace. Cheers at the woman's futile attempts to bite his face.

Joy Division. "Love Will Tear Us Apart." No question what was to follow. Indeed, the Maestro drew a knife nearly the length of a machete and began slashing the woman. She fell away from him, raining black blood on the stage, then swung helplessly back into range. Another series of strikes in time with the music. The set list continued with more downbeat love songs. The Maestro caught each dangling corpse and sawed through them, sometimes tearing whole limbs free and tossing them down to the stage. The platform swayed with his efforts and he rode it deftly, like a ship captain in a storm. Indeed, the rain was coming down hard by the time Leona Lewis's "Bleeding Love" reached its crescendo.

Then, quiet. The slimes swayed about the Maestro. He caught the hair of the woman he'd first attacked. But he dropped the blade and fished a long, thin spike from a pouch on his belt. Knotting the woman's hair around one of the cables that supported the platform, he unspooled wire into his hands. He was threading a needle. He crossed to the other end of the platform and seized one of the dead men.

Wild clapping and cries of glee as the Maestro began sewing the two undead together. He joined their moldy lips in a permanent kiss. Actual "awws" from the audience, like they were watching *Lady and the Tramp.* With that couple fused, the Maestro went to work on the next. Metallica's "Master of Puppets" tore through the silence as he stripped the clothing from the next pair and sewed the inside of the woman's thighs into the hips of the male, making it look like a sexual death grip. He stitched the man's face into her mottled cleavage. The faux-lovers spun away and their moaning was greeted with applause.

"If I Had a Heart" ended it. As always, the dead fell to the stage and assistants nailed all exposed extremities to the floor. Chain-link fencing fell like a curtain to separate the audience from the dead. Then the carrion were loosed. Vultures and crows, ugly things with stiff, filthy feathers and battle scars. They fell upon the dead in a frenzy. Had probably been starved for days before the event. They picked the slimes' bones clean to a standing ovation.

By comparison, the Maestro's earlier Doors revue had been tame. Jim Morrison's body of work accompanied a living—or unliving—garden, shackled slimes with vines weaving through their ribs and blossoms growing from their eye sockets. Various colored spotlights panned over men whose skin had been replaced with moss and children overtaken by fungus who toddled about like walking dolls. "Light My Fire" saw the players doused in accelerant and, with a wave of the Maestro's glowing wand, immolated; "Riders on the Storm" broke in early and water showered down on the ruined and writhing forms. Then the birds.

Labyrinth had been the name of the one show Miranda refused to attend. She'd caught wind in advance that Eli had made some suggestion to the Maestro and inspired the idea of a show where drugs were served to the audience in order to "disintegrate the fourth wall and, perhaps, a fifth."

Though she didn't see it, Miranda got plenty of recaps from those who had. They dizzily recounted slipping into a psychedelic fantasia while Radiohead blared and the Maestro unveiled a cadre of slimes who'd been surgically altered to look like mythical beasts. Oh, everyone raved about the Minotaur and how much his head resembled that of a bull. And able to walk on those legs, broken and reset like a satyr's to complete the look. The Gorgon had been another favorite. Several attendees flew into fits of panic and/or exultation when the woman took center stage, her skull split and overflowing with undulating serpents. The snakes were harmless, of course, but no one knew that at the time. An older woman had found one's fangs planted in her ankle and suffered a stroke. As far as Miranda was aware, the woman was still half-paralyzed. But she had called the show "a revelation."

A female slime who appeared to have been bronzed was wheeled out and, from a speaker embedded in her throat, Jefferson Airplane's "White Rabbit" sent the audience into orgiastic hysterics. It was the grand finale, though many of the attendees didn't leave until they awoke the following morning.

So tonight's presentation was titled "The Long Eye." Miranda could only imagine the mutilations that were to come. The lights in the hall went down and people around her murmured in fevered anticipation.

A narrow beam of light fell upon the Maestro. He wore vermilion tux and tails and a mask adorned with glittering jewels. He waited for the applause to die before he spoke.

"The long eye, it stares past and through the door. Toward futures, over moors and preachers' signs—and, cresting o'er the banks of time, it looks through its own eye."

He raised his wand and its little light bloomed. "Friends," he said softly, "the strange dead." Then he spun and raised both arms to summon the stage lights.

A song Miranda recognized as VAST began thrumming in the walls. God—a woman filled with bees stood there, chained to the floor. Her head was covered and its shook from side to side as people clapped. She was on a platform, and the Maestro wheeled it forward so everyone could stare through their opera glasses at the hive in her viscera. Miranda shut her eyes.

"We don't have to stay," Salt said in her ear.

"I do," she said.

The bee woman stayed onstage as the next piece was wheeled out. It was a man—maybe—who'd been made to look like an invertebrate, although he stood, likely with the help of some brace. His mouth had been forced wide by a metal appliance. He looked like a worm, or…

A leech.

Razors glimmered in the man's maw. The Maestro pressed against his swollen throat and the razors began rotating. The Maestro pushed the leech over to the bee woman and forced the leech's face into her underarm.

A Perfect Circle took over for VAST. The leech's head jolted. The Maestro hitched the two platforms together and rotated the scene for the audience. There was blood spilling from where that razor-filled mouth had been fastened to the bee woman, and there was something else too, runnels of yellowish goo.

Honey?

Miranda couldn't help but groan aloud at the sight as the leech was pulled away from the wound, strings of honey and spit and gore falling to the floor. Bees teemed at the edges of the ragged hole under the woman's arm. They began buzzing about the woman, and the Maestro, who waved gaily at them with the wand. Some followed their pilfered honey into the mouth of the leech. Pearl Jam kicked in with "Do the Evolution" while appreciative laughter filtered through the hall.

Another man was wheeled out. This one was bent at the waist over a bar. Every orifice in his head was sewn shut. The Maestro turned his ass toward the audience, and they exclaimed at the sight of dozens of maggots wriggling in the half-devoured cavity of the man's rectum. The Maestro slapped one rotten cheek and smiled broadly. He raised a finger to still the audience. *Wait! There's more.*

Turning the slime back around, the Maestro drew a scalpel and whiskered it across each sealed opening—mouth, nose, eyes and ears. The man's head shook back and forth. His jaw dropped and eyelids lifted to reveal nothing underneath—not until the flies began boiling out, swarming about the dead man's head in a cloud. The bees, agitated, streaked out over the audience. People screamed and clapped.

Behind the Maestro, a naked female slime walked out from backstage. She was stiff and looked like a dried-out husk. She was neither restrained not crippled. A few people gasped in shock, but no one raised their voice to warn the Maestro. They just watched. It had to be part of the show, Miranda thought. The Maestro swatted flies from his face and searched his pockets for something. The woman closed in on him. The Maestro was frowning as her hands extended toward him.

Then he snapped his fingers and whirled. He caught the woman's arms and flung them aside. He grabbed her shoulders and shook her violently. Entire chunks of flesh fell from her arms and chest and back, and as her bones were exposed, so were what had to be hundreds of little round beetles. How long had they been tunneling through her meat to turn her into this fragile jigsaw horror?

Salt hissed. "Skin beetles, for Christ's sake. Do you know what those things do to fabric?" Others nearby echoed the sentiment with grumbled curses. A few actually stood and backed off from the stage.

The Maestro looked out over the crowd and saw those retreating. He shook his head and held out his hands to placate them. The dead woman crumbled and beetles were spreading in every direction.

"Friends!" the Maestro sang. "Nothing to fear! Please!" He ran to the rear of the stage and shouted something. A new piece was brought forward.

Two slimes had been joined at the middle, a surgical wonder, torsos fused as if one had simply been passed through the other. They formed a seamless X, and their reshaped arms and legs constituted the eight limbs of the spider.

The head of the monster was actually eight heads. They were infants. Miranda lowered her head between her knees, but the sight was burned into her retinas—eight heads sewn together, mouths agape but quivering, eyes lifeless but blinking. Their brainstems must have been hooked up to a current to make them appear alive. Infants...how did someone come across one infected newborn, let alone *eight?*

Rosewood DiPontiac sanctioned all of this sickness. The drugs, the dead. Iain's own goddamned father. He may have very well sanctioned Iain's death. Miranda couldn't help herself and looked up to the Senior's box. Eli and DiPontiac were both on their feet marveling at the spider.

She hadn't been sure if she wanted the Senior dead. Now she was.

#

Eli sat on the lip of the fountain he intended to demolish. In the light of streetlamps, he watched algae and mold drift lazily across the pool. In its center, a marble archer aimed his arrow heavenward. The wolves at his feet vomited brown water into the pool.

"Sir," a voice said. Eli started and whirled to face the speaker.

"I'm sorry," Hansom Fete said, recoiling from him. "There's an outsider at the west gate. I don't know his face, but he has the password."

"Is this about the calf? Because I already slaughtered it."

"No, this man's from a different group. The Tribe?"

Eli took a moment to cycle through the possible implications. He reached into a fold in his robe and rested his hand on the butt of a revolver. "Take me to him."

The young man at the gate looked weary. He stood with a horse who appeared equally exhausted. "How long have you been riding?" Eli asked.

"Maybe two weeks," the man said.

"And you're from the Tribe."

"Yes, sir."

"And you came here...why?" Eli let the cordiality drop from his tone.

"Uh...Max Korn sent me. He said you needed to hear this news. That you'd want to hear it." The man shuffled his feet and looked back at the horse. The animal offered no help.

"What is your name?" Eli asked.

"Caliban."

"I hope this is good news, Caliban."

It was. Oh, it was!

#

This time, the little old man led Eli past the red and blue rooms to the Maestro's bedchamber. There, the man himself lay flat on his bed, staring at the ceiling through a featureless white mask.

The little man left, and Eli leaned against a dresser by the door. "Maestro?"

"I have no excuse," the man mumbled.

"Come again?"

"Is my father angry?" the Maestro was dressed in baggy bedclothes, his feet bare. It looked as if he'd kicked the sheets off the bed. Eli stepped closer. The man's eyes were red-rimmed and unblinking. The mask was stained with what must have been tears.

"Why do you think he's mad?" Eli said. "The show went well. The spider was incredible."

"I saw the people walking out," the Maestro said. "The cadaver beetles. I should have scrapped that piece. I wanted to contain them—to make it a static display—but it would have been too similar to the beekeeper. Why didn't I just get rid of it?"

"That's of no concern. The hall will be fumigated."

"People *hated* it," the Maestro snarled.

"Art isn't safe," Eli told him. He didn't know what he was talking about, but it sounded like something the Maestro would respond to.

The Maestro sat up slowly. "Brother Eli. Did you know that leeches aren't bugs?"

Eli shook his head. The Maestro stood. "Well, someone told me. Some*ones*. *After* the show. Like it matters. Apparently, it does. Apparently, I'm the idiot. It wasn't a fucking bug show!" The Maestro grabbed an oil lamp from his bedside table and hurled it against the wall. Thank God it hadn't been lit.

"Maestro," Eli began.

"What do they think of me up there?" The Maestro pulled off his shirt and rummaged through a trunk for another. He bore great, star-shaped scars across his back. Finding a black top, the Maestro yanked it over his head. He went to a small vanity in the corner and looked through the masks which lay atop it.

"They love the shows," Eli said. The Maestro, back to Eli, removed his mask. Eli craned his neck to see if he could catch a glimpse of the man's face in the vanity mirror. No such luck. The Maestro donned a dark leather mask. Like all the others, it was in the style of one attending a masquerade ball, and had silver stitching around the eyeholes which made them expressive. Angry.

"Do they? Do the love the shows?" the Maestro scoffed. "I should have gone out on my own long ago. That's the real test of an artist. Here I am in a studio beneath my brother's old house. People applaud at my father's direction. He doesn't come here, you know. Never."

"He's running an empire."

"So am I," the Maestro snapped. "The dead surround me, as they surround us all. And I give them new life."

He sighed dramatically. "The spider wasn't supposed to be the end. I have a caterpillar. She would have become a butterfly right there before their eyes. The rigging took weeks to design. But beetles devour fine fabrics, they say. And leeches aren't bugs."

"A caterpillar?" Eli tried to picture it, humoring the man. "Like a centipede?"

"No, a centipede's an entirely different thing. And tasteless if you ask me." The Maestro sat before the vanity and dropped his head into his hands. "What am I to them?"

Eli approached him. "What are you to yourself, Maestro?"

"Irrelevant. I am my work. I give it away every time I step out there."

"Maestro, you know the word *omnicuta?*"

The seated man froze. He spread his fingers and looked at his reflection, then at Eli. "I coined the term," he said. "It isn't just a legend. I've seen them."

"That's what I had heard." Eli pulled a chair over, asking, "May I?" and sat next to the Maestro. "Flesh-changers. I heard many tales of them when I was younger. And I've heard people say you claim to know all about them."

"Tell me why," the Maestro said. Eli had never been this close to him before. His eyes were glassy, pupils large. The Maestro's teeth clacked together. "Tell me what you know."

"I have reports that some associates on the outside have captured an *omnicuta.* A young woman."

The Maestro's mouth hung agape. Eli began to stand when the Maestro caught his wrist.

"Where is she?"

"I'm going to have her brought here. It will take time. A month, maybe. But she's in good hands."

The Maestro's grip tightened. "Tell me about her."

"I've told you all I know." Eli gingerly pried his wrist free. "Am I'm going to deliver her here. Now what can you tell me?"

The Maestro stood. He glanced down at his pajama bottoms, then grabbed a formal robe from a hook on the wall. "Excuse my manners. Yes, the *omni.* Follow me."

He took Eli to the red room, where he began searching through cabinets filled with disorganized scraps of paper. "I've had two of them on my exam table," the Maestro said. "They're exceedingly rare. And we don't know why they are the way are. Chicken-egg thing. I've never had enough time with them."

"You used them in shows?"

"No, never," came the reply, accompanied by reams of paper being thrown onto the floor. "My interest was purely academic. I knew of them long before my first show. Back when I was a field doctor."

"You really *were* a doctor?" Eli said, adding, "Not that I—that you couldn't—"

The Maestro didn't appear to have heard him. "I was delicate in my vivisection, but they'd eventually succumb to shock. Nothing I could do. You know the most extraordinary thing about them?"

The Maestro turned with a fistful of paper. "They're *infected.* It's the bugs that enable them to change. Yet they live."

"Could it point toward a cure?" Eli asked.

"I doubt it. We went backwards and forwards through the genome when the outbreaks started. I couldn't say why these people adapt while others die. Whatever's happening, it's as much the nanos as it is the host. Do the nanos decide?" He shrugged, the smile wide on his face. He was jittery, excited, completely healed from the injuries of the evening's folly. "Maybe it's the new evolution. Mutation in tandem with technology, inseparable. After all, our evolution was largely technological for ages. Medicine. Computers. Chemicals."

He waved the thought away. "I'm getting off track, aren't I?"

Eli asked, "Do you believe they can fully control their abilities? Or is it more of an unconscious thing? Extrasensory?"

The Maestro paused. He pursed his lips. "Are you asking whether you can train them, Brother Eli?"

"I'm just saying, imagine an *omnicuta* loyal to our faction."

"I imagine that would be thrilling for some," the Maestro said. "Our own super-spy, I suppose. But I thought you were bringing me a specimen for research."

"Yes, yes. Of course! These are things the Arches will want you to look into."

"My father."

"I haven't spoken to him yet, but I will. I'm sure he'll want to know all about it."

The Maestro looked uncertain. He glanced around the room. "I don't want to be told what to do."

"These things would be part of your research anyway, I'm sure." Eli pressed his hands together and held them out pleadingly. "Maestro, your *work*. Something to benefit the people."

"Ah." The Maestro stuffed the papers he was holding into his robe. "To show them I'm more than a carnival barker. Very good, Eli."

It was the first time he'd ever said *Eli* without *Brother*. Eli wasn't as pleased as he'd thought he might be.

"Look, my motives aren't hidden," Eli said. "Yes, the Arches. Yes, espionage. That doesn't change the fact that this will be your operation. We're all on the same team. I'm not jerking you around."

The Maestro nodded. "That would be best." He removed his mask.

Eli's breath caught in his throat. Yet he forced himself to remain still as the Maestro walked over to him.

"I wear all my wounds on the outside," the Maestro said. "That's art. And yes, it's very unsafe."

"Maestro," Eli said. The man interrupted and told Eli his name.

Eli repeated it back. He then said, "Friend. *Brother*. We're brothers."

The Maestro smiled. It was a subtle thing, but ungodly all the same.

"How terrifying," he replied, and replaced his mask.

NINE | NEW FRIENDS

"So they know," Andre said.

Claire nodded.

It had taken a long while for him to pry the truth from Claire. She'd obviously been upset, and every time she came back from talking with Max, she seemed worse. At first, Andre feared they were hurting her. Later, it became clear that it was something even deeper. They knew the thing that had been a secret between Claire and Andre all these years.

The Tribe had left Raylene a week prior. Now they were camping in a forest, and Andre had no idea where they were beyond that. They hadn't heard any booms, nor encountered any knights. The slimes had been few and far between, easily evaded.

The flap of Claire and Andre's tent peeled back. Hina leaned in. "Dre. Let me see your hand."

He held out his left palm and she undressed the wound. He'd been attacked by a hawk when he was sent to gather kindling. The trees were thin and there hadn't been a nest in sight, but he figured Mama Hawk knew better than he did. He'd managed to smack her in the head and get away, but not before a talon raked through his open hand.

"It's healing all right," Hina said. She produced fresh bandages.

"How many of those do you have?" Andre asked. "Don't waste them on this."

"It's fine." Hina knelt and rewrapped his hand. "We've got plenty. When I was in the service, we never had enough first aid supplies on hand. I had to try and use leaves to make tourniquets. Spoiler alert, it didn't work."

"Guess you've moved up in the world," Claire said without a trace of civility. Hina seemed to take it in stride, winking at her before going back to Andre's hand.

"Rules and regulations aren't my thing," Hina said. "When you throw out the playbook and just do what circumstances call for, things move along a lot smoother."

"So you and Max follow common sense," Claire spat. "I'd hate to see you lose it."

Hina narrowed her eyes at that. Her retort was cut off by a yell from outside.

"We got rebs!"

Hina ducked out of the tent. The baying of dogs—they were actual dogs Max had, nasty things—sounded throughout the camp.

Andre slipped over beside Claire. "What does Max make you do? Change over and over?"

"He shows me pictures," Claire said. "He wants me to try and look like them. The same pictures again and again. They want to use me."

"I wish you'd told me sooner."

"You're always off running errands. Collecting firewood, feeding the hounds."

Andre took Claire's hand in his. "You know I only do that to keep us safe. You know they only trust me to do it because they know I won't run."

"I don't feel safe," Claire said. "I wish you would run."

"Not leaving you behind," Andre said. "Now, if we can—"

Both stiffened at the crack of a rifle. "Damn." Andre crept over to the tent flap and peered out.

It looked like the raiders had taken three people. Max Korn held a smoking rifle; he'd fired up into the trees. He paced now before the captive trio. An imposing black man, an olive-skinned teen girl, and an older boy who could have been the girl's brother but—

I know him, Andre thought, and searched his memory. When he found the face in his mind, he began grinding his teeth. *He's no reb. God, let me get my hands on him.*

"Names," Max demanded.

"McCall. Colonel," said the black man. He had to be six foot five and he was built like a wall. He began reciting his serial number and Max turned from him.

"That's enough from you. Girl."

"Tavia," the teen stammered.

"What do you do for the people, Tavia?"

"I'm a courier." The girl rolled up her shirt sleeve. She must have been showing Max her tattoo. All the couriers had numbers assigned to verify their legitimacy. Max looked and nodded.

"And you?" he said to the third.

Claire knelt next to Andre. "You think their camp was attacked?"

"That guy's not one of ours," Andre said. "The third guy. He's the *feder* who came to the Field the morning of the attack. The one Potter turned away."

Claire pulled Andre away from the flap. "There's something else I want to talk to you about."

"What?"

"Some of the Tribe are wearing knight armor," Claire said. "I've seen it more than once. They hide it but I've seen."

"Well, they probably took it off dead knights," Andre said. Claire's eyes fell as if she had expected no better from him. "What?" Andre sat and crossed his legs. "Claire, you want to talk to me? Talk to me. I've got a feeling you know more than I do."

"Why would they hide the armor?" Claire asked. "Another thing. Back on the hotel roof, some of them weren't using silencers. Like they weren't afraid of attracting attention."

"Why worry? Guns beat swords," Andre said. "Which goes back to the likelihood that, if they ran afoul of knights, they killed them and took their shit."

"The knights firebombed military camps with slimes, right?" Claire insisted. She must have been turning this over in his head for a while. "Why would the Tribe think they're only carrying swords? They could have robbed our armory, right? And they have slimes? And bombs?"

"Okay, slow down." Andre held out his hands. "Tell me exactly what you think is going on."

"I think the so-called knights *are* the Tribe."

Andre chewed his lip. Possible? Sure. But there was no smoking gun here. Just some ballsy raiders with stolen armor. He sure as hell hadn't seen any slimes or bomb-making materials around here. But Claire looked like she'd already convinced herself.

Meanwhile, he knew that guy outside was the missionary who'd visited the Field. If Andre could talk with him—"talk with" him—then he could find out what was really going on.

"I believe this is the Church," he told Claire.

"I'm telling you this is some sort of trick," Claire said. "Goddammit, what's with you? Ever since the hotel. Are you just going to give up and let these assholes lead you around on a leash?"

That stung. Jesus, Claire was the one who was different. Couldn't blame her—it had been a long time since Motor City Mountain, and Andre had been watching her back ever since. This was the first time in her adulthood that she'd really been waist-deep in the shit.

"I've seen a lot of things in my time," Andre said.

"Don't pull rank just because you're older."

"It's not about age, it's about experience. These raiders aren't the mafia. They're thieving hobos. There's no conspiracy out here in the middle of nowhere. We're just caught. And I know you want it to be more than that—I get it. But we're caught is all. "

Claire glared at him. "It *is* more than that. They know about me. They probably came for me."

"Whoa. How would they have known before actually meeting you?" Andre gave her a look that he hoped was more sympathetic than patronizing. "Listen to what you're saying. Doesn't make sense. It's all coincidence."

"You talking to Claire or Clarissa?"

"I'm not talking down to either of you."

"Really? So you've got all the experience. *Corporal.* And you know all about this raider group you've never seen before in your life. And me, the one they've been interrogating for two weeks, the one who's seen every inch of this camp while you're picking up fucking sticks—I don't know a thing. Right? Not even worth listening to."

"Fucking hell," Andre snapped. "I did listen. *It doesn't hold up.*"

He pointed out the flap. "You'll see. That *feder* knows."

He pushed the flap open wide. Max was still talking to the three captives. "Okay," he said. "So are any of you going to be trouble?"

"If you mean me," the big man said, "no. But let these two go. They're civilians. They're not from my base. I found them out there."

"Oh, I have questions for them, too," Max said. "If you don't mind, Colonel McCall, I'll make the decisions here."

"They can't tell you anything. They're practically kids." McCall swept his arm around the camp. "Just more mouths to feed. Assuming you're gonna feed us."

"Okay." Max sighed, and shot McCall in the head.

The colonel folded down the ground and was still. The dogs began howling again. "Get these two situated," Max said, gesturing to those still standing. Neither of them made a sound as they were led away.

#

"Vikram," the young man said in a hoarse voice.

"Andre."

He was playing nice for now, seeing what he could get from the *feder* before the thumbscrews had to be applied. Andre sat between Vikram and the girl, Tavia, in a small clearing. Hina had changed his dressing again and was now attending to Tavia's sprained wrist.

Andre saw the number tattooed on her skin—*0232*. There was something familiar about that, too, as there had been about Vikram's pinched face. Something about the Field.

"We were waiting for you," he said.

"What?" Tavia looked up at him. So did Hina.

"You were bringing something to Fairfield."

Tavia nodded with a frown of apology. "I lost them."

"What's that?"

"Schematics for your power station."

Andre turned to Vikram. "And how did you two hook up?"

"She was with McCall when he found me," Vikram said.

"What happened to your buddy?"

"My *botar* is dead." Vikram turned his palms upward and studied them. "We were attacked by dead in the woods. He saved my life."

"Well, we're glad for that," said Andre.

"Quiet down," said Hina. "Vikram, is it? Go over behind those bushes and strip. Need to check you for bites."

The young man turned bright red. "I'm not bit."

"Got a Bible to swear on?" Hina smirked at him. "I can get a man to examine you if you'd prefer."

"I can't disrobe in front of *anyone.*"

"Must make laundry day a bitch," Hina cracked. "Get over there and wait for me."

"Miss, I really can't."

"No religious exemptions here. You're not going to be trouble, are you?"

Vikram's face went from crimson to a ghastly pallor. "No, no, I don't mean to be trouble."

"Good." Hina finished wrapping Tavia's wrist. "Head over there. Tell you what, you can close your eyes and think about baseball. I won't be offended."

In spite of himself, Andre couldn't help but enjoy the way she was working Vikram over. The kid would definitely fold under questioning when the time came.

#

"You said you worked with animals," Max said to Claire. "Ever work with dogs?"

"I'm not going near those things."

It was during their morning session. They'd already gone through the pictures—a red-haired woman with green eyes, an androgynous male with short blond hair, a black girl with an ugly scar on her forehead. Claire hadn't had any trouble shifting from one to the next. Now the pair sat in a field away from the camp.

"They're not so bad," Max said. "My boys know how to read a situation. Their bark's far worse than their bite. Generally."

"They learn all their cruelty from their master," Claire muttered.

"They're disciplined, not sadistic. They know how to read people too. I bet they'd roll over and show you their tummies."

"I don't serve you."

"You depend on me."

"And you don't depend on me?" Claire cocked her head and her flesh rippled, turning mottled and sickly. Her eyes grew full black.

Max smiled at the change, but his body language bespoke his unease.

"Whatever it is you want from me," Claire said, "you know it's mine to give."

"Oh, Claire. You're young yet. And you could learn something from my boys." Max drew a pistol from his bomber jacket. "If I were to walk over to the pen and shoot one of them right now—I won't, but if I did—the others wouldn't so much as flinch away from me. Nor would they mourn their brother. That's a discipline you need to learn. Survivors survive alone, always."

He pointed the gun toward the camp. "Now, if I were to shoot Andre in his stomach, I'll bet you would just fall to pieces. Just the suggestion makes you sick, doesn't it?"

Claire's complexion returned to normal, though the color was missing from her cheeks.

"What you have is mine to take," Max said, "and your survival is my choice. Be grateful now and then."

He pressed the barrel of the gun against Claire's head and pulled the trigger. A hollow click.

"If you've got the gift, expect the grift." Max laughed and put the gun away. "I've got low friends in high places, girl. Do right by me and you'll be just fine. Now, come meet the pups."

He strode away from her. Claire sat shaking in the grass. She wasn't shaking from fear. She was furious. Because she knew he was right.

#

At dinnertime, the captives sat apart from the rest of the group, picking at week-old deer meat. It had been slathered in salt and tasted like an old shoe. Everyone was ravenous nonetheless.

"Saw you playing with the dogs today," Andre said. "I've never gotten that close."

"We weren't playing," Claire shot back.

"Well, they were having a good time," Andre said through laborious chewing.

Claire turned her back to him. "What did you say you were delivering to the Field?" she asked Tavia.

"Diagrams for the power station. I don't think they matched exactly to your layout, but they were the closest we could find."

Claire nodded. "We were so close. Could have had electricity. Then they come along and smash us." She gnawed the last bits of meat from a rib bone and tossed it. "Like they don't want us to be able to make our own way. Who'd do that?"

She glanced back at Andre. "The Church," he said in a flat tone.

"They'd have you think so," Claire replied.

"It makes sense," Andre grumbled. "I'm not in the mood for this again."

"Why would the Church want to hurt our infrastructure? They use it as much as we do. We're hardly in competition," Claire said.

"You could say the same thing about raiders," Andre told her. "For Christ's sake. Where's the motive?"

"There must be others in on it."

Andre stood. "I'm done."

Vikram, who until this point had been staring fixedly at his lap, spoke softly. "If any of you think the Church attacked your camp, it's not true. I was there."

"We know that," Andre said. "You were scouting out the site."

Vikram's face twisted in surprise. *"What?* No! She's the one who's right! We work together with you."

"Potter wasn't interested in working together, was he?" Andre said. "Bet that smarted, even if you weren't really there to spread the good news. And what *is* the good fucking news, anyway?"

He took a step toward Vikram, who shrank away, and backed into the waiting arms of a Tribe member. "All right," declared the burly man. "That's enough of that." He started off with Vikram in hand.

"Where are you taking him?" Claire shouted.

"Somewhere he can't start anything," the man called back. Vikram gawked helplessly at the other captives. The man took him into the trees.

Claire closed her eyes and waited for the gunshot. None came. Maybe they were just going to choke the life from him. Or feed him to the dogs, as Max had once threatened to do with Andre.

Claire looked to him now, but Andre was shaking dirt from his hair and refused to meet her eyes. It felt like things between them had changed irreversibly. It felt like the end, of everything.

Yet Max would drag the end out as long as he wanted. As long as he chose to. *I have to kill him. I want to.*

She'd never done such a thing, had never even considered it—in this moment, she felt she had no say in the matter. Like Max had said, all the choice was his. He'd brought it to this.

Stop with the theories, the Church frame-up, the armor. Start thinking about what matters right now. And that's getting out of this camp.

#

Max stopped with the pictures and had her spend mornings with the dogs. She did as she was told. She didn't stop the backtalk entirely—didn't want to raise suspicion—but she kept it to a minimum. Let Max think she was growing afraid of him. Soften him up.

The hounds had no names. They acted as one entity when she commanded them. They'd all chase down one stick and tear it to splinters. There was no fetching among these "pups," only killing. They all sat when she said to. They all stopped in their tracks when she said so. Granted, they'd always look past her to Max, to make sure the orders were official. But as the days went on, Max paid less and less attention, and the dogs began focusing on Claire.

Their pen had been hastily erected using chicken wire and wooden posts. Had they the notion, the dogs could have easily broken out. Despite their uniform behavior, Claire began seeing character quirks among them. The dog whose left ear was clipped was usually the first to reach a stick and the last to walk away from the kill. She named him Cap. The girl with the spots on her belly, who always rolled onto her back when Claire first arrived, became Baby. A particularly lanky mutt who always brought up the rear was christened Scraps. Claire made sure to keep an extra bit of food in her pocket so he'd be able to get something while the others gorged themselves. They mostly ate bone meal and berries.

It was about as good as anything the humans got. At least the prisoners.

One morning, several men rode into the camp on horseback. They were greeted as fellow Tribe members. Claire listened in as they reported to Max. They'd been scouting ahead and said it looked like smooth sailing. Max directed them to put the horses up with "the others." Claire had never seen any horses around the camp. She watched from the corner of her eye as the horses were led off. They were taken in the direction of a thick grove where she knew Max's tent to be.

The morning after that, Claire was lobbing sticks across the pen when she heard the rattling of chicken wire and turned to see a slime pushing the fencing down and stalking toward her. He had a gaping hole in his chest from which jags of broken ribs protruded. His heart and lungs were gone. Yellow eyes fixed on her and the thing stretched his scarred arms.

"God," Claire breathed. She turned to the dogs, who were still attacking the stick. "Heel!" she hollered.

They wheeled around to run to her, then froze. Hairs rose along their backs. Cap began barking furiously.

God, what was the command? How did she get them to attack? Was it *kill?*

"Hold," Max yelled, and the dogs turned as one towards the voice. "Right there," Max told them.

The slime was closing the gap between himself and Claire. She had nothing to fight with but a handful of pencil-thin sticks. Max stood alone, just outside the pen, and watched with his arms crossed.

Terror seized Claire and the little branches slipped from her hand. The dogs began whining. "Hold," Max repeated. "Stay."

What was he doing? Was he trying to get her killed?

"Change," Max ordered. This time, he was speaking to Claire.

The lumbering slime's bony fingers snatched at the air. It was desperate for her. *Change? Change?*

"Better get a move on, girl," Max said.

Max was behind her with the dogs. The slime was right in front of her. If she bolted to the right, she'd end up in the camp. To the left was the field where Max had shown her pictures and played with her ability. Beyond that…

If Andre wasn't willing to flee, someone had to. Claire feinted right and the slime lurched after her. She dug her feet into the earth and sprinted in the opposite direction.

"No!" Max bellowed. The dogs began barking as one. *"Get her!"* Max yelled.

The dogs swarmed around Claire and cut off her escape. Lips pulled back, they gnashed their teeth and flung spittle at her. Claire found Cap's eyes and called his name. He snarled at her.

"Cap! Cap!" She looked over her shoulder. The slime was coming for her again. "Cap, get back! Back up!"

Cap was still growling, but his stance changed. He took a step back, then forward. The other dogs did the same.

"You get her!" Max shouted.

The slime grabbed Claire's hair and yanked her back. She threw her fist at him and struck his jaw with her wrist. Pain bloomed in her arm. She ignored it and tore her hair free. Fresh agony spread throughout her scalp. The slime came away with a generous fistful of hair. Claire threw another punch and this time landed a shot to the slime's temple. He staggered sideways.

Max had jumped the fence and was gesturing wildly at the dogs. "Get her *NOW!*"

Cap leapt. Claire cried out, but the dog flew right past her and sank his teeth into the slime's thigh. The dead man groaned and swatted at the dog. Dogs, now; the one Claire called Lenny took hold of the slime's other leg. The rest of the hounds were closing in. The slime fell, and they tensed as if they were one body, ready to pounce from all sides.

"No! Wait!" Claire cried. She didn't want the slime wounding any of them in his struggling. She clapped her hands. "Get back!"

She searched the ground and spied the pile of branches from which she got the sticks. She ran over and grabbed the thickest one. Max stood motionless. The dogs parted as Claire advanced and, as the slime sat up and began to rise, she swung the branch into the back of his neck.

She put every ounce of strength she had into the blow, and she felt it; a sharp ringing shot up both arms and into her shoulders and neck, and then there was nothing, not even the strength to stand, and she fell upon her knees.

As for the slime, the branch shattered across his neck, and his head snapped back with such force that, had he been any more rotten, his head might have just flown off. He dropped for the last time.

Claire sat very still. The dogs came to her and sniffed her face, making excited sounds. They'd done it, all of them. And she was okay. Wasn't she? Cap shook blood from his snout and panted in her face. It looked like he smiling, and Claire made herself return the expression.

There was a crack. Cap slumped down in her lap.

Max stepped over to Lenny and shot him too. Claire screamed. *"NO! WHY! THEY'RE NOT INFECTED!"*

Other Tribesmen had come from the camp to see what all the noise was. They stood outside the pen and watched as Max aimed his pistol at Claire's head.

"I told you to change," he said.

"FUCK YOU!" Claire screamed, and jumped to her feet. She grabbed at the pistol. Max yanked it away, then came back with it and brought the butt down on her ear.

Claire raked her nails across his face. "That hole in his chest, huh? Is that where the bomb was supposed to go? You *fuck?"*

He grabbed her throat. She twisted his arm and sank her teeth into it. He brought the gun down once more.

The world turned red and the roar of rushing blood filled Claire's head. She was aware of falling back down, then of being dragged. It felt more like floating, then it didn't feel like anything.

#

Hina held a wet rag to Claire's head. "When she wakes up, you make sure she stays awake. Sit her up and watch her. She's probably got a concussion. If she passes out or starts slurring or anything not normal, you call for me."

Andre nodded.

"Are you okay? Can you do this?"

"I'll do it," Andre said.

Hina closed the tent flap at her back and sat beside Andre. "It didn't use to be like this. We didn't do this. We didn't take prisoners. We didn't..."

"What?"

Hina pushed the rag into his hand. "Go sit over there and put her head in your lap like I was. Keep it elevated."

Andre did so. Hina removed Claire's shoes and propped her feet up on a small lockbox.

She held Claire's feet like she was counting her toes. Then she said, "I can't keep doing this."

When she lifted her eyes, they were different. It was if a great burden had been lifted her, a heavy cloud that had broken apart and let the light back in.

She told Andre, "Once Claire's better—and she will be better—I'm going to help you. Don't ask how. Don't ask anything and don't say anything. Just take care of this girl."

Andre nodded again. "I should never have stopped. God forgive me."

"Don't worry about God. He's got nothing—nothing—to do with this." Hina gave Andre a long, strange look. "You understand what I mean?"

"I think I do."

"I'm going to try to help all of you. Tavia and Vikram too. Is that going to be okay?"

"Yeah."

"Okay. Watch her. Get her talking if you can. Keep her awake."

Hina left the tent. Andre held Claire and waited for her to wake up. There were things he needed to say and, he believed, things he needed to hear.

#

She drank a little from a canteen, but she said she couldn't eat. Andre placed a bedroll beneath her head so that he could sit next to her.

"What happened with us?" Claire mumbled. "This is ruining us, both of us."

"All I can say is that…" Andre's throat grew thick with grief, and he lowered his head until the feeling passed. "Back at the hotel, I nearly lost you. Twice. Maybe three times, I don't even know. I've felt like I'm right there ever since. About to lose you."

He cleared his throat loudly. "I'm not going to cry. Trust me, it's really gross."

Claire smiled. "You know I wouldn't mind. But it'd be fine too if you just want to tell jokes. I miss that."

"I miss things being funny," Andre said. "Look, someone's promised to help us get away."

"The nurse? Hina?"

Andre nodded. "Keep your lips zipped."

"You kinda like her."

"She's your age," Andre said.

"So? I'm not your daughter. And you sure as hell ain't no dad."

"Up yours," Andre said.

"I love you, though," Claire told him.

"Thanks."

#

Max Korn, whose real name was Chuck Farris, sat outside his tent at twilight. Down a long slope, the Tribe's horses stood quietly in a field, watched by armed guards. Max leaned to grab his flask, then relented. There was a dull pain in his bowels and drinking probably wouldn't help.

Another horse rode into the field, its rider waving to the guards. Caliban had returned. Good. They'd be rid of that little bitch before long. Max expected that House-Major to pay handsomely for Claire. Between that what the Church still owed, he'd be able to set up his own little fiefdom far away from all these lunatic factions. He had dreams of building a boat and finding a nice island. Something modest. He didn't really want to be a king. Just a chief was all. Max looked at the bite on his arm. He'd refused to let Hina dress it, preferring to give it some air and let it scar over. It told a story, after all. The wild shape-shifter he'd enslaved. It would become the stuff of legend, a tale inscribed in flesh.

Goddamn, his guts ached. He wiped gummy sweat from his brow and crawled into his tent to await Caliban's report.

TEN | EASY

"Paper covers rock." Andre pushed Claire's fist away. "You're never gonna stop with that rock, are you?"

"I just want to lie down," she said. "I don't want to sleep. Come on."

"It's not a question of whether you *want* to sleep. You're concussed."

"You are." Claire's shoulders slumped in defeat.

Andre heard the shuffling of leaves outside and covered his penlight with his hand, casting himself and Claire into total blackness. "Shhh."

The tent flap opened. Hina held her own flashlight up to her face. "We have to go now," she whispered.

"Already?" Andre looked worriedly at Claire.

"Max is fucked up. Fever. I think he's drunk, too. You need to clear out before he takes it out on you." Hina handed Andre a leather sheath containing a hunting knife. "Two hundred paces toward the moon. There'll be horses tied there. I'm going to send Vikram and Tavia too."

"What about you?"

"I'm going to tend to Max. Keep him and the others occupied." Hina placed her hand on Andre's shoulder. "Two hundred paces." To Claire, she said, "You good to walk?"

"Why not?" Claire sighed.

Hina ducked out without another word. Andre didn't like leaving like that, so abrupt and uncertain. He knew he had no choice, and so he secured the sheath on his belt and took Claire's hand. "You hold onto me."

They slipped through the flap into the night. There was no one to be seen outside their tent, and no light shining through the trees. There were, however, faint voices audible. Claire grabbed onto Andre's arm, and they started in the direction of the full moon.

The sky rumbled. Andre couldn't see any clouds through the forest canopy. The storm couldn't be too far off, though. If it came this way, the noise would provide much-needed cover. He just hoped the others didn't make a racket getting to the horses.

Vikram. Andre wanted to believe Claire's theory about the Tribe, but he still did not want that *feder* as one of his charges. Andre didn't even want to think about him, which made him remember he was supposed to be counting his steps. He turned to Claire. "How many—?"

"Thirty-one," she whispered.

Andre nodded. "Thirty-two."

Claire mumbled something he couldn't make out in response, then her weight slumped against him.

#

"What in the goddamn hell took you so long?" Max rasped at Hina. She entered his tent, where a few other members stood vigil, and knelt beside the reclining chief. His face was red, though probably more from anger than pain. He was unable to sit up due to stomach pain, which was pissing him off more.

"Sorry, I had to find the right size dropper," Hina said. She unscrewed a small bottle and dipped an eyedropper into it. "Stick out your tongue."

Max did. It was coated with a thick slick of white. Hina grimaced and administered the medicine.

"When was your last bowel movement?" Hina asked.

"The fuck business is that of yours?" Max grunted. He rolled onto his side and cradled himself. "I feel like I'm being fucking ripped apart. Isn't anyone else sick? What the hell happened to me?"

She noticed the wound on his arm, still scabbing over, bore a dark red tone. "Max, I need to clean that bite."

"Forget the fucking bite. I've been poisoned. One of those fucking rebs did it. Maybe it was even—" His buggy eyes bored into Hina's. "That little bitch must have given me some virus. Go check her. She probably got it from the dogs."

"I already checked her out."

"Go get her."

"She's unconscious," Hina said. "Max, I'm seriously concerned about that bite."

"So am I, now." Max tried to sit up and clutched at his abdomen. *"God!* Isn't that shit you gave me supposed to do something?"

"It'll take a minute."

Max shook with coughing and fell back into the fetal position. "I can't throw up," he moaned. "I tried. And no I can't go to the fucking bathroom. Everything feels locked up. Like I'm full of concrete. My chest is tight. Everyone back up and let me breathe!"

The other men around him obliged. Max swung feebly at Caliban. "You don't even need to be here. We're done."

Caliban slunk out, and one of the other men said, "Should we talk to the rest of the Tribe?"

"About what? I'm not dying, Bill." Max clenched his jaw. He shut his eyes and the lids danced. "It just hurts like a fucking bitch. And I know it's from that girl."

"Then will you let me treat the bite?" Hina demanded. Max heard the exasperation in her voice and gave her a look of murder.

"You do as I say," Max hissed.

"I'm trying to help you." Hina took hold of his wounded arm. "At some point, I'm going to have to take care of it, one way or the other. The bite becomes infected, you get sicker. The way you are now, you could die."

"I said I'm NOT dying," Max retorted, "and don't you tell anyone out there anything different. Don't any of you go running your mouth and don't get any ideas. I AM this tribe. I have all the connections. Everything falls apart without me, you understand?"

"I'm going to go get some antiseptic," Hina said. "I'm going to clean and dress the bite. And I'm going to give you something to help you sleep."

"Only if you take it too," Max said, scooting back from her. "Bill, you stay here. She's going to take whatever she gives me."

Hina walked out. Against Max's outraged protests, Bill followed.

"Hey," he said quietly. "This looks bad. Almost looks like..."

"I know," Hina said, "but it can't be that. I'm going to go get the stuff I said."

"All right. Well, don't worry about taking the sleeping medicine. Just take a...you know, a fake dose."

"Placebo. Right. Thanks, Bill."

Max bellowed Bill's name, and Hina rushed off.

\#

Andre held Claire under her arms and kept his eyes on the moon. "Come on, hon. Seventy-nine. Eighty. One foot in front of the other. Stay with me."

"I can't stay awake," Claire mumbled.

"Yes, you can. Count with me. Eighty-three. Eighty-four."

Claire wobbled and threw out a hand to steady herself, finding a tree within reach. Andre tried to pull her along but she planted her feet. "I need a minute. I can't see straight."

"We're almost halfway there," Andre pleaded. Hell, maybe they were halfway there. "Two hundred paces" wasn't very exact. He hoped they hadn't wavered off course. It looked as if the moon was directly ahead but who the hell knew? If they were off by a few feet, they might walk right by the horses.

He held Claire and looked back from where they'd come. He could still hear distant voices, but there were no footfalls. No sign of Tavia and Vikram.

If those two reached the horses first, would they wait? Or would they gallop off on their steeds and give the whole thing away?

Jesus. I'm relying on them as much as Hina. "Claire, let's go."

"I really need—"

She started at a sound from the woods. Someone was approaching. Andre drew the knife and let Claire go. "Hold on," he said, and she wrapped her arms around the tree.

There were at least two people coming right in their direction. The leisurely, noisy pace couldn't mean the other captives. Andre crouched behind another tree and readied himself. He knew how to slit a throat on paper. This was…*this is going to be bad.*

Claire pushed away from the tree on uncertain feet. Andre waved his arms at her. *What the fuck are you doing, Claire?*

She pulled her hair back into a ponytail—a black ponytail—and her eyes glittered in the moonlight as they changed. She pulled the bandage from around her head and tossed it. The flesh of her face didn't just change in tone—it was as if tissue or fat was moving along her jaw and into her chin, shaping it to look like—she looked *exactly* like Hina now.

A man and woman stepped through the trees. Claire said, "Thank God. Do you have a light? I dropped my medicine."

Andre stayed behind his tree, cloaked in shadow, and watched. Claire didn't sound exactly like Hina, but it wasn't a bad impression. That wasn't part of her power, just Claire being Claire. Andre held still, his legs like coiled springs, as the two Tribesmen turned their backs to him. A small torch flared to life in the woman's hand.

"Max needs it," Claire said, bending to sweep her hands through the grass. "He's got a fever."

"He does?" the man exclaimed. He fell on his knees and began helping in the search.

"Are you okay, Hina?" the woman asked.

"I will be once I find the friggin' meds," Claire snapped.

"I mean *you* sound sick," the woman said. "You have a cold?"

Claire looked up and past the woman. "Now would be a good time."

"Huh?" The woman crossed her arms. "What's going on?"

Andre brought a softball-sized rock down on her head. She folded like laundry, and he seized the kneeling man by his shoulder. Before the man could cry out, he took a shot to the forehead and crumpled.

"Couldn't do the knife," Andre said, grabbing Claire as she limped past the unconscious forms. "Stay like that in case we run into someone else."

"I think we'd better just start running," Claire said in her own voice.

#

Four horses stood in a small clearing, quietly fussing to one another. They weren't saddled, but they behaved like they were broken in. Andre helped Claire mount one.

She glanced around from her vantage point. "This feels too easy."

"We have to trust Hina," Andre said.

She pursed her lips, then nodded. "The Tribe might have planned to let you go, but not me. Four horses. She gave me a horse." She shed her façade and was Claire again.

Andre untied the reins binding Claire's horse to a nearby tree. He freed a young paint and climbed onto its back. "Why would they want to let any of us go?"

"So you can tell everyone else about the knights."

"Okay. I'll take your word for it."

A small silhouette came crashing through the trees. The horses snorted and backed off. A breathless Tavia looked desperately at Claire and Andre. "Vikram's hurt," she gasped. "His leg's hurt!"

Andre slid off his horse. He walked past Tavia—she turned to follow and he stopped her with one hand, using the other to loose a third horse's leash. He cupped his hands next to the animal and said to Tavia, "Get on, quick."

"But Vikram! Are you going to get him?"

"Andre?" There was fear in Claire's voice.

"We have to hurry," Tavia said, edging toward the trees.

"Listen," Andre said, cocking his head toward the direction Tavia had come from. Several voices could be heard. They were some distance off, but they sounded frantic.

He grabbed Tavia by the waist and lifted the teen onto the horse. He got back onto his. "You know how to ride, right?" he called back to Tavia.

"Yes, but—"

"We don't have time!" Andre said. He kicked his horse in the ribs and snapped the reins. "Come on!"

Then he was off, and Claire was half a gallop behind him. Andre ducked his head to avoid thin, low-hanging branches. He felt a few catch in his hair and break off. Andre chanced one look back and saw that Tavia was keeping pace with Claire. He urged his steed on, and soon they broke out of the trees and onto a wide expanse of flat earth.

"Let's go! Ha!" He didn't look back again.

#

Claire slowed a bit to Tavia wouldn't lose her in the woods, but after they were out, it was Claire who was fighting to keep up with the courier. The kid knew how to handle a horse. She seemed to have let go of the thought of Vikram as soon as Andre demanded it. For Claire, it was a little different.

Had Andre abandoned him because there was no time, or because he didn't care to try and save the missionary? She didn't know how much, if any, of her theory Andre was buying. She didn't even consider it a theory anymore. And even though it appeared that Hina's helping them had been legit, Claire couldn't help analyzing their escape from every angle.

Maybe that was how it was with Andre and Vikram, that lingering mistrust. Maybe it was smart to be skeptical. The difference was, Hina was in the clear. Vikram had just been caught trying to get away.

#

Max forced himself to walk from his tent to the clearing where Vikram was being held, along with a horse. He used a branch as a walking stick and hobbled past his subordinates. Someone wouldn't meet his eyes, and others looked like they were ready to stick a knife in his back.

Maybe they already had.

He approached Vikram and leaned on the branch to catch his breath. "All right," he rasped. "Who got you the horses?"

"I really don't know. I don't. I just followed the others." Vikram was kneeling to hold his leg. A trap made from a sapling and a little wooden stake had taken a nice chunk out of his calf. It was wonder none of the other captives had sprung such a trap. Again, maybe they were helped. Maybe? Oh, of *course* they had been. And it was no fucking coincidence that Max's guts were suddenly on fire.

"Vikram," he said through his teeth, very quietly, "I know you're a child of God. And I know God doesn't like a liar. I sure don't. In fact, that's the thing I hate more than anything in the world." He leered at the young man. "I am not feeling very merciful tonight."

He glanced back at the Tribe. "Does anyone want to say anything?"

No answers from anyone. He focused on Hina. She was, after all, his nurse. And he was turning fucking inside out from the agony in his nerves. She had a lot of contact with the captives too. And now, here in the somber silence 'neath the light of that big ol' moon, she wouldn't look him in the eye.

"See, there are so many things wrong with this picture that I just can't believe this was someone's innocent mistake," Max said. "Some of you are familiar with what the next stage of the plan entails. Very few of you know the entire thing. But you all know our code. We all stand to reap the fruits of our labors. There's literally no reason for any one or more of you to fuck it up. And yet..." He tightened his grip on the branch and stood as tall as he could. He took the branch in both hands. "I just can't help but see this as an act of treason. Treason against all your brothers and sisters here. We have traitors in our midst."

He whirled and smashed the branch over Vikram's back. Vikram let out a choked cry and sank to the forest floor. Max planted the end of the branch in the small of Vikram's back.

"Vikram, I'd really like to know. A name. Give me one name."

"I swear I don't know!" Vikram screamed.

Max's teeth squeaked as he ground them inside his head. "Someone here tried to help him escape," he yelled. "Would you save him now? Would you step forward before I drive this stick through his back? How much do you believe in your treason?"

He applied pressure. Vikram wailed like a child whose arm was being twisted to the breaking point.

"Stop!"

Max did not relieve the pressure, but he looked back with a pained smile. "Yes?"

"Max," said Bill, "come on. This isn't you. This isn't any of us. We can talk through this."

"Bill," Max sneered. "Billy. I would really never have guessed."

"Whoa! I didn't do anything," Bill said, raising his hands. "I'm just trying to calm things."

"Caliban," Max wheezed.

Caliban stepped forward with terror in his eyes. "S-sir? I just got back from Salome."

"I know. I'm not accusing you, son. You might be the only one I can trust, given the particulars you and I know." Caliban relaxed at that.

"So, draw your pistol, please," Max told him.

Caliban fished through his trousers and withdrew a small gun. Max pointed to Bill. "Kill him."

"I swear I didn't do anything!" Bill exclaimed. He stared hard at Caliban. "I didn't do a goddamn thing. You know me."

"I gave an order," Max said. Vikram squirmed beneath him. Members of the Tribe backed off from Bill and Caliban.

"Max, you know me, too!" Bill spun around. He couldn't seem to find a friend in the crowd. Max nodded impatiently at Caliban.

"It was me!" Hina shouted.

Caliban had his gun leveled at Bill's face. Max stared at him for a moment to see if he'd go ahead and pull the trigger anyway. Then he motioned for the gun to be lowered.

"Hina," he said in a sing-song voice. He pulled the branch off of poor weeping Vikram, if only because he needed the support again. "Go ahead, then."

She shrugged. "I let them go. I gave them horses."

Max returned her shrug. "Just like that."

"You've lost it," Hina said. The air was sucked out of the forest and everyone stood rigid.

"She says I've lost it." Max paced in a circle around Vikram, the branch creaking and cracking. "When we're closer than ever before to comfort and prosperity. Retirement from this life." Now that she'd look at him, Max addressed her directly. "Claire is worth an honest-to-goodness king's ransom. Forget what we've earned from the Church. I mean we could be done with all of this by Christmas. Does anyone remember Christmas? Do any of you old fogies like me remember creeping down the stairs as a child on that morning? When magic was real." The pain suffusing his marrow had so overwhelmed his senses that it felt more like a warm tingle at this point. "If we could just live in a world without begging or stealing or starving, that would feel like magic to me. And we can have that. But, but but *but,* we need Claire."

He turned his attention to Bill. "Billy. You want things to calm down? Start by taking Hina there and tying her up. I want her blindfolded and gagged and wrapped up in a tarp. Alive, of course. We still need her."

Bill took Hina's arm. His eyes said he was sorry, but that was as kind a gesture as she'd be able to hope for. Max spoke to the rest of the Tribe. "We ride tonight! I want that girl unharmed!"

ELEVEN | BAD

The rain came just as the shadow towers of a dead city became visible on the horizon. Claire was no longer feeling drowsy, but dizzy was another story. The sound of the churning black overhead, and cold droplets slapping her face from all directions, didn't help.

Andre stopped his horse beneath a skeletal billboard. "We could lose them in the city. But God knows what's already in there."

"They're coming for me, I promise," Claire said. "The city."

Andre nodded. "You good with that, Tavia?"

The girl made a weird movement with her head that was something between a nod and a shake.

"How old are you?" Claire asked.

"Sixteen. Ish."

"And you travel alone? The brass really trusts you. You must have proven yourself."

"I've been around," Tavia replied, sitting up a little straighter. "I know how to fight, if that's what you mean."

"That's what I mean," Claire said. "Hopefully, it won't come to that."

They walked the horses along the edge of a shattered highway and into the suburbs surrounding the city. This place was much larger than Raylene. Every house and business looked as if it had been raided a hundred times and then kicked in by the elements, with collapsed roofs and black glass. Some of the roads were in good enough shape to travel on. Others had fallen in or become weed gardens. Claire didn't expect any animals to jump out at them from the shadows, not in this weather, but all the same, she eyeballed every dark hole that might be something's den.

They passed the leaning gates of what had apparently once been the Arbest Zoo. What sort of captive beasts had survived the collapse? Were they still here? Their offspring's offspring, rather, Claire thought. Predators that originated from a foreign land but knew nothing of it. For them, this urban decay would constitute their natural surroundings. They'd be well at home while the descendants of their human owners were the fish writhing on land.

They had no guns. Andre had a knife. She hoped he wouldn't hesitate to use it on non-humans.

Lightning illuminated the street. At an upcoming intersection, a slime stood inert, face raised to the sky like a suicidal chicken. Andre motioned for the other riders to give the dead man a wide berth. The slime didn't even notice them as they passed by. Claire's horse gave him a curious sideways look. Claire did, too; the man was dressed like a policeman. Maybe he thought he was directing traffic. Maybe he'd been standing there for years. Looked threadbare enough, literally soaked to the bone.

The rain let up a little. It looked like the storm was moving on. Tavia rode up next to Claire. "Do they still scare you?"

"Depends. Some of them aren't so slow."

"You mean the ones who run?"

"No, I mean some of them aren't so dumb." Claire thought again of the zoo and how its inhabitants might have adapted. The nano-driven dead had claimed places like this for their own. Some of them were well acclimated to it.

Thunder boomed. In her mind's eye, Claire saw the shrike scrabbling over crumpled vehicles. She saw a corpse speared on a metal rod, its legs stripped of meat. The shrike didn't bite right into them. She tore the meat off with her hands, then ate it. Claire had watched from underneath a car, where she'd been forced to stay for nearly an entire day until she was sure the coast was clear. The memory became sharper, more vivid, and she saw the face of the staked corpse.

The face was pale, slightly bloated. Its skin glistened with moisture, giving it the appearance of porcelain.

Claire called her horse to a stop and sat there, transfixed by what her mind was showing her. She knew it was her mom. There was no question, even if she could not call to mind an image of that same face when it had color and life. Her memory offered no scenes of being held, of how the woman spoke or sang. She couldn't even remember the sound of a scream or sob from those purple lips. All she had was that broken porcelain figure in the middle of the MCM.

"Claire?" Andre said. The rain increased again, and he was gone. Claire shut her eyes and tried to summon another memory, any memory that wasn't a nightmare. Why was this all the world would allow her?

Everything you are is mine.

The shrike, who shouldn't even have had a voice to recall, had told Claire that in a dream. The dream where she'd seen the man in the truck, her father. His face was a blur. He had not said a word. Only the shrike had. And her voice had been the creaking of brittle floorboards. It had been the din of angry insects pouring from a hive. The surreal shriek of steel being twisted and torn. Her essence was fear and pain shaped into something with a face, with a bloody black mouth that spoke prophecy.

Everything you are is mine. The shrike had eaten both her parents. The shrike was the wicked witch, and Claire was a fairy-tale castoff lost in a haunted wood.

When Andre touched her, she screamed, and the rain drumming on her head swelled to a roar that felt like it was inside her. Andre grabbed her arm to keep her from falling off the horse.

"Claire!" he barked. "What is it?"

"They died," Claire said, rain and tears dribbling over her lips and falling onto her clenched hands. "She killed them, and that's all she'll let me know."

"Claire, look at me." Andre examined her eyes. "Does your head still hurt?"

"The shrike," she said. Andre sat back on his steed.

"She killed my mom and dad. She almost got me. I could hear her moving around in the Mountain—I knew it was her because she didn't move like the others. The others avoided her. She would hunt for me when it was light. She knew I was still there. And—I think, when I would make myself look like one of them, I think she could almost tell.

"You never saw her eyes," Claire insisted, shaking Andre by the shoulder.

"I believe you," he said. "But she's gone now, long gone. That was fifteen years ago. She's dust."

Claire stared back toward the intersection where the dead cop stood. "How do you know?" she said.

"Let's get out of the rain before we catch pneumonia," Andre said. "Tavia, keep an eye out for a building that looks secure."

The teen nodded. *She's probably spent many a night in abandoned buildings,* Claire thought. She wondered if the courier had ever heard stories of the MCM and what was there.

#

The windows of Gabriel Toy Co. were covered by boards, and the boards were coated with moss. The entryway had a rolling metal shutter covering it which, while rusty and dented, was holding up. Andre used the knife to pry apart what remained of the locking mechanism, then raised the shutter. The actual door behind it was heavy wood. It wasn't easy to force open, and that was good news in Andre's book.

This was one place that hadn't been completely ransacked. The shelves were lined with sodden boxes. Andre heard rain pattering on the floor somewhere in the back. Hole in the roof. Not a problem. They could keep warm in here. Hell, there was a bin filled with teddy bears right by the smashed register. So long as they weren't infested with bugs, they'd make nice bedding.

Andre shone his penlight down the center aisle. Muffled thunder clapped and Tavia muttered, "Must be one storm after another. Summer's almost over."

"Oh, it's over." Andre read the faded lettering on board-game boxes and packets of playing cards that were probably fused together. "Follow me, folks."

He passed the video games and action figures and stopped before the girls' section. *Never thought I'd say this, but God bless sexism.* The make-believe kitchen utensils and play clothing here might actually come in handy, unlike the oversized plastic tools in the boys' section. That made him think of model kits. They'd have real tools. Maybe even something to make fire.

He spotted Claire holding a ragged plush toucan. "I think I had one of these," she said, reading the attached tags.

"I can't believe all this stuff," Tavia said. She'd gone over to an endcap loaded with plastic dinosaurs. "This must have been awesome."

"I like the quarter machines up front," Andre said. "I collected sticky spiders."

He moved to the next aisle. There was a clatter at the far end. Andre put the light on it and saw a LEGO set lying on the floor, colored bricks scattered.

"Let's go up front and move the checkout counter to the door. Start a barricade."

"What if it's bolted down?" Tavia asked.

"The counter? Good point. See if you can find any building kits. Like robots or cars. They have tools."

He walked past the LEGO mess and panned the light over the back wall. "I'm going to see if there's anything useful in the storeroom. Claire, want to come with?"

Claire joined him, still holding the toucan. She set it atop a jigsaw puzzle. "Don't let me forget that."

They found the door marked EMPLOYEES ONLY and gave it a push. It was definitely barricaded from the other side. Andre called Tavia over. "Okay, there might be trouble behind this door. We need weapons. Something heavy you can wield with one hand."

Tavia nodded and disappeared down an aisle. She came back with bike gloves. Andre raised an eyebrow, but Tavia handed them out and said, "You want a good grip, right?" Then she went back into the aisle.

She returned with a trio of metal softball bats. They were child-scale, which made them perfect cudgels. "You've done this before," Andre said as he took one.

"Been around," said Tavia.

Andre braced his shoulder against the door. "It's giving a little. I don't think there's anything nailed across. Probably just furniture. I'm gonna try and get this open with one shove. Ready?"

Claire and Tavia raised their bats.

Andre threw his weight against the door. It groaned and opened a full foot before stopping. The clatter of falling shelves could be heard. The sound of dripping water became louder. "There's our leak," he said. "The room's probably a wreck. But there might be an office or—"

A chattering sound came through the gap in the doorway. It was a rapid clicking. Andre jumped back. "The hell?" he breathed, then turned to the women and pressed a finger against his lips.

The chattering stopped. Then it started again. Metal groaned on the other side of the door. Andre had no idea what the sound was. Maybe it was something spilling off one of the shelves. But there was no mistaking the low grunt that came next.

It was a sickly, throaty noise. It was followed by more in quick succession, an animalistic sort of "Hrh. Hrh."

Then it became "Hoo."

More chattering. Multiple sources. Andre grabbed the door handle and began pulling it closed.

A gnarled black hand came around the door and grabbed at his. Andre screamed and released the door. He brought his bat down but missed the hand and instead blew the handle right off the door. "Fuck!"

An entire arm snaked out, gray and wrinkled and covered in patches of black hair. The hand's overgrown nails swept back and forth through the air. Whatever they were, they were all hoo-hooing now.

Andre and Claire exchanged a look of disbelief. "No way."

The chimp at the door shoved its shrunken, hairless head through and its rotted jaws opened to display huge, jagged teeth. It roared.

Andre smashed its brainpan and yelled, *"Get outta here!"*

The three sprinted down the center aisle. Andre's legs were numb, flopping along like wet noodles, and he felt like any second he was going to hit a puddle and do the splits and break his goddamn pelvis in half. The storeroom door thudded repeatedly, and he could hear the chimps shoving shelves aside to get it open.

Must have been from the goddamn zoo. How'd they get infected? Had one bitten a slime, or had the slime bitten the chimp? Who cared? Andre dove across the checkout counter, knocking the register to the floor, and threw open the front door. *"Comeoncomeoncomeon!"*

Claire and Tavia raced past him. He leapt to grab the bottom of the shutter and missed. Andre came down in a slick of rainwater, fell hard on one knee and felt splitting pain.

"DO IT!" Claire screamed, pointing past him into the store. A half-dozen rotting chimps were coming down the center aisle. Of all the dead Andre had seen, all the corpses and all the slimes, this was the most awful. He forced himself to his feet and snagged the shutter. It came down with a crash that rivaled the thunder, and then the chimps slammed into it from the other side and it rattled in its frame.

"Go around back and get the horses!" They were tied under an awning, and Andre hoped the chimps hadn't come out the roof and after them. He had no idea how infected animals would behave. He'd never believed a word Johnny Idaho said about those test monkeys. *Never a dull moment.* Andre followed Tavia and Claire around back. The horses appeared unharmed, though they were stomping their hooves in response to the thunder. The humans mounted up and set off down a side alley at a brisk gallop.

"Shit!" Claire snapped behind him. "I forgot my fucking toucan!"

"I'll get you another one, I swear to God!" Andre yelled. Lightning rippled through the clouds, and he looked back to see if they were being followed. No sign of the chimps. They must have been too busy at the storefront.

But up ahead—directly ahead—loomed a pair of slimes. Andre's horses reared back and nearly dumped him. He jumped off and fell upon the first undead with his bat. Claire caught the second with a single blow that turned its head halfway around. Andre stood and grabbed at the reins of his horse. It tried to lunge away from him, saw its retreat was blocked by the others, and whipped its head back so that the reins lashed Andre across the face.

Claire grabbed them and stepped in front of the horse. "Hey! Whoa!" She reached for its head but it didn't bite. Instead, it lowered its snout, and Claire patted the water from it. "Hey," she said softly. "It's okay. You're okay now." She stroked its mane and picked out the tangles. "We're okay, beautiful boy. Who needs a toucan."

Andre felt laughter bubbling up in his chest. It felt unreal. He let out a chuckle and turned his face up to catch a few drops of rain.

"You ready to ride?" Claire asked. Andre saw she was talking to him and nodded. "If he'll have me."

#

Max was lagging behind the other riders. He pressed his face into the back of his horse's neck. The pain wasn't really pain anymore. He thought it was the certainty of death that had relieved his suffering. Pain was an inconvenience for the living, sure, those spoiled on life. But it was leading him by the hand toward an ending, and he didn't mind so much.

Hina and Vikram had been roped together and placed on the back of the same horse. Caliban led them along. Bill would be up front. Someone called back to Max, saying there was a city in sight. He waved half-heartedly. Didn't care anymore about the girl. He felt as if his little private island was already within reach. The sound of rain became the gentle sloshing of waves, and the rock of the horse's gait was the lazy sway of a hammock. The smell of the animal was the smell of salt and sand.

He heard someone's voice nearby. "Max? Max!" A hand nudged him. He slipped off the horse sand fell into warm shallows. The surf came and its foam enfolded him like a blanket.

Later, his hands lifted him out of the sopping grass and the world turned about him so that he was upright beneath the stars. There were no shapes or sounds of life to be seen. Smells were still there, smells like dirty water and like his sick and horse-skin. The wet dripped from his fingertips and from the tip of his nose. There was no cold. Cold was only a memory and memories were dissipating fast. There was only hunger now. Hunger was an uneasy feeling on both sides of his flesh, a tugging that made his feet stumble and splash in the grass.

He didn't mean anything anymore. It was just the hunger, and the hunger pulled its limbs onward and forward toward black towers which blotted out the stars. Hunger was the endless space beyond. Black towers had doors and floors and bore the promise of meat. It needed the meat like meat needed breath. That was all there was to know.

Walking now. Things turning and moving inside. Making room.

TWELVE | FEED

Sharp stones had been used to carve letters into the side of a crumbling brick building. Early dawn's light revealed the words: *Lilith is the only forever.*

Andre cast a wary glance around the block. The graffiti looked old, but that didn't mean there weren't still loons-in-waiting. Lilith was some wackadoo cult thing, he knew that much. Cults, of course, tended to burn out far more quickly than churches.

"Hungry?" Claire asked him.

"Not even thinking about food," he lied. He asked Tavia, "You go for any of this religious stuff?"

"I'm a Satanist," she said. Surprising as it was, it was far from the worst possible answer and Andre just nodded.

"You worship the Devil?" Claire asked.

"No, I don't go for any of that. It's more like a philosophy." Tavia had dismounted her horse and was seated on a block of concrete. "Like, everything we do to survive, to live, there are always people who will tell you it's wrong. Just being human is evil to some people. Then why are we frickin' here?" Tavia took off her shoes and made an effort at wringing them, then set them aside. "I mean, I don't think you should hurt anyone. Unless they hurt you."

"And then you...?"

"Destroy them," Tavia said mildly.

"I'm sorry about Vikram," Andre said out of the blue. Not that it hadn't been eating at him like his empty stomach. He thought it worked better as a throwaway line. Maybe no one would even say anything.

Tavia did. "Well, it wasn't your fault. We had to go."

Claire repeated, "We had to go." She glanced in Andre's direction, and he looked down.

"I hope he'll be okay," Tavia said. "He was really nice. I don't care that he's a Church guy or whatever."

"Some Satanist," Claire said.

"You've got the wrong idea," Tavia said. "Besides, you said the Church was being framed for the attacks. Right?"

"That's what *I* said."

"So there's no war. And I'm not about to waste my life going after churchy people. I just want people to keep their peanut butter out of my chocolate."

Claire laughed. "Where did you ever get a line like that?"

"My dad," Tavia answered.

Claire smiled. "I'm glad you can remember him."

"He's still alive," Tavia said. "He's at Fort Lassiter, way back east. I'm going to go back and you should come with me."

"If we're going to ride on, we should go now." Andre gestured toward the horses. "If we're going to stay and hope the Tribe passes us by, then we have to cut the horses loose. Those dogs are tracking them, not us."

"We need to eat," Claire said. "At least I do. My head's swimming."

"I vote we hunker down here," said Andre. "I think they'll lose us and follow the horses. If they decide to turn back, we'll be gone."

"Or we get going now," Tavia said. "We might find some wild game outside the city."

"You mean besides the monkeys?" Andre said. "It's a long shot. And all we have to hunt with are bats."

"You have a knife."

Andre drew it and tossed it to Tavia, handle first. "You want to carve spears, go for it. As for me, I'll bet there are edibles all around us right now."

Tavia said, "We ought to at least try and find food on the road. It'd be a shame to send those horses off and be stuck on foot, and snacking on leaves."

"It'd be a shame to keep them and get caught," Andre said. "It could happen here in whatever town this is, or it could happen a hundred miles down the line. Those horses are marked. And hey, leaves aren't that bad. Ever had a grub wrap?"

"Not by choice," said Tavia.

"I like the sound of Fort Lassiter," Claire said. "But I don't think we're going to get there today."

"Of course not." Tavia grabbed her drying shoes and beat the dirt from them. "I just don't want to give up a horse unless I have to."

"You could always go on ahead by yourself," Andre said. He didn't mean it, either as an insult or a sensible option, but Tavia seemed to take it as the latter.

She slipped her shoes on and placed her hands on her hips. "You both are staying?"

"I think it's safest," Andre said. "Don't go. Not on that horse."

Tavia dropped her hands. "Oh well. Nothing bad is forever." She tossed the knife back to Andre. "And everything good ends."

#

They set the horses loose without any ceremony. For their part, the horses trotted off without so much as a look back. *They're ready to get out of town,* Andre mused. And they'd live.

The trio headed for a throng treetops visible over the smaller buildings. They came upon a cobbled street that had probably once been a pedestrian walkway and was no completely overrun by plant life. They began picking through the foliage for something they could eat.

"I can't tell if these are blueberries," Andre muttered. Tavia knelt beside him and placed the bunch of shriveled fruit in her palm.

"Forget it," she said, and dropped them in the dirt.

She'd seemed so meek upon first meeting. Perhaps that had been by her own design. That or Andre was feeling and thinking overprotective, still fearing that at any moment he might lose one of his fragile charges. He reminded himself that neither Tavia nor Claire were his charges, and far from fragile. The weathered fatigues he wore didn't mean anything right now.

A crow cawed nearby. Andre's hand went to the bat lying by his feet. Tavia did the same. Together, they crouch-walked toward the sound. Low-hanging branches thick with leaves shielded them from view. Andre poked the bat into the leaves and pushed them aside.

Crows meant one of two things—dead meat or undead meat. In this case, it wasn't what Andre had hoped for. A slime was hanging, nude, from a tall branch on a sycamore. The crow was perched on the dead man's shoulder, worrying at the papery flesh of his temple with its beak.

A second crow lighted on the opposite shoulder. The two birds exchanged caws and then set to tearing at the man's face. There was very little tissue left there. One of the eyes was gone and the other, sunken and yellow, moved slowly downward to observe the newcomers.

"Claire," Andre whispered. She came up behind him.

The slime's jaw, barely attached to the skull with a few strands of black sinew, wavered as the thing tried to moan. A sound like autumn leaves being raked escaped its dry gullet.

It hadn't been hung by the neck. The rope was secured beneath its ribcage. Its hands were bound in the front while its legs dangled uselessly.

"Like a scarecrow," Claire said.

"Is it a trap?" Tavia whispered.

Andre believed someone had placed the slime here as some sort of crude alarm system to protect their berry crop. However, the state of both the plants and the slime indicated no one had been tending garden in a while.

"I think we're good," Andre told the others. "There's no one watching over this place."

He fingered the contents of his pockets. Hadn't found many edibles yet. "Let's hurry up and finish all the same," he said. "We still need to find shelter."

Shelter came in the form of an apartment building a couple of blocks away. Along the way, they stopped to drink from a long-abandoned birdbath filled with rainwater. They rinsed the berries and splashed the rest of the water on their hands and faces. Then they went into the building to sweep it. All clear.

It was midday when they settled down in a third-floor suite. Andre pulled a ratty ottoman over to the window and parked himself there to watch the street. Tavia sorted the berries and gave Claire the lion's share. "Is your head any better?"

"I think it will be once I eat," Claire said, gratefully accepting the food. "How's your wrist?"

"Oh, the sprain healed fine." Tavia flexed her arm to demonstrate. "I noticed you limping off and on when they first brought us to the camp. Same thing?"

"Yeah, sprained my foot." Claire gestured to Andre. "He nearly got his head taken off."

"Just grazed me," Andre said.

Tavia whistled. "I feel like I'm always living on borrowed time."

"Borrowed from who?" Andre said. "You've earned it. You're playing with house money. It's the slimes who are in the red."

The Tribe, too, he thought. They owed the people they'd hurt. And whoever was behind this whole conspiracy, assuming there was one. Andre wanted to believe there was a God who'd someday balance the books and make sure everyone got their due. But then, where did the slimes fit in? Maybe Andre was being punished for something, but surely not Claire. Nope, it fell to Man to settle his own accounts.

Sarge had said something once that, at the time, all those years ago, hadn't resonated with Andre. But it did now, and more with each passing day. *"I've met four or five leaders of exemplary character in my time, and a hundred antichrists. Once they've used us all up, they'll go to war with each other. And the last man, on the last day, will be one of them. A bug-eyed psycho playing with himself and laughing."*

#

Alone on the street—yet far from the only one there—Claire searched desperately for a face she knew among the milling crowds. These pale, hunched wraiths were barely people at all. They wore kerchiefs on their heads like little burial shrouds, and their clothes hung long and loose from withered arms. Pruned faces hid beady eyes and deeply etched scowls within their folds. They were all old crones, and they jostled against her in passing like she didn't exist. Somehow, Claire knew that was best. She was afraid to move for fear that they would take notice of her and then fix those little black eyes, like crows' eyes, on her. She didn't want to be part of this world. Claire stopped looking for familiar faces and instead focused on finding an escape route. Every narrow building had a stoop upon which stood or sat the miserable crones. There were no alleyways between the brownstones. They were like teeth, closed tightly around her. The air was stale and dry. Claire covered her mouth to keep from coughing.

"Oh. *Oh.*"

Dread surged through its own veins and turned Claire's bones to ice. She ignored the voice at her shoulder. She felt the woman's tiny body nudging hers.

"Oh?"

The woman stood on her toes and spoke into Claire's ear. Her mouth smelled like a coffin. *"I know you're there."*

Claire couldn't help it. She glanced down into that pitted face and it smiled toothlessly.

"Isn't it awful?" asked the crone.

"Don't you just want to be dead? *Really* dead?"

Claire backed away. She collided with another crone, who cursed and fixed a dark glare upon her. "Why are you *here?*" the hag snapped. "You have nothing here."

More faces turned in Claire's direction, each more hateful than the last. She steeled herself and began pushing through the crowd while their voices rose in pitch. Each's voice was tremulous, sick.

"Wouldn't it be nice to be dead?"

"We all want you to be dead like us."

"So do you."

Claire stumbled on the lip of an askew manhole cover. She grabbed it and shoved it aside, dropping her legs into the hole. She didn't feel a ladder.

"You're going to live in *shit?*"

"Stupid, stubborn child!"

"You killed them!"

Claire fell through space into a stone tunnel, splashing down in a few inches of fetid water. She ran from the open manhole before their voices could reach her again.

The walls had a very weak greenish luminescence. Claire was able to navigate her way down the snaking corridors and began looking for a way back up. There had to be a street somewhere up there that wasn't haunted by those things.

The walls began to give off a red glow. She took that to mean progress and continued on. The sewer was uncomfortably warm and the smell unbearable, but the silence made up for it. Red turned to blue. The tunnel's walls smoothed, and Claire reached out and felt cool plaster.

It was a hallway in a house. Moonlight streamed through an open window. Claire tried to first door and found it locked. She stepped back and was moving to the next when suddenly the knob rattled and turned from within.

A purple porcelain face loomed from the darkness of the room. Claire froze.

"Mommy?"

This wasn't right. This wasn't a good place.

The emotionless porcelain face seemed to be trying to smile. Tiny cracks webbed out from the corners of its mouth.

Claire ran to the window at the end of the hall. Despite the blue light pouring in, she saw no moon in the sky, nor any detail below. *This isn't a house!*

She turned. The porcelain lady glided down the hall toward her. Her nightgown whispered across the floorboards. Claire was ready to scream.

Then a door to the lady's right flew open, and the shrike lurched out with an enormous pair of shears in her hands. With a baleful cry, she shoved them into the porcelain lady's gut.

The lady froze in mid-air. Blood began pouring down the oversized blades.

Claire opened her mouth, but not to scream. She tried to call to her mother, and the porcelain lady tilted its head and offered a smile before its face shattered to dust.

The shrike yanked the scissors free and ran at Claire. "AUUUGGGHHH!"

Claire jolted awake. The scream that had been caught in her lungs tore free, and she sat bolt upright in bed.

The bedroom door flew open, followed by a silhouette in electric light. "Oh my God, Claire! What is it?"

It was her, really her, in the flesh. It was her face. Claire's scream died and she gasped for breath. "Mom. Oh, Mom, I'm sorry. It was—"

The shrike stepped into the doorway. Claire saw the shadow of the scissors, saw the blades spread wide. She leapt from the bed.

Something clamped down on her ankle. She felt terrible pressure, then heat, and toppled to the carpet like a ragdoll.

Claire rolled onto her back and saw that her foot was gone below the ankle. A *second* shrike crawled out from under her bed, bloody scissors clacking.

The thing seized the stump of Claire's leg and began dragging her into darkness. Claire let out one final scream before the shadows suffocated her.

#

Claire's eyes opened. She immediately shoved herself back across the floor, away from the forms towering over her.

"Don't scream!" Andre said, dropping to one knee and clapping his hand over her mouth. "You're okay! It's us! Just don't scream."

Claire's chest heaved with the effort of swallowing the scream down. She scanned the empty apartment room. There were no dark corners or under-places where a shrike could hide. She sighed and sagged against the wall.

"They're in the city," Andre said. "We heard shots not too far off. Are you okay?"

"Bad dream," she muttered. And she'd awoken into another one. Nightmares within nightmares. Maybe part of her did want to be dead. It would make sense, wouldn't it? She should want to die.

"How long did I sleep?" she asked Andre.

"A few hours. It would've been longer, but you started yelling and I had to wake you."

"The gunshots didn't?"

"Maybe they spooked you in your dreams, but you were gone, trust me."

Several shots were fired in rapid succession. Then more. Andre slid to the window and peered over the sill. "I don't know what they're shooting at, but they'd better not draw any extra attention."

#

They'd all been ready to fire, guns trained on the entrance, when the toy store's shutter was lifted. They knew there was someone in there. Bill had expected them to get the drop on whoever it was.

But when they saw the chimps, when the animals spilled out into the sunlight and the first ripped into the nearest guy's face, everyone had sat stock-still in utter disbelief. Bill had to look away and will the feeling back into his arms before he could line up a shot. *"Fire!"*

The chimps were near-skeletons but somehow they still moved, and fast. There were six or seven. Bill couldn't get an exact count any more than he could get off a single good shot. It was like they were *everywhere.* One leapt up onto a nearby rider's horse and began slashing at her with its claws. She fell back and off the saddle, blood spurting from her throat.

Bill shot the chimp. It recoiled, righted itself, then locked its ravenous glare onto him. It jumped.

#

Caliban held Hina and Vikram in a bank building half a block away. The two prisoners sat tied back-to-back behind the tellers' counter. Caliban ran to the window when the shooting began.

"What is it?" Hina demanded. She'd managed to work her gag loose after hours of gnawing.

"I don't know. Just be quiet!" Caliban hefted his rifle and checked his ammo belt. The dogs were in the bank too, and began howling madly, jumping at the doors and trying to get out.

"No! Stay! You be quiet!" Caliban cried. A hail of gunfire.

"Let me help!" Hina said.

"Everyone shut up!" Caliban shouted.

"You need to get the dogs into the vault!" Hina argued. "Let me fucking help, Caliban!"

"No! You're with them!" Staring out at the street, Caliban suddenly yelped and backed off from the glass.

A rotting chimpanzee lurched into view and pressed its face against the glass. More shouts sounded, and the thing leapt away.

"What was that?" Hina said in a flat voice.

"Dunno," Caliban mumbled.

"That wasn't 'them.'"

"No."

The hounds continued attacking the doors. Caliban swore and ran over to Hina. "You get the dogs. Try anything and I swear I'll shoot you."

He untied her from Vikram, then began undoing the knots binding her arms and legs. "Hurry," Hina urged.

He got her arms loose. She snatched the rifle right off his back and slammed the butt into his face. Caliban staggered back with a wordless exclamation, then touched his hand to his bloody nose. Then he dropped.

Vikram peered over his shoulder. "What's happening?"

"Sit tight," said Hina, freeing her legs. "There's some kind of monkey thing going on out there."

"Monkey…what?" Vikram began struggling. "What's a monkey thing?"

"Just cool it! You and I are busting out." Hina called to the dogs, but they didn't pay her any mind. She'd let them out as a distraction. Hopefully, the Tribe was distracted enough already with…well, with whatever a monkey thing was.

#

Bill fired point-blank into the head of the chimp that had landed upon his horse's head. The horse was whinnying and bucking like crazy and Bill missed a few times before scalping the little slime. The chimp somersaulted off the horse, stringy loops of brain matter flying from it, and hit the asphalt.

It had bitten the horse several times. A flap of skin hung over one of the steed's eyes. Bill dismounted, unsure whether the animal could be infected now. It was like all the rules had gone out the window.

Most of the other Tribesman were still on their horses and mowing through their ammunition. Bill saw one other chimp with its head blown off. The rest were still leaping amongst the panicked horses. "Fall back!" Bill hollered. "Forget it, just go!"

A chimp bounded toward him. He took off running around the side of the toy store. What would Max have done in a situation like this?

An open dumpster up ahead. Bill vaulted over the side and landed in a soggy, rancid mess. He pulled the lid down and held it.

The chimp began beating on the dumpster with a series of hellish screams. The lid threatened to bounce right out of Bill's grip. He tried to brace himself, but his feet keep slipping in the shit beneath him.

The chimp's assault ceased. Bill heard the baying of hounds. *Thank God.* He heard the chimp hop off the dumpster and scamper away.

#

Caliban rose shakily to his feet. First, he saw that Hina and Vikram were gone, as were the dogs. Then he saw that the assholes had left the front doors wide open.

Caliban dropped behind the counter. Rifle gone. He still had a pistol with—nope, the holster was empty. That evil bitch! Didn't he deserve a fighting chance?

He crept between loan officers' desks and through an open door and a sliding partition of titanium bars. The vault was there, and it was open too. He wasn't stupid enough to lock himself inside. He'd just pull it partway closed and huddle down behind the shelves. No reason anything would come poking around. Right?

#

Bill sat in that hot slurry until the sounds of gunfire and the hounds had both stopped. He lifted the lid just enough to survey the alley. He saw a corpse at its mouth—it looked like a child, had to be a chimp. He opened the lid all the way, gingerly resting it against the side of the store.

Bill climbed out and advanced, rifle in hand. It was slick with waste, but he had his finger curled around the trigger, stock braced firmly against his muscle, and wasn't about to miss another shot.

He made it to the mouth and peered around the corner. They'd fallen back, all right. They were gone. One wounded horse stood there, motionless, surrounded by several bodies. He counted five dead chimps in all. Ten people.

The sun had dipped behind some clouds and the world was slate gray. Bill walked out to the middle of the street. Not one sign of life besides that horse. That was probably his horse. He'd have to put it down. Bill let out a long sigh. The others, they would have turned and headed back toward the city limits. Unless they'd decided to ride through, then they would have headed the other way.

Bill looked west, then east. It dawned on him that, for the first time in his life, he might be completely alone. The buildings on either side seemed to close in as the clouds swallowed the sunlight. He swatted a fly from his brow and gritted his teeth. "I got this."

Someone behind him said, "Hmm." He spun and saw a man walking toward him. The horse regarded the man coolly, stepping out of his path.

"Max?" Bill started forward. "We thought you were dead, man! We even—" He thought back to checking Max's pulse on both his neck and wrist. He thought back to shaking the limp body and then placing it facedown in the waterlogged soil. There hadn't been time for a grave, let alone a proper sendoff. So here Max was. But he didn't look upset. Just hungry.

Bill raised the rifle. "Son of a bitch. No way. How'd you turn?"

He lined his sights up with Max's face. "That girl," he muttered. "Guess you were right. Sorry bub."

The rifle clicked. Nothing. Bill almost laughed as he dropped the barrel and fished through his cargo pants for rounds. He began walking backwards, pulling one pocket inside out, then another, and another. Wasn't that a bitch. He'd have to beat Max down with the stock. Bill told himself it wasn't Max anymore. He turned the rifle in his hands and wielded it like a bat.

Max was right on top of him. The dead man swept the rifle aside and seized Bill's head in both hands, his eyes wide and lifeless.

"MAX!" Bill felt teeth sawing into his forehead and struggled, but Max's grip was unyielding. Max's gnashing teeth raked down into Bill's eyelid, then tore into his nose. It came away in a fountain of blood, and Max relinquished his grip to shove the prize into his mouth.

Bill teetered backwards. Max stared blankly at his feeble retreat, then lurched to grab hold of him again. He ripped into Bill's cheek, then his neck, and Bill hit the asphalt. Max dug greedily into his belly.

THIRTEEN | KILL

Caliban approached the toy store as if he was on autopilot. His hands were so cold. He barely felt the blood-slick barrel of the rifle as he picked it up. He opened the jacket of the nearest corpse and fished through it for bullets.

The corpse's jaw popped. Its eyes lit on him and hands flailed.

Caliban jumped back with a moan. The slime answered him with one of its own, sitting up. One ear dangled comically by a thread of tissue, and it bounced as the corpse got to its feet.

Caliban aimed the rifle and fired. It was one of the few with a suppressor, and it quietly spat a round into the slime's nose. The dead man wheeled around, and Caliban put another round in the base of its neck.

He spun several times to see if any of the other bodies were stirring. One of the dead women had an ammo belt. He crept forward, then pounced to snatch it away. Damn thing was fastened around her. Hissed curses fell from his mouth as he yanked the belt free and secured it around his waist.

He recognized the next body as that of Bill. Half of his face and most of his throat was gone. His neck appeared to be broken clean in two. He wouldn't be getting back up.

And the other dead things…they were, in fact, actual chimps. Lord, didn't those things have retard strength? There were two dead humans for each of the half-size simians. Hopefully, there weren't more.

Caliban needed to get indoors and barricade. He hustled down the street.

#

Max watched from the alley. He chewed absently on a chunk of meat. Then he started after the man.

#

It had been a long while since any shots had been fired. Andre sat vigil at the window.

"When do we move?" Tavia asked.

"Night. Assuming things stay quiet."

A howl pierced the air. Claire sat up and rubbed sleep from her eyes. "Was that a dog?"

Andre shrugged. "I don't see anything. Wait, yeah I do. Come here."

Claire went to the window. A lone hound stood in the street. It looked in one direction, then the other, and let out another desperate howl.

"That's Scraps," Claire said. "They left him behind."

Andre saw the look in her eyes and said, "Claire, we cannot."

"He's lost. He doesn't know how to survive on his own."

"He's a dog, he'll figure it out." Andre returned her pleading gaze with a firm shake of his head. "We can't have him tagging along. The noise. The smell. He might bring the others back on us. I think we're in the clear so long as we sit tight until dark."

Tavia joined them and looked down at the dog. "He's right," she sighed. "It's a bastard thing to say but he's right."

Claire turned and headed for the door. "Don't!" Andre yelled.

"I'm not going there. I'm just getting away from you two." She opened the door and took a step out, then stopped. "Shit."

"What?" Andre stood. Claire turned and pressed a finger to her lips. Past her, there was a thin trail of slime in the corridor.

Andre grabbed his bat. *We searched this place top to bottom. The entrance is barricaded floor to ceiling. Where the hell did this come from?* Only one way to find out—he stepped into the hall and studied the trail. It grew thinner and spottier to the left, going around a corner. Their new friend was probably that way.

Tavia and Claire armed themselves and followed him. Andre moved to the corner and stepped quickly around it, bat raised.

A man in a bloody bathrobe stood there staring at a wall. He glanced over at Andre, and his rotten cheeks split like Swiss cheese as he sang his greeting.

Andre dashed his skull and drove him to the floor, stomping on his neck until it was pulp. "How the hell did we miss him?"

They went back and followed the trail to its source. It was a freezer in one of the other apartments. Someone must have stashed the body there ages ago. Old coot had probably sat there in the dark without complaint until he heard the three of them mucking about.

"No more surprises," Andre said. "Let's go through the building again."

#

Surprise.

Another dead senior came tumbling out of an armoire. He'd been bound with extension cords, but they were piled around his feet now. They tripped him up as he ran at Claire, and she was able to sidestep and smash him in the back of the head.

He hurtled toward a window across the room. Claire knew she had to stop him, but every molecule in her body was committed to *not* running to the slime. She watched the man pitch into the glass and through it.

Andre and Tavia rushed into the room. They looked out the shattered window. The man was deader than dead on the sidewalk below.

Another howl split the air. Andre sighed.

#

Caliban followed the sound of the dog. He spied the mutt standing in the middle of the street, sniffing at a corpse. The body was surrounded by glass. Caliban eyed the building and saw the open window.

He knelt on a stoop and loaded the rifle to capacity. If it was the Tribe, good. If it was the escapees—better. He'd take Claire to House Salome himself. All those rewards would be his. They wouldn't be divvied up amongst a bunch of people who hadn't stuck their necks out the way he had.

What if it was Hina and the *feder?* That wouldn't be as good as Claire, but it'd be pretty goddamn good. Before the bank, Caliban hadn't known if he really had a nerve to shoot Hina. Now he wanted it.

#

After the jumper episode, Tavia resumed searching other apartments. She headed down to the first floor. In the lobby, it was immediately clear that the barricade had been breached. A desk had been shoved aside and lay overturned next to a fallen couch.

She flattened herself against the wall and listened for movement. Other than the stairwell she'd come by, there was another one across the lobby, and a maintenance door next to the building entrance.

A slime wouldn't have been able to worm its way through that furniture. They had fit everything tightly together like they were raising a barn. Getting through would have taken human agility and thinking.

The intruder must have gone up the other stairs. Tavia went to the access door and pried it open, bat at the ready.

No one there. The door swung into the back of her head and sent her careening into the stairs.

Someone came through the door and placed a boot on the small of her back. "Be quiet," said a man's voice.

Tavia looked back with a grimace. She didn't recognize him. He wore filthy and otherwise nondescript clothing. Could have been a Tribe member, but not one she'd ever seen.

He pressed a rifle between her shoulder blades. "Face forward."

She obeyed. "Where's Claire?" the man asked.

"Why?"

"Listen, kiddo. I can find her myself if that's how you want to play. I'm trying to avoid a scene here. You know what I mean by a scene, right? Like where you die?"

He took the rifle and the boot off of her, along with her bat. "Get up."

She started to stand and he pulled her roughly against him. The rifle muzzle came to rest against her ear. "We go up. Yeah?"

She didn't say anything. The man said, "With or without you. Make up your mind. If I have to kill you, I'll kill the guy too."

"What do you want with Claire?"

"It's not what I want, it's what *they* want. Start climbing."

#

Andre met Claire in the corridor outside their apartment. "All clear?" he asked.

"As far as I can tell," Claire said. "Who puts a corpse in an armoire?"

"Maybe it was the guy's wife. Or kid. Couldn't bear to let him go, finish him off."

The door to the stairwell opened before them. Caliban pushed Tavia into the hall.

"Don't say a fucking thing," Caliban told them. "No negotiating. Here's the deal. You don't have guns. I do. Claire, you come over here and I let this one go. Then Claire and I leave. That's deal one. Deal two is that I kill you, Andre, and this one, and I take Claire."

Claire had known that, if the Tribe caught up to them, this very moment would come. That foreknowledge had done nothing to prepare her for it.

"How do I know you won't kill them anyway?" she said.

"You don't." Caliban pushed the rifle into Tavia's head. "I didn't even have to make the offer. I did it because I'm not a bad person. It's on you if I'm forced to snuff them."

"How about you let Tavia go?" Andre said. "Like you said, you've got the gun. You don't need to be holding her."

"Did I say something about negotiations?" Caliban screwed up his mouth in mock confusion. "I know I said something…"

His face hardened. "CLAIRE. NOW. Or I kill this little bitch."

Claire looked at Andre and said, "It'll be all right."

"What—?" he stammered. She knew he wanted to tell her to forget it, that there was still a way. But they both knew that any more fussing around was likely to get Tavia killed. Andre stood, helpless, and said nothing. Claire lowered her head in apology and started forward.

A sharp bark made everyone jump. Caliban turned to look behind himself with a bewildered expression.

Scraps had entered from the stairwell. His tail wagged excitedly at the sight of the people.

Tavia threw her weight back against Caliban. He was caught off-balance and fell into the wall. Tavia broke free of his grip and bolted toward Andre and Claire. *"Knife!"* she cried.

Andre's hand drew the blade and put it in her hand. She turned just as Caliban had regained his footing and was taking aim. With an underhand throw, Tavia sent the knife into his gut like a spear.

Caliban paused. He lowered the rifle and looked down in amazement at the knife. It was buried to the hilt.

He pointed the rifle at Tavia.

"Kill!" Claire shouted.

Caliban raised an eyebrow and turned the rifle on her. Looked like all deals were off the table.

Claire stood where she was and said again, *"KILL!"*

The dog jumped onto Caliban's beck and ripped into the nape of his neck. Caliban let out a howl to rival any hound, and the rifle swung away from Claire before discharging into the wall. Andre moved in quickly and seized the gun, throwing a fist into Caliban's nose. Scraps still clung to Caliban's back by his jaws. Caliban backed into the wall and the dog fell away with a squeal.

Caliban clutched at the knife handle. He glanced up and into the rifle's barrel.

"New deal," said Andre.

Caliban snorted and spat blood, but his eyes were wide with fear.

Andre said, "You can exit down those stairs, or out the back of your head. You make the call, cowboy."

Caliban grinned red. "I was never gonna let you go."

Andre nodded in understanding. He pulled the trigger.

Scraps ran to Claire. She hugged him and swept the blood and debris from his back. Andre sat down on the floor, and Tavia joined him.

"I'm pretty sure he was alone," the girl said. "We need to redo the main barricade, though."

Scraps walked over to Andre and sniffed his face. "I guess we keep the dog," he said.

"He's a hunting dog," Claire said. "And he learns fast. More pros than cons."

Tavia considered this and patted Scraps on the head. "I vote keep."

"You don't need to argue for him," Andre told Claire. "He made the case for himself."

To Tavia, he said, "Nice knife throw."

"I worked at a sideshow for a while," she replied.

"You've done a lot in your short life, haven't you?" Andre rested his arms on his knees. "I'll bet you've got stories."

She did, young Octavia, the Girl Without Fear; and she told a few while they repaired the barricade, swept the building one last time, and waited for dark.

#

With twilight came time to pull the barricade down. "Let's hit that garden again," Andre said.

They headed out into the night. Claire had fashioned a leash for Scraps from the extension cord that had once bound a dead man. The dog kept quiet, smelling the breeze and checking every shadowy recess.

He suddenly became rigid and pointed straight ahead. Andre brought the rifle down from his shoulder.

It was a single slime walking toward them. Andre shouldered the gun and brought out his bat. "I got him."

As the slime came within striking distance, they all recognized the face, the beard, the bomber jacket. Maybe Max recognized them too, because he slowed and looked from one face to the next.

Claire stepped past Andre. "I got him."

She changed, and Max stood in place and gawked.

Tavia grabbed Andre's arm. "It's all right," he whispered.

Now pale and withered, Claire stood inches from Max. He looked absently at her, then at Andre and Tavia. His eyes focused.

"Wait," Claire said. Max looked back at her and now he was clearly confused.

"I just wanted to thank you," Claire said. "You taught me a lot." And then she decided, for him, his fate, and sent his brains across the street.

Claire changed back before facing Tavia. "I *am* a sideshow."

"You're awesome," Tavia breathed.

FOURTEEN | ZOMBIE LAKE

It was near dawn when they heard the first reports of gunfire. It was definitely from within the city, but sounded a fair distance away.

"Bastards are still here," Andre muttered. Scraps whimpered and Claire pulled him to her side.

It's because of me, she thought. Faint shouts bounced around the brick-and-steel corridors. The trio slipped into a park overgrown with tall weeds and headed toward the muted glow in the east.

Coming up against an iron fence, they followed it until they reached a gate that had been secured with chains and padlocks. The chains looked like they were ready to crumble to red dust at the slightest breeze. *Atlantean,* read the ornate signage above the gate.

"Looks like a…golf course?" Andre guessed. He yanked at the chains, and surprisingly, they held fast. The fence was too tall to climb, and topped with little spires besides. Then there was the matter of Scraps. The dog sniffed along the fence and looked anxiously at Claire.

She knelt. "You know what…" she reached through the fence and snapped her fingers. "Go ahead." And the thin little hound did, slipping through with ease.

"Maybe he can find the keys," quipped Andre.

"We can use the trees," Claire said. Several of them, neglected over the years, had sprouted thick branches which reached right over the fence.

Despite the fatigue of the hours since their escape, Claire was able to pull herself up into a tree and rest against it, legs dangling. Andre ascended a different one and made his way over the fence. "Quickly," he said, and dropped out of sight.

Claire scooted along her branch, the fence's spires scraping the bottoms of her feet. Scraps sat below and watched as she lowered herself and let go of the branch. The dog practically body-checked her as he greeted her with a barrage of licks.

Once everyone was over, they started up the road which led from the gate into the property. If it had been a golf course, it was a nature preserve now. Birds chirped in the enormous trees along the road. The tall grass rustled with activity, and Claire saw a mouse race across the road. An owl cut down through the air and vanished in pursuit of its prey. Sloping gently upward, the road led them to the top of a hill where, sure enough, a golf cart throttled by weeds sat derelict.

"Stay sharp," Andre said. He stooped to study the road. There were creeping threads of vegetation woven all across it. Claire figured he was looking for signs of human activity, alive or undead.

"Okay." He started forward again. A distant pop reminded them that the Tribe was still on the hunt. Hopefully, the previous day's storm of gunfire meant that they'd roused some slimes and had their numbers reduced.

They crossed an open field toward a small, squat building. The sun was coming into view, and it revealed the building to be a restroom.

"I don't want to think about what's in there," said Tavia.

"This is why I told you all to go to the bathroom before we left," Andre said. He made a confused sound and fell into the tall grass.

Claire ran to where he'd been and managed to stop herself just before pitching over the edge of a drop. It was relatively shallow, filled with sand and rocks. Andre lay on his back at the bottom. "Sand trap," he coughed.

"Are you okay?"

"Yeah. Never had much luck with these things." Andre sat up and turned, beating sand off his pants. Granules slid over his boots in tiny avalanches. A dark rock poked up from the sand behind him. And moved.

"Andre!" Claire pointed to the shape.

He turned and said, *"No shit,"* in a mixture of awe and horror. The thing, which was now clearly a hand, spread its bony fingers and grasped at the air.

"No thanks." Andre scrambled up the side of the trap and Claire grabbed his hand. They stood with Tavia at the edge and watched the hand mill around.

"It ain't getting out of there," Andre said.

"How did it get *in* there?" Tavia wondered.

"Storms or a busted water main probably turned these traps into quicksand at some point," Andre said.

"You're damn lucky," said Tavia.

"Don't remind me." Andre resumed his trek toward the rising sun.

Scraps hadn't made a sound during the entire thing. Claire patted his head and led him on.

#

It wasn't just a golf course; it was an entire lakeside resort. A string of bungalows and a restaurant stood next to the clubhouse, all of it seemingly abandoned. "I'm not in the mood to clear another big building today," Andre said. "Let's just do the clubhouse and get some shuteye."

The lobby was secure. Same for staff areas and a small bar. Out back, abutting the bungalows, was a swimming pool which had become a mosquito-infested swamp. Past the bungalows, the lake was visible. A few boats sat idle on the placid water.

Andre led the way into the basement. There were several large tarps covering what looked like machinery. "Huh." Andre looked them over with his penlight. "We've got some heavy-duty generators here. No way they're gonna work." Nonetheless, he pulled a large switch and took hold of the hand crank beside it. "Especially if they run on gas. Forget it." He started cranking. "Then again, I—"

The machines began to hum. Everyone jumped back. Lights flickered overhead and Andre grinned widely.

The lights came on and stayed on. Tavia clapped her hands and Andre went back to examining the generators. "They're solar," he said. "Son a bitch. Building must be covered in panels. Can't believe they still work. Wiring and all! This is…this is good. Great."

He told the others, "Let's head back upstairs and make sure we're not sending up any smoke signals to the Tribe."

"And make sure we didn't wake up any slimes," Claire said. "At least it's morning, so even if outside lights came on, they're not going to be so obvious."

"Right. But we need to shut off anything nonessential. Which means pretty much everything."

As soon as they got upstairs, they heard warbling music. "Shit." Andre ran across the lobby to the staff rooms. "Controls have got to be in here!"

The music was being piped outside, too. Claire went to a window to watch for signs of life. There were loudspeakers mounted on poles around the pool. The song was unpleasantly light, something about a guy trying to find his salt.

"Pool," she called. "It's coming from the pool."

The music stopped. Claire and Tavia headed after Andre and found him in a room with a long board covered in switches. He was flipping most of them downward. He thumped his fist against a nearby monitor, sending dust into the air.

"Not a bad setup," he said. "Now this is a place where we can wait out the Tribe."

He punched a button on the monitor and it came on. The screen was snowy, but there was a menu visible. Andre shook the dust from the attached keyboard and tried navigating through the options. "Orientation," he read, and pressed Enter.

"Welcome to The Atlantean," a voice crackled through a small speaker. A middle-aged man in a suit appeared on the snowy screen. "I'm Mark-Paul Gosselaar, and I'm here to introduce you to some of the unique amenities of this five-star resort."

"Who's that?" Tavia asked.

"I have no idea," Andre said.

Mark-Paul Gosselaar told them all about the world-class golfing, Chef Roman Pablo's renowned cuisine and the spa on the other side of the lake. "And why Atlantean?" the man posed. "The real treasure of this resort is what's under the water. Let's have a look."

The screen showed what looked like a tunnel made of glass. Fish swam past Mark-Paul Gosselaar's smiling face. "The observation walkways cover the lake bed from shore to shore," he boasted. "And at the center of it all is the exclusive Atlantean Café. You'll want to make your reservations far in advance. Enjoy Chef Roman's finest dishes surrounded by the pristine beauty of the lake and its colorful wildlife." The café was a small room situated beneath a dome, where several well-dressed actors laughed as they cut into their fish fillets under the mystified gaze of the trout outside.

Mark-Paul Gosselaar began talking about timeshare opportunities, and Andre killed the video. "I'll bet there isn't much to see down there now." He searched the control board. "Let's have a look."

The monitor had returned to the menu screen. After a stuttering delay, it switched to grainy black-and-white footage of an underwater tunnel. The lake looked dark as pitch. Even the tunnel's powerful lights failed to pierce the murky water.

"How about that café?" Andre threw another switch. They saw a shadowy mess of overturned tables and shattered dinnerware. A single skeleton dressed as a maître d' sat slumped against the side of the dome.

Andre began cycling through the rest of the security cameras. There was another skeleton lying in one of the tunnels. Cameras along the shoreline showed a mostly-decayed body in a life vest lying on a dock next to a sign about boating hours. The body was that of a child.

"So the place must have been in season when the shit hit the fan," Andre said.

"Where are all the people then?" Claire asked. "There ought to be slimes all over the place."

"My guess is they left when pickings got slim," Andre said.

"And whoever managed to survive in here locked them out afterward." Tavia scratched Scraps behind his ears. "There must still be a few slimes about, though."

Andre switched to the next camera. The view was partially obscured by foliage, but it looked like there was a silhouette standing at the edge of the water. They all stared for several seconds. The shadow didn't move. Andre went to the next camera.

Nothing on that one. Nor the next. The one after that showed the entrance of the day spa. Two slimes stood inert on the sidewalk.

Next was another shot of the lakeshore. Another two slimes. One turned away from the camera and walked into the trees.

"Good news is, they're all on the other side of the lake." Andre went to the next camera. The screen was blank. The next one showed a dead man holding a golf club. He appeared to be entangled in some weeds near the sixteenth hole.

The next shot made them all cringe. A shrunken face glared directly into the camera. It appeared to have fallen from its perch and lay sideways on the ground. "Why is she staring into it?" Tavia cried.

"I don't know. She's clear across the lake. Don't worry."

"We'd better make sure we don't have any lights on tonight," Tavia said.

"That reminds me." Andre flipped down all the switches for the underwater lighting. "Let's see what kind of supplies are around here."

#

They sat in chairs in the lobby and ate the last of their berry haul. "Tomorrow we do the bungalows and the restaurant, okay?" Andre said.

"I wonder how many dead are in the woods," Tavia muttered as she chewed.

"We'll handle it," Andre said.

"Were you always Army?" Tavia asked him.

"Believe it or not, I was a comic."

"You mean you drew comic books?"

"No, I did comedy. Jokes. How do you know about comic books? They were gone before you were born."

"My dad collects them," Tavia said. "When he'd go on supply runs, he would always pick up any one he found. He taught me to read with them."

"What kind of comics?"

"All kinds, I guess. *Spider-Man, Spawn, Archie.*"

"That Archie was a badass."

"Did you read comics when you were a kid?"

"Sure." Andre sat back in thought. "EC reprints. They did *Tales from the Crypt, Haunt of Fear.* You know I tried writing a comic-book movie once. Me and my girlfriend had this idea about—you know supervillain teams, like the Sinister Six?"

"Yeah," Tavia said, leaning forward. Claire watched all this with a slime, Scraps lying at her feet. This felt...not *normal,* exactly, but good.

"Okay," Andre said. "So our idea was these supervillains who roll on their boss, the head guy, and then have to go into witness protection. So they have to give up their evil identities and act regular. It was a good idea but we never finished it." He laughed. "There was a guy based on the Incredible Hulk called the Red Rager."

"I don't get it," Tavia said.

"Good."

"Why didn't you finish it?" Claire asked.

"Well, it was really more Molly's idea than mine. And we broke up." He shrugged. "It happens."

"You've never mentioned her before," Claire said.

"I didn't exactly mean to. She's just part of the story." He sighed. "I dicked her over pretty good. I was into some heavy stuff. Drugs, you know."

"Devilspit?" Tavia asked.

"Sort of. Same kind of shit." He shifted uncomfortably.

Claire gave him a sympathetic eye. "It's okay, you don't have to keep talking about it."

"No, it's fine. You know the weirdest thing? The collapse, the slimes, that's what finally sobered me up. You can't make it in this world unless you're completely tuned in. Then again, you look around and ask yourself, what's the point?"

He picked at his teeth. "I guess, for me, the point is you guys."

Scraps sat up and looked around. He made a low growl.

"What is it?" Then Claire heard it, too—the other hounds.

"Goddammit," Andre snapped. "Fuckers can't just fuck off?"

"They want me," Claire said. "We have to go."

"We can't go out there in the dark," Tavia argued. "Let's just hide. Lock ourselves in the basement and shut off the power."

"What if they decide to stay?" Claire said. "We can cross the lake on a boat."

"They could see us," Andre said, "and I bet the slimes will too."

He grabbed his pack and the rifle. "We obviously have to use the tunnels. Let's see if we can find a map. I don't even know how to get down there."

"You're kidding," Tavia said.

"You saw them, they're still intact. All we have to do is run across the lake. No one will spot us through that soup." He hoisted the rifle onto his shoulder. "And once we get to the other side, we put a few holes in the tunnel. No one follows us. This is gonna be some *Ten Commandments* shit."

#

The entrance to the walkways was past the bungalows, next to the boat rental center. A locked vestibule, which they quickly breached, led down a carpeted flight of stairs to a room with various paintings of aquatic life. The scenes were all oceanic. It wasn't exactly the most honest advertisement but there wasn't any more time for wit. They opened the next door, a thick metal hatch, with a sucking sound. Stale air flooded the room. They entered the first tunnel.

Andre had turned up all of the underwater lights, including some outside the tunnels. The water was still dark brown, and the only visible things were plants growing along the surface of the walls.

Their footfalls echoed down the tunnel. Tavia had found a map and led the way, ducking around corners and racing through dark patches so fast that Andre kept telling her to slow down.

They entered the Atlantean Café. The maître d' offered a wide smile. They ignored him and entered the next passage.

Tavia shrieked and stumbled as something slammed into the wall from the outside. A slime's face pushed through the murkiness and pressed its blind eyes against the glass.

Claire helped Tavia to her feet. Scraps snarled at the slime and she told him, "Back off. Come on."

They continued on. Another bloated yellow face hit the glass on the opposite side of the tunnel, and its eyes followed them as they passed by.

Another, and another, as they entered the next section of walkway. Claire began to realize where all of the resort's people had ended up. One face after another mashed against the walls, hands pawing hungrily.

There was a loud CRACK. One of the slimes was banging a rock into the glass.

"It's okay!" Andre yelled. "Just keep going!" They were now running a gauntlet of the dead, soundless, slow-motion attackers at every turn. More cracking sounds. "We're almost there!" cried Tavia.

A loud groan echoed all around them. "Oh God," Claire gasped.

"Just ahead!" Tavia increased her speed and collided with the door at the end of the tunnel. She began wrenching at the handle.

The groan built in volume and the walls started to shake. Claire looked back and saw only the slimes pressed against the walls. No water. No break. They were at the door. They were okay.

The next sound that boomed through the lake sounded like a judgment drum from the heavens.

Andre and Tavia pulled at the door. "It's flooding!" Andre shouted.

The door began to open, but it was fighting them hard. Claire joined them. Together, all three pulled on the handle. It squealed and bent back.

"NO!" Tavia threw her arm into the open gap just before the handle came free and the door slammed back into place.

Her face turned bright red and she swooned. The door held her firmly in place. Andre and Claire grabbed the edge of it. Claire felt like her arms were about to tear from their sockets. She looked back again. This time, she saw the water. Thick and dark and roiling, it poured into the tunnel, and it was seething with the dead.

The door opened on Tavia's arm and she fell limp. Andre pulled it all the way back and shoved Claire through, then grabbed Tavia. They made it through just as the water hit.

#

This is what it's like to be struck by a train, Claire thought. The air knocked from her lungs, limbs powerless against the current, she flew weightless through a surging, roaring wave of darkness. Things slapped against her, the flailing dead, but none could take hold. She struck something hard and uneven. Stairs. They'd broken through the last door into the stairwell. She opened her eyes and the lake water stung them. Gravity returned and she was lying on the stairs. She rolled back and forth until she was able to right herself, and she lifted her head out of the water and let the stale air rush into her body.

Something bit into her arm. She couldn't yet scream, and could only look down to see what had her. It was Scraps. He kicked his frail little legs as hard as he could, trying to drag her to safety. In the end, she picked him up and placed him on the stairs.

Andre was above them, holding an unconscious Tavia. He offered his free hand and Claire waved it off. She climbed out of the water. A slime slapped at her ankle with a pulverized hand. She kicked it away. Her chest burned as she struggled to breathe. She followed Andre up the stairs and into the vestibule. He shut that last door behind them and sagged against it.

Claire sat and breathed, clutching her dog. Tavia's broken arm looked like a wet sock filled with rocks. Andre patted her cheeks and spoke to her. She didn't respond. "Did she take in water?" Claire asked.

"No. I think she's just in shock." Andre hugged her, careful about the arm, and glanced around. "Rifle's gone. Fuck it."

Claire listened for the scrabbling sounds of the dead on the other side of that door. There were none. Most of them had probably been ripped apart. She wanted to go back in there and stomp their heads. A reassuring lick from Scraps brought her temper down.

Tavia's eyelids raised. "Hey." Andre took off his shirt and began tearing at it. "Gonna make you a sling. Tavia? Do you know where you are?"

"Out of the lake, I guess," she mumbled.

"Yeah, we're out. Thanks to you. Just sit there and take it easy."

The other door, the one that led outside into the night, rattled. Scraps froze, ears pinned back.

There was a knock.

Andre shut his eyes and lowered his head. "God damn them."

The door jiggled and jostled in its frame, then opened. Rifles poked into the vestibule.

"Claire," a voice said. It was one of the women from the Tribe.

Scraps growled, but it was a feeble effort, and he looked uncertain about what to do. Claire wasn't about to order him to attack. She smoothed the dog's hair. "Why can't you just leave us alone?" she asked the darkness.

"We'll let the others go if you come with us now."

Andre stood up. The rifles followed him. "That other girl looks hurt bad," the woman said. "She needs someone to look after her. But it ain't gonna be us. So, soldier, you oughta sit yourself back down."

"I'm not letting you go," Andre said to Claire.

"It's not up to us," she said. "We tried."

There was a gunshot from outside. "We need to get a move on!" a man yelled.

Claire got up. Scraps stood nervously in front of her. "We'll take him too," the woman said. "He's ours. Come on."

"Max is dead," Claire said, knowing it was a futile thing to say. But she couldn't just walk out of here. "We're all free. You don't have to do this."

"You're coming with us."

Claire reached back and touched Andre's hand. He was shaking with anger. He couldn't look at her through his bleary eyes.

"We're not going to have trouble, are we?" the woman asked.

Claire's hand dropped, and she walked into the dark.

#

Some time later, when it was light, and the birds were out, and clothes were nearly dry, Andre and Tavia walked out the rear gate of The Atlantean. The Tribe had entered and left through there, and it hung wide open. They'd quietly dispatched a lot of the slimes while waiting for their bounty to appear.

Tavia shuffled along, eyes half-closed. She had to be in terrible pain. Andre felt dead.

"I'll get you to Lassiter," he said. "Then I gotta come back."

"My dad will send a party," Tavia said. "They'll kill them all."

"Can't have a war," said Andre. "I gotta do it myself."

Tavia walked away from him without reply.

#

He let her walk far ahead of him. A few times, she disappeared around a bend, and he half-expected her to be gone when he got there. Their wills were pulling them in opposite directions. He knew the Tribe had scouts hanging back who would shoot them if they headed after Claire. He knew Tavia was right about getting help at Fort Lassiter. He just didn't care about right or wrong anymore. He'd sat there, impotent, while Claire was led away. They had plans for her. What plans? He didn't want to imagine, yet he had to know.

He caught up with Tavia and gave her the knife. "Every step is leaving her further behind," he said. "I'm sorry."

"I can take care of myself," she said. "I'll try and get them to send someone for you."

"Good luck," Andre said.

"You can have all my luck," she said. "You need it. Take care."

FIFTEEN | LOOSE ENDS

Eli and his guards met Hansom Fete in the receiving tunnel. Fete appeared more nervous than usual. He knew this wasn't a drug drop, nor one of the Maestro's special deliveries, but Eli hadn't told him what to expect tonight. Truthfully, Eli wasn't one hundred percent certain himself. The potential of the moment was thrilling, even frightening. He'd thought that he already held the keys to Pandora's Box but, tonight...tonight Pandora herself came to him.

More guards came down the tunnel, escorting a couple dozen hobo-looking goons. The hallowed Tribe. Eli didn't recognize any of them, but they'd known the secret words. And they had her. The young woman had a burlap sack over her head, hands bound behind her back, and shuffled forward at the prodding of the guards.

"Untie her," Eli said. A guard freed her hands and they dropped limp at her sides.

Eli came forward and took one of the hands. The girl's entire body tensed. "Easy," he said, and tugged her toward him. "Come along."

"So..." one of the Tribe women said. "I'm Karen. We lost Max. But he told us about Claire."

"And what did he tell you?" Eli asked, handing the girl's hand off to Fete.

"He told us her worth. We've lost a lot of people, actually, to get her here."

"I don't really care," Eli replied. "As to her worth, what did Max quote you?"

Karen looked like she didn't want to be the leader anymore. She and the others murmured.

Finally, she said, "He didn't say, exactly."

Eli motioned to one of their armed escorts. The guard came to him. "What do they have?" Eli asked quietly.

"Guns, ammo. Horses, dogs."

"Take it all. Kill them." Eli stepped back. "Mister Fete, take Claire to the stables."

"The stables, sir?" Fete began to whine but it was cut off by the guards firing en masse into the Tribe's numbers. The sound filled the tunnel and Eli's head vibrated. He leaned into Fete's ear and shouted, "The stables, please, thank you."

#

The gunfire still echoed throughout Claire's skull as she was planted on a wooden stool. The sack was removed, and she saw a thin man in strangely elaborate garb, flanked by two armed men in similar dress, but with a more military look. She smelled manure and heard the grumbling of livestock and knew where she was.

The men stood silent as others led the Tribe's horses into the stable, taking them down a dark corridor to the stalls which would, presumably, be their new homes. She heard the hounds carrying on outside and prayed they wouldn't be shot.

A man whose robes bespoke some authority came in next. When he spoke, she recognized him as the one who'd given the kill order. "You all wait outside," he said, and reached up to light an oil lamp hanging from the ceiling.

He looked Claire over. He knelt close to study her face, and though her hands and feet were free, she held stock-still. She was trapped, no doubt about that. Were these...could these be Church members? Could she have been wrong about everything?

"The *omnicuta*," the man said. Claire didn't know the word. She stared at him and waited.

"I'm Eli," he said. "This is my house. Well, these are the stables. You won't be kept here, don't worry."

"What about the dogs?" she asked.

He looked confused for a second. "Oh, well, they're mine now."

"You won't hurt them?"

"Why would I do that?" Eli shrugged off her concern. "You mean because I hurt those people? They weren't your friends, were they?"

"No."

"I thought not. But you're fond of the mutts. Fair enough. They'll be just fine." Eli grabbed another milking stool and sat himself across from Claire. "Why do you think you're here?"

"They wanted to sell me to you." Of course, Max had denied such a thing was ever on his mind. The Tribe had gotten what they deserved. Claire was taken aback at having just thought that. And yet she still felt it.

"And what makes you hot property?" Eli asked.

Claire saw that he already knew and said, "Because I can change myself."

He smiled broadly. "That's good. It's good that you're being straight with me. That fosters trust. Now, Claire, you may be worried that I'm going to turn around and sell you off myself. The fact is that there is no higher bidder. I am the end of the line. This is your home now."

She thought of Andre and Tavia, of whether they'd managed to make it to Fort Lassiter. They would have no idea where she was. She felt miserable and selfish for wanting nothing more than to see Andre's face, to set things back to how they'd been in Fairfield. This new home of hers, no matter what it held or what they offered, was a nightmare purgatory.

"We'll get you situated in your new digs," Eli said. "Stand up."

"What do you expect me to do for you?"

Eli crossed his arms. "Whatever I say, for a start."

Claire stared straight forward and through his ridiculous garb. "What is it worth to you?"

Eli grinned. "Oh, I like you. The only thing more exciting than an underdog who is a purebred bitch." She snatched her hair and yanked her to her feet.

Claire willed her hair to turn white and brittle. Eli let go and staggered back. She fixed her dead, black glare on him.

He regained his composure and clapped. "That is *perfect*. You're perfect. I love it. Come on." He seized her wrist this time. "I want you to meet your new roommate."

#

Andre sat atop a treeless hill and scanned the barren earth below. He didn't see hoof prints or anything else to indicate he was on the right track. He gnawed on a rubbery bit of plant root and searched himself for the will to get back up on his feet.

Something stung his neck. He slapped at it and felt a long thing, quivering there. It was stuck fast in his skin and, thinking it was some kind of bug, he tore it away and crushed it in his fist.

He opened his hand and saw a little handmade dart there. A bead of blood fell onto his palm. He dropped the dart. "Damn."

He turned, expecting to see a Tribesman, but saw no one. The brush on the hill was scarce, no hiding spots. How far away was his sniper? His head began to feel cloudy and suddenly he didn't much care.

He felt grit against his face and realized he'd fallen. Shadows fell across his eyes and he was lifted and carried through an increasingly hot and thick sea of voices. Even when the sun went away and his body was placed upon cool rock, heat filled him and wept from his pores.

When his head cleared, he had no idea how long he'd been there. Andre rolled onto his back and stared at the ceiling of a cave. A few clusters of bats twitched and mewled overhead. His limbs were terribly weak and he found himself unable to sit up. He could only look from side to side. There was torches mounted in the walls, and waters dripped from certain points in the ceiling. He was drenched in sweat and tried to pull himself over to the water. No luck. A little gray lump near one on the puddles turned. It was a frog and it regarded him coolly.

A figure covered head-to-toe in a cloak entered from some passage beyond Andre's view. The figure stood over him as if in judgment.

"Who are you?" Andre managed.

"Nobody," whispered a sexless voice. "Don't touch the frogs. Poison."

The figure fetched a torch and returned to Andre. Now he could see a thin, haggard face. The figure's gender was still questionable but that was the thing Andre was least curious about.

"I'm a soldier," he said. "I don't intend any harm. I'm alone."

"We know these things."

"I'm trying to find a woman who was abducted. She needs help."

"These things don't matter."

"They matter to me," Andre said. "So, if you're not going to let me go, why don't you tell me what the hell you want?"

"Soldier," said the figure. "Why do you fight?"

Andre felt woozy again. He didn't want to believe his fate depended on a fucking quiz. He very subtly tested his limbs. His strength was coming back by degrees. He took in the room. Torches, sparse pools of water, killer frogs, creep in a cloak. A very dry-looking cloak.

"I fight to help people," Andre answered.

"How does that help?" the figure replied.

"It's about saving lives. And making those lives better." Andre flexed his fingers.

"Quality of life isn't an entitlement," said the figure. The voice dropped an octave. "None of us are entitled to our next breath. The greatest thing is to be humble. To give that up."

"I don't understand," Andre said.

The figure walked over to the wall and returned the torch to its mounting. "The only certain thing in life is death," the figure said. It produced something long and narrow. Andre tried to raise himself on his elbows and failed.

"The test, the great test," said the figure, "is to see who stubbornly and pointlessly clings to this life and who embraces the next step.

"The undead are merely a symptom of Man's hubris." The figure knelt and traced the long object along the back of the gray frog. "Some people think the undead's purpose is to wipe us out once and for all, but I disagree. They're the next level of human nuisance."

The figure approached Andre. "Do you think you know now what my purpose is?"

"You're a suicider," Andre gasped, making no effort now to hide his attempts at sitting up. "You think we all ought to be dead. Why don't you start with yourself?"

"That's the question each and every single one of you asks," said the figure, and it whipped the long object at Andre. The dart stuck in his abdomen. He moaned as his head began to thicken again.

"I am ordained of Lilith to carry out the great work," said the figure. "Once you're all gone, then I'll go to my reward."

"Lilith," Andre mumbled.

"The mother of death," the figure said. Andre's vision swam and doubled. No, it wasn't his vision—there were more cloaked figures entering the chamber.

"Your death will be of particular significance," said the lead figure, "and you should thank us for it. You go into the belly of the beast."

"*Semidiós,*" sang one voice from the rear of the pack. The call was taken up by others.

"Son of Lilith," said the lead figure, propping Andre up. "Come meet your brother."

#

"This isn't the Church," Claire said.

"Heavens no," answered the Maestro.

Claire was strapped to a chair in a room filled with sickeningly red light. She closed her eyes to try and ward off a headache.

"It's so different to have a living guest," the Maestro said. "You know how they get me the slimes? They lace corpses with curare. Slimes eat it, they become paralyzed. Sometimes the effect never quite wears off. As if they weren't difficult enough to work with."

The Maestro moved around Claire. "You look pained. Is it the lights?" he asked. He rounded the room, and when Claire looked up, she saw he'd removed all of the colored shades. "That's better," he said. "Much better in fact. I see you now. Yes...*I know you.*"

The Maestro sat himself on a gurney and clapped his hands on his knees. "I had a feeling about you. And here you are. You don't know me, but you do. You're going to get such a kick out of this." He swung his legs like an excited child. "How have you lived so long? You use your ability, yes?"

Claire didn't know what to make of this masked man, didn't know what to say that wouldn't set him off on another manic tangent. She feared that sooner or later one of those tangents would involve the polished surgical horrors hanging on the walls.

The Maestro seemed disappointed at her silence. "Maybe it's all a blur. Never quite yourself. I know, I know." He lowered his voice and spoke in a conspiratorial tone. "Detroit. Motor City Mountain."

Claire shook her head. "How could you know? Do you have Andre?"

The Maestro leapt off the gurney. Claire screamed and he threw out his hands, saying, "No, no, it's all right! It's fine! Everything is fine!" He turned one way, then the other, then said to her, *"Andre? Dozens?"*

He pressed his fists against his mouth and chuckled. "They called him Dozens. A corporal. He's alive?"

Claire pulled against the straps. "Just tell me if you have him!"

The Maestro recoiled. "Claire, please! I'm the one at a loss here. You know far more than me about so many things. I haven't seen Andre since he left me there."

"Left you...?"

"Did he ever even mention me? Christopher Mink? Hmm?"

The name seemed vaguely familiar. Claire tried desperately to recall the context.

"I'll bet you and I share the same nightmares," the Maestro said. "Maybe we've even seen one another in them. Do you remember me?" He pulled off his mask.

Claire screamed louder than ever. The man's face was nearly fleshless between his bloodshot eyes and his smiling mouth. It was like handfuls of meat, like clay, had been dug out of his face, leaving only a thin purple layer of dermis stretched over the cheekbones. His nasal cavity was an open crater. He grabbed the arms of her chair and leaned in. *"Tell me you remember,"* he pleaded, a sickly antiseptic smell wafting from his wounds.

"I'm sorry, I don't," Claire said, turning her head away. The door was making her eyes water. The Maestro stepped back and said softly, "Don't cry."

She didn't correct him as to the source of her tears, instead feigning complete shock and hoping he would put the mask back on. He did, but reluctantly.

"I remember you," he said. "I saw you crawling around that first night. I saw you change. I guess I was just another body to you. She had me pinned like a moth."

Claire stammered, "She?"

God, no. Not this.

The Maestro pulled off his surgical gown, the removed the vest and shirt underneath. His torso was a patchwork of scars. He fingered a particularly ugly circle of gnarled flesh in his side. "That's where she stuck me. I screamed. I know I screamed. Andre was the only one who got away. He left me. But he took you out, and now you're with me." He clapped his hands together. "I think that's a wonderful thing. I think it was supposed to work out this way."

"Are you going to cut me up?"

The Maestro looked from her to the instruments around him. "Cut? Oh, I don't know yet. But I won't hurt you. That I can promise. I'm a doctor. I have the proper tools and experience."

He sat back on the gurney. "She never bit me, was the oddest thing. She'd just peel me, like an onion. You see?" Claire saw, and nodded queasily. "Left me so curious. I was able to pull myself out of the Mountain during a storm. Lightning stuck, there was fire. Parts of me were still open and bleeding but a lot of it was scabbed over. I did my best to keep things intact. I don't know how many dozen—ha, Dozens—dozen surgeries I had to do on myself. No anesthesia. Fear and pain trigger the release of natural aids. And I was always afraid, and hurting."

He pulled his shirt on and buttoned it over the scars. "Does Andre know what you are?"

"He knows what I can do."

"Others?"

She shrugged.

"Some of these questions come from Brother Eli. I don't do politics. But I'll admit I would be interested to see Andre again. Talk shop. Old times." He went to the wall behind the gurney and selected a long steel saw.

"Please don't," Claire said.

The Maestro started and put the saw back. "Oh, I wasn't about to. I was just thinking." He passed through a curtain and out of the room. A moment later, music began to play. Frenetic drumming and a nasal voice that sounded as strained as she felt.

The Maestro returned. "I was saying…yes, I was still so curious about her, the dead woman, as curious as I was about you. I came back later. It had been almost a year. You, of course, were gone. But she wasn't."

"I've come to understand certain terrible and beautiful things about her," the Maestro said. He moved to the curtain. "I've waited a lifetime for this. So have you."

"What—what do you—?" Claire wrenched against her restraints. *"Don't tell me you have her! Don't show me! Don't do it please!"*

"She can't reach you, Claire," the Maestro said. He began pulling the curtain back and blue light entered the room.

"She killed my parents! She'll kill me, you, she'll kill us all!"

The Maestro whisked the curtain all the way back.

The shrike slammed against the bars that contained her. Claire changed without thinking, pure instinct turning her flesh to mottled alabaster. The Maestro clenched his hands together and stared in wonder.

The shrike was more withered and hideous than ever, but she was still standing. There were incisions all over her body, held together by steel wire as they would never heal. To think this man had held her for over a decade, keeping her viable, fighting the rot and…thinking of Claire?

"I'll tell you what makes her what she is," the Maestro said. He walked toward the cage and the shrike bared her jagged teeth. "She must have been pregnant when she turned. The fetus turned as well. Development ceased but…well, he's still in there. Still a part of her. I've seen him. Oh, she was furious when I opened her womb. Nearly got loose."

The Maestro smiled at the shrike, then Claire. "I wanted to know why she fed the way she did. Why the other slimes feared her. And you see, it's the baby. She's still caring for it. She's still *feeding* it."

He returned to Claire, leaving the curtain open. "He'll never be brought to term. I'm sure he'd fall apart if I excised him. But isn't that remarkable? Doesn't that make you think? Life, even in its most unnatural, perverted form, adapting. You adapted too. Did you know the bugs are in you?"

"No," Claire said, eyes on the shrike. "That's a lie."

"It isn't. I've studied others like you. This time we're going to find the answer. What makes you so darn special?"

He placed a hand on Claire's. "We're going to make beautiful music together."

#

Tavia stood at the unmarked boundary outside Fort Lassiter. If a stranger ignored the sentries and stepped past this point, they'd be shot. She began yelling passwords to the guards mounted atop the wall, but someone called back "It's Tavia!" and the big doors retracted.

Her father came running. He nearly stumbled in shock at her emaciated appearance, the bloody sling containing her arm, and a haunted look in her eyes. He placed a hand on her cheek. "Say something."

"Hi," she croaked.

"Water!" he yelled. "Medic!"

With Tavia on a stretcher and a splint on her arm, she was carried into the camp and placed in a cool tent. "Ice," her dad told the medic.

"Yes, sir."

"Baby," Tavia's dad said, and tears fell onto her skin. "I didn't think I was ever gonna see you again. We just found out about the attacks out west. I shouldn't have sent you."

"You said you wanted to send the best," Tavia said.

The medic returned with a bowl of ice slivers. "Here you are, General." Tavia's father took a handful and pressed it to Tavia's head, then the sides of her face.

"Only you could have made it back," he said. "You're still the best."

"I never made it to Fairfield. It's gone. I met people but…"

"I understand, baby. Just rest."

"No. They were taken by raiders. There's this woman, Claire. She's got…" Tavia considered her words. "She has intel."

"About the Church?"

Tavia shook her head. "It's not the Church, Dad."

"Our main supply line was attacked by knights," he said. "We lost a lot of good people. Your friend Reggie."

Tavia sighed. "Fuck."

"Hey." But her dad let it slide. "The knights were carrying orders from the *Goni*. And they had explosives."

"Claire says it's a frame job."

"Well listen. I don't know who this Claire is, but I can tell you I interrogated one of those knights myself, and he was the genuine article."

When the man had taken Tavia hostage in the apartment building, he'd said: *It's not what I want, it's what they want.* She couldn't say with any certainty who *they* was. But Claire had been so adamant about it, and she was the one *they* wanted most.

"Dad, I'm going to tell you. About Claire. Promise you'll listen, and no matter how much you don't believe it, believe that *I* believe."

The general sat back. "I'm listening."

END OF BOOK I

CHECK OUT OTHER GREAT ZOMBIE NOVELS

DEAD ASCENT
by Jason McPhearson

The dead have risen and they are hungry...

Grizzled war veteran turned game warden, Brayden James and a small group of survivors, fight their way through the rugged wilderness of southern Appalachia to an isolated cabin in the hope of finding sanctuary. Every terrifying step they make they are stalked by a growing mass of staggering corpses, and a raging forest fire, set by the government in hopes of containing the virus.

As all logical routes off the mountain are cut off from them, they seek the higher ground, but they soon realize there is little hope of escape when the dead walk and the world burns.

CHAOS THEORY
by Rich Restucci

The world has fallen to a relentless enemy beyond reason or mercy. With no remorse they rend the planet with tooth and nail.

One man stands against the scourge of death that consumes all.

Teamed with a genius survivalist and a teenage girl, he must flee the teeming dead, the evils of humans left unchecked, and those that would seek to use him. His best weapon to stave off the horrors of this new world? His wit.

CHECK OUT OTHER GREAT ZOMBIE NOVELS

DEAD PULSE RISING
by K. Michael Gibson

Slavering hordes of the walking dead rule the streets of Baltimore, their decaying forms shambling across the ruined city, voracious and unstoppable. The remaining survivors hide desperately, for all hope seems lost... until an armored fortress on wheels plows through the ghouls, crushing bones and decayed flesh. The vehicle stops and two men emerge from its doors, armed to the teeth and ready to cancel the apocalypse.

TOWER OF THE DEAD
by J.V. Roberts

Markus is a hardworking man that just wants a better life for his family. But when a virus sweeps through the halls of his high-rise apartment complex, those plans are put on hold. Trapped on the sixteenth floor with no hope of rescue, Markus must fight his way down to safety with his wife and young daughter in tow.

Floor by bloody floor they must battle through hordes of the hungry dead on a terrifying mission to survive the TOWER OF THE DEAD.

CHECK OUT OTHER GREAT ZOMBIE NOVELS

900 MILES
by S. Johnathan Davis

John is a killer, but that wasn't his day job before the Apocalypse.

In a harrowing 900 mile race against time to get to his wife just as the dead begin to rise, John, a business man trapped in New York, soon learns that the zombies are the least of his worries, as he sees first-hand the horror of what man is capable of with no rules, no consequences and death at every turn.

Teaming up with an ex-army pilot named Kyle, they escape New York only to stumble across a man who says that he has the key to a rumored underground stronghold called Avalon..... Will they find safety? Will they make it to Johns wife before it's too late?

Get ready to follow John and Kyle in this fast paced thriller that mixes zombie horror with gladiator style arena action!

WHITE FLAG OF THE DEAD
by Joseph Talluto

Millions died when the Enillo Virus swept the earth. Millions more were lost when the victims of the plague refused to stay dead, instead rising to slaughter and feed on those left alive. For survivors like John Talon and his son Jake, they are faced with a choice: Do they submit to the dead, raising the white flag of surrender? Or do they find the will to fight, to try and hang on to the last shreds or humanity?

CHECK OUT OTHER GREAT ZOMBIE NOVELS

Z BURBIA
by **Jake Bible**

Whispering Pines is a classic, quiet, private American subdivision on the edge of Asheville, NC, set in the pristine Blue Ridge Mountains. Which is good since the zombie apocalypse has come to Western North Carolina and really put suburban living to the test!

Surrounded by a sea of the undead, the residents of Whispering Pines have adapted their bucolic life of block parties to scavenging parties, common area groundskeeping to immediate area warfare, neighborhood beautification to neighborhood fortification.

But, even in the best of times, suburban living has its ups and downs what with nosy neighbors, a strict Home Owners' Association, and a property management company that believes the words "strict interpretation" are holy words when applied to the HOA covenants. Now with the zombie apocalypse upon them even those innocuous, daily irritations quickly become dramatic struggles for personal identity, family security, and straight up survival.

ZOMBIE RULES
by **David Achord**

Zach Gunderson's life sucked and then the zombie apocalypse began.

Rick, an aging Vietnam veteran, alcoholic, and prepper, convinces Zach that the apocalypse is on the horizon. The two of them take refuge at a remote farm. As the zombie plague rages, they face a terrifying fight for survival.

They soon learn however that the walking dead are not the only monsters.

www.ingramcontent.com/pod-product-compliance
Lightning Source LLC
Chambersburg PA
CBHW031957170626
46807CB00006B/2536